The Chef's Secret

ALSO BY CRYSTAL KING

Feast of Sorrow

The Chef's Secret

A NOVEL

Crystal King

ATRIA BOOKS

New York   London   Toronto   Sydney   New Delhi

ATRIA
BOOKS

An Imprint of Simon & Schuster, Inc.
1230 Avenue of the Americas
New York, NY 10020

This Atria Books hardcover edition February 2019

ATRIA BOOKS and colophon are registered trademarks of Simon & Schuster, Inc.

For information about special discounts for bulk purchases, please contact Simon & Schuster Special Sales at 1-866-506-1949 or business@simonandschuster.com.

The Simon & Schuster Speakers Bureau can bring authors to your live event. For more information or to book an event, contact the Simon & Schuster Speakers Bureau at 1-866-248-3049 or visit our website at www.simonspeakers.com.

Interior design by Kyle Kabel

Manufactured in the United States of America

10 9 8 7 6 5 4 3 2 1

Library of Congress Cataloging-in-Publication Data

Names: King, Crystal, author.
Title: The chef's secret / Crystal King.
Other titles: Feast of sorrow. English
Description: First Touchstone hardcover edition. | New York: Touchstone, 2019. | Includes bibliographical references and index. | Identifiers: LCCN 2018025073 (print) | LCCN 2018026648 (ebook) | ISBN 9781501196447 (eBook) | ISBN 9781501196423 (hardcover) | ISBN 9781501196430 (pbk.)
Subjects: LCSH: Cooking, Roman—Fiction. | GSAFD: Historical fiction.
Classification: LCC PS3611.I5723 (ebook) | LCC PS3611.I5723 C44 2019 (print) | DDC 813/.6—dc23
LC record available at https://lccn.loc.gov/2018025073

ISBN 978-1-5011-9643-0
ISBN 978-1-5011-9642-3 (pbk)
ISBN 978-1-5011-9644-7 (ebook)

For GrubStreet
You opened a door into a new world for me.

The Chef's Secret

CHAPTER I

Giovanni

Roma, April 14, 1577

Word traveled fast at the Vaticano, even during the darkness of night. Within an hour of Bartolomeo Scappi's passing, serving women from all over the palazzo had come to the chef's bedside, crying for the man they had loved and respected. They keened and wept, tearing at their hair, their skin, and clothing, their wails filling the gilded halls. Francesco Reinoso, the Vaticano *scalco*, ordered the staff to bring candles, and soon they filled the room with their glow, lighting up the shadows and illuminating the faces of the mourners. As papal steward, Francesco always kept things in order, even when his best friend was before him on the bier.

I sat in the corner and watched, lost and helpless, as two of the kitchen servants helped my mother, Caterina, and her maid bathe and dress my late uncle Bartolomeo. Of course, these women needed not take on this macabre task—the servants who reported to Francesco were more than capable, but they insisted, such was their love for my uncle. The heavy odor of rosewater hung in the air as they perfumed Bartolomeo's skin. It broke my heart to breathe in the scent. It was a smell he had loved, using the floral essence to flavor thousands of dishes in his kitchen.

For the last eleven of my thirty years, I had worked as an apprentice to Bartolomeo, a lion of a man who spent his days fussing over pots of boiling meats, scribbling elaborate seating arrangements on thin parchment, directing kitchen servants on which pies to bake and how many ducks to cook. Being related to Bartolomeo Scappi was a great honor. As the celebrated private chef to several popes, he was lauded in circles all over Italy, and countless *cardinali*, nobles, kings, and queens had fallen under the spell of his cuisine as I had. I always thought him invincible. And he had been, until five days past when sickness broke his spirit and laid him low. During his illness, I eschewed my duties in the kitchen and remained by his side, ever my uncle's *braccio destro*, his right hand, as he often referred to me. He was more to me than my maestro; he was also the father I never had, my own having died of plague before I was born. To see him stretched out before me, his eyes closed, his skin so pale and cold, seemed inconceivable.

"Giovanni," Francesco said, laying a hand on my shoulder. "We are ready to move him."

I nodded my assent and watched with a heavy heart as eight men lifted Bartolomeo's body onto a stretcher to carry him to the nearby Cappella Sistina, where the vigil would continue. I followed. As I entered the chapel adorned with breathtaking frescoes of the pagan sibyls and figures of the Old Testament, I thought how fitting it was for my uncle to lie beneath the magnificent paintings of Michelangelo, a man he once called friend.

Throughout the night and into the early morning, everyone the chef knew came to the chapel to pay their respects, light a candle, and share their condolences.

Relief flooded through me when Valentino arrived. He was my dearest friend and knew me better than any other. When I was nine and my mother had decided she was tired of Tivoli and moved us to Roma, I came to know Valentino Pio da Carpi and we became friends despite our difference in station. One of Valentino's great-uncles was Agostino Chigi, the famously wealthy Roman banker. Between the Chigi wealth on his mother's side and the riches of the Carpi family on his father's, Valentino was a man who would want for nothing in his life. But the money had never mattered to Valentino. He loved me like a brother. And I him.

I caught his eye as he entered the chapel, which was full of flickering candlelight that illuminated the frescoes covering the walls and ceiling. I had been in the cappella dozens of times, but always during the day. At night it held a strange magic that was difficult to explain. The paintings seemed larger, the saints even more beautiful and imposing. I was glad Pope Gregory had allowed special dispensation for the chapel's use. How Francesco had managed it I did not know and did not ask.

My best friend lived in a magnificent palazzo not far from the Vaticano. His mother, Serafina, accompanied him, the shadow of her cloak masking most of her face. Valentino led her through the ornate gilded door in the marble screen at the end of the chapel and across the black and white circles of tile. I stood to greet him.

"Gio, oh, Gio. We came as soon as we heard." Valentino shook his head as he neared, his long dark hair falling into his eyes. "Your sorrow is my sorrow." He pulled me close in a strong hug.

"Thank you for coming," I said. "Francesco sent for you?"

"Yes, God bless that man. Always making sure the world is running, even when his own heart must be breaking." Serafina pushed past her son and enveloped me in an embrace, her frail arms full of surprising strength. She smelled like lavender. "I loved your uncle," she whispered in my ear. "He never failed to make me smile." Her tears wet the collar of my vest.

As she pulled away, her hood slid back to reveal her soft, elegant features, which still held a hint of the beauty she must have been. I was thankful for her compassion. A boy of Valentino's standing should not have befriended an apprentice like me, but Serafina never blinked an eye, accepting me graciously into their home and their lives. It was part of what made me love her so much—she was generous almost to a fault, caring for her servants as though they were family, never minding what the rest of the aristocracy thought.

Valentino glanced over to where Bartolomeo lay. "How is your mother doing?"

My mother sat next to her brother, staring at his silent form, her fingers rubbing her rosary beads. She had been close to Bartolomeo, and if my grief felt like weights upon me, I could not imagine how much heavier was the burden she bore.

"As well as can be," I said. "You know how close they were."

Valentino put a hand on his mother's shoulder. "Go to her, Mamma. She told me once how much she admired you. Perhaps you can give her comfort."

Serafina nodded and walked away, wiping her eye with the back of her glove just before she put a hand on my mother's shoulder. The two women held each other and sobbed.

Valentino smiled a little. "Women are always adept with tears, are they not?"

"Agreed. But so am I today."

"They are honorable tears, for an honorable man. But what happened? How could he have become so sick?"

I shivered. "The doctor said Bartolomeo was no force against *la polmonite*. His lungs would not clear."

Valentino lowered his head. "Today is a dark day. You'll bury him at alla Regola?"

"Yes, of course!" a gravelly voice answered him from behind.

Virgilio Bossi, one of Bartolomeo's dearest friends, the man who first helped him find work in Roma. The *chiesa* of Santi Vincenzo e Anastasio alla Regola was the guild church of the Company of Cooks and Bakers, of which Virgilio had been maestro since before I was old enough to walk. His personality was bold, a match to Bartolomeo's, and his hair and beard always appeared wild and slightly unkempt.

The burly man clasped me on the shoulder. "There could be no other resting place for someone as celebrated as Bartolomeo Scappi! Your uncle's service to the guild will be greatly missed. We will honor his legacy as befitting."

Virgilio's wife, Simona, dabbed at her red and puffy eyes with a fringed handkerchief. When she saw Bartolomeo's body, she let out a cry, rushed to his side, and threw herself upon his supine form. Her sobs came in gulping gasps. My mother and Serafina moved to comfort her.

"*Dio mio!*" Virgilio swore. He leaned in to me and Valentino, lowering his voice. "Forgive her dramatics. She has been distraught since she heard the news. Your uncle, may he rest in peace, he could charm the ladies, could he not?"

I could not help but chuckle, especially when Valentino made his own snort of laughter. More than one noblewoman had mooned after the charismatic cook. "That he did." I swallowed hard. "Tell me, Virgilio, what needs to be done for the procession and the funeral? I am at a loss."

Virgilio grew serious. "Do not worry about a thing. It's all taken care of. I arranged it with Bartolomeo years ago. Even the marble has been inscribed."

My mind reeled with the thought of my uncle so prepared that the marble of his headstone was already engraved. I shut my open mouth, working to regain my composure. "What do you mean?"

Virgilio unfastened the button of his cloak and a servant appeared at his elbow to take it from him. "Gio, your uncle is one of the most important men in our entire company. He deserves a fine procession and a grand funeral. The guild is honored to send him off to God like the king of cooks he was."

Virgilio was right: Bartolomeo would have wanted a grand show. He was the master of spectacle. To imagine less for him at the end seemed unthinkable. "Thank you," I managed, choking back another bout of tears.

We discussed the arrangements. Virgilio suggested that members of the guild with the closest relationship to Bartolomeo should carry the bier in the procession. He had already sent men to the chiesa to cut the marble floor where my uncle would be buried. Virgilio had only to ask the priest to arrange the requiem mass and eulogy.

I was relieved that I could rely on Virgilio and glad he had already set many of the wheels in motion.

Finally, he gathered up his wife and made to leave. "We will come for him late morning. Try to get some rest, my boy."

A hand tapped me on the shoulder. Cardinale Gambara's elegant red and gold cape rumpled around his shoulders, and there was a crease on his cheek as though he had fallen asleep in his clothes and was roughly awakened. The look in his eyes showed a mixture of sympathy and sadness.

"Your uncle was the best kind of man, Giovanni. He made many people happy with his food and his friendship. We are fortunate to have known him. Now he will know God, so be comforted."

I didn't trust myself to speak.

Valentino nudged me, and when I looked away from the cardinale, I found Pope Gregory in front of me. Instinctively, I dropped to my knee and bowed my head. The pope held out his hand for me to kiss his ring. The embossed gold was cold and hard against my lips. It made me think of the headstone that would soon mark the legacy of Bartolomeo's life. Pope Gregory said a blessing over me and gestured for me to rise, then kissed me on both cheeks.

"May the Lord shine his face upon you, Giovanni, and may you shine your light on the world in his name."

"Thank you, Your Eminence."

"Your uncle was a man of admirable service to the papacy. We know you will continue his good work as our *cuoco segreto*."

"Yes, Your Holiness, it would be my honor."

"Excellent." Pope Gregory gave me a weak smile, then turned his attention to the cardinale.

I sat down, shaking. I had not had many audiences with Gregory, and although I myself did not adhere much to religion, the aged pope always made me nervous. He was a stern man, given to little excess. He had ruled the church and much of Italy with an iron fist for the past five years, implementing drastic reforms to rout out Protestant heretics and designating a committee to update the Index of Forbidden Books, those banned for being anticlerical or lascivious. Bartolomeo had often told me in confidence how little he cared for this pontiff, who was only slightly better than his forbearer, Pope Pius V. Both men subsisted on bread, gruel, a little meat, apples, and water, and the dearth of elaborate banquets that had made Bartolomeo famous— replete with pies packed with birds, peacocks dressed to look alive, statues made of sugar and marzipan, and the intricate, delicate molded gelatins filled with cherries and other fruits, common in the times of Pope Julius III and previous princes in the cardinalate—had left my uncle despondent. Only on rare occasion did the pope let Bartolomeo and me work for other nobles, as we did at the Easter banquet held by the Colonna family a few weeks back.

Instead we cooked bland daily meals, meals uninspiring to a chef of such genius. Still, the pope held a strong liking for my uncle and his work for the church over the years, respecting his knightly title of count palatine and the civic and honorific position of mace bearer, both bestowed upon him by Pius V. These positions elevated him beyond mere chef and guaranteed him specific entitlements as a respected member of the pope's cabinet. After the banquets of the past disappeared, Bartolomeo and his staff, including me, were left with little to do, but for some reason I had never discerned—money or perhaps security—Bartolomeo chose to remain loyal to the papacy.

Now it was my turn to swear loyalty to the pope, to be his cuoco segreto, his secret chef, his private cook. An immediate future of barley soup and apples awaited me. I sighed.

Valentino and his mother left shortly afterward, placing kisses on both my cheeks before they departed. The remaining friends, servants, and wailing women trailed out after them. Soon only Caterina and I sat by Bartolomeo's side.

The image of my uncle lying upon the pillow in death was one I would never forget. He wore a mask of peace, a slight smile turning the corner of his lips. My heart, my head, every part of me ached for the hole my uncle had left.

I pulled up a chair next to my mother. She gave me a grateful smile and leaned her head against me. We sat together in silence, looking through bleary eyes at the no-longer imposing figure on the bed before us.

My mother spoke first. "I don't think I've ever seen him so quiet. His voice was always booming. He always talked so fast."

"He was forever excited about something," I agreed.

"Even the small things. He was always so enthusiastic. He had a way of making you want to believe everything he said, even if you knew it was outrageous."

I squeezed her shoulder playfully. "Didn't you?"

"Didn't I what?"

"Believe everything he said."

"Mostly," she said. Then quieter, "Mostly."

* * *

At some point, Francesco returned for us. He must have been as tired and saddened as we were, but there was no evidence on the man's fine-lined face. He was, as always, expertly coiffed, his flat black hat flopped in perfect array atop a head of silvered hair.

"I arranged for a room for you tonight, Signora Brioschi," he said. My mother lived a short distance away, across the Tevere, not far from the ancient Pantheon, but to return so late was perilous. It had not occurred to me she would need a place to sleep, but of course Francesco had thought of everything.

"*Grazie*, Francesco. You are too kind." Caterina kissed us both and departed with one of the maids.

I was grateful for Francesco. He always had everything in order, even when things felt like chaos. We had been colleagues for over a decade, first serving together under Cardinale Michele Ghislieri, he as a steward and me as an apprentice chef. When the cardinale took on the mantle of Pope Pius V, Francesco and I followed him to the Vaticano, where my uncle was working as *maestro della cucina*. I became Bartolomeo's apprentice and *secondo*, and Francesco took on the prestigious duties of papal scalco.

I thanked Francesco for his help that week. He had assisted with some of my supervisory duties while I attended to Bartolomeo in his illness. The other chef who had reported to Bartolomeo, Antonio, was responsible for the main Vaticano kitchen, which serviced the staff and the various clergy living in the palazzo, but he often lacked confidence and needed supervision, a role that now fell to me. As cuoco segreto, I would also oversee the pope's private kitchen.

Francesco waved a hand at me. "Of course, Giovanni. It is the least I could do for you and Bartolomeo. We are lucky Easter celebrations are past."

I nodded. "Lucky indeed. Everything depended upon him during those meals. He was a true master. I feel like I hardly learned a tenth of what he knew."

Francesco shook his head at me. "Do not underestimate yourself, Giovanni. I saw all those sugar sculptures. Few could have orchestrated such a spectacle!"

I thought back to the dinner, and as I recalled the various dishes going out to the table, I realized I was pulling at my hair, fingering the curls. It was a nervous habit for which Bartolomeo always scolded me. "Stop that, boy! You'll get hair in the food!" To him I was always boy, although I was already nineteen by the time I became his apprentice.

"Your uncle gave me something meant for you."

Francesco drew a cord out from the pouch tied to his belt. He handed it to me. Two bronze keys were attached.

"Keys to the strongboxes in his *studiolo*. He was failing when we talked, but I am under the impression he did not want you to read the documents under those locks, just to burn them. He lamented he hadn't yet done it himself."

I was puzzled. I knew the small strongbox on the desk in his studiolo well, but I could not picture a second one. Nor could I imagine what could be so terrible that Bartolomeo would want it burned.

"I know what you are thinking, Gio. I won't tell you what to do, but Bartolomeo was extraordinarily concerned about those documents falling into the wrong hands." He raised an eyebrow at me. "He said there were lives at stake."

"Lives at stake?" I was incredulous.

He nodded. "That's what he said."

"I don't understand. He could have asked you to do this for him."

Francesco looked to the ground. "He did. At least at first I thought he did. He was not himself, Gio. He thought I was you."

He hugged and kissed me, and departed, leaving me with the two keys, heavy and cold in my hand.

CHAPTER 2

Giovanni

Roma, April 15, 1577

When Bartolomeo Scappi was knighted in 1549 and became papal count palatine, he was granted a set of rooms at the Vaticano, an apartment where he slept and a studiolo adjacent to the kitchen. At first, he used the apartment only on feast days, preferring to sleep in his house across the street. But as he aged, he began to appreciate the apartment's proximity to the kitchen, the big bed, and the view of the garden and Roma beyond. I lived in a small house near the Vaticano but sometimes slept in one of the rooms allotted to Bartolomeo, which is where I went after I said good night to Francesco.

I leaned over to the bedside table, and in the dim moonlight found my pocket watch, a newfangled item Bartolomeo had given me a few months earlier for my thirtieth birthday. I turned the bronze oval over and over in my hand, fingering the finely engraved laurel leaves decorating its case, my heart heavy. It was past one in the morning.

I lay on my bed, exhausted but sleepless. There were only a few more hours until I had to be up for the funeral procession. I knew I should sleep, but memories flooded my mind, and nothing I did would bring me solace. Finally, I rose and made my way to the window, opening the curtain to let a sliver of moonlight in, enough to help me to light the candles. My fingers found the keys on the cord around my neck. I had told myself to wait, to sleep now and look for the strongboxes later, but I could not stop thinking about my exchange with Francesco. I took off the cord and stared at the keys. The steward's warning that lives were at stake lingered. My uncle was not one to be melodramatic, so hearing words of this sort gave me pause.

But, I decided, not pause enough to stop me from discovering what was in those strongboxes. As I lit a lantern and slipped on my shoes, I thought about what Francesco had said about Bartolomeo wanting me to burn the contents. I rationalized that I would look over the items first, then carry through with my uncle's wishes. Surely, if our roles were reversed, he would do the same, without question. Curiosity was a trait difficult to quench in us.

I hurried through the dark corridors, arriving a few minutes later in the pope's private kitchen, which sat adjacent to the much larger kitchens that serviced the entire Vaticano.

Two papal Swiss Guards were stationed at the doors to the pope's kitchen night and day, and no one unfamiliar passed through. Poisoners were a worry to any pope. The guards bowed their heads in deference as I drew close.

"Maestro Giovanni, our condolences to you. Your uncle was a good man," the first said.

I started at the formal title he used; Bartolomeo had always been the maestro. "Thank you," I murmured, uncomfortable. "I couldn't sleep. I thought spending time in his studiolo might comfort me."

"Of course, of course. Please." They moved aside.

As maestro, Bartolomeo had a private office attached to the kitchen. I had rarely been in the kitchen when it was empty. Usually the stoves were ablaze and dozens of servants, their white blouses carefully tucked behind their aprons, were bent over tables, fires, and sinks, preparing meals. On most days, the aroma of baking bread and meats simmering in cinnamon and fennel broth assaulted the senses, but that evening there was only a lingering smell of pork and the hiss and spit of the flickering torches. Sadness gripped me.

The office door opened with a squeak as familiar to me as it was to all the other kitchen hands. It had meant Bartolomeo was content enough with the flow of the service for him to retreat to his studiolo to work on recipes or on his correspondence.

I set my lantern on a nearby table, then went around the cold room lighting candles. Although it had only been a week since Bartolomeo had been there, the stale scent of dust permeated the air. Curiosities from his travels to Milano, Venezia, Ravenna, and Bologna lined the shelves amid volumes of poetry, philosophy, and cookbooks written by friends and competitors alike.

I faltered when I reached my uncle's desk. A notebook of recipes lay open on the sloped writing surface. My stomach lurched at the thought of Bartolomeo's unfinished second book, which he had been working on in earnest for the last seven years, ever since the wild success of his 1570 cookbook, *L'Opera di Bartolomeo Scappi.* I closed the folio and set it aside.

The small strongbox on the corner of the desk was half buried under piles of notes, recipes, and kitchen records. The little key slid into the lock with an audible *click.* Inside was a bound leather journal and a few letters, each with a broken red wax seal, but no stamp.

I removed the little book, settling into the curved high-back chair where Bartolomeo so often sat to write. My fingers stroked the worn cover. I hesitated, thinking of Francesco's words, but decided there would be little harm in reading the journal before I burned it.

My heart pounded as I unwrapped the cord and thumbed through the book, flipping past scores of little drawings and passages in his neat and compact handwriting. The last entry was dated seven days before he died, when he was just starting to feel sick and had not yet taken to his bed.

April 7, 1577, Evening

I am ill but determined to mend quickly. As I write this, my very last entry, Giovanni is making me a licorice potion and a thick pea soup, just as I set forth in my cookbook in the section for convalescents. I rarely need to turn to my own medicine, but here I am, coughing hard enough my brain may burst.

How did I get to this point? Every day my bones creak a little more with age. If it were not for Giovanni, I do not think I could manage the kitchen.

With such age comes wisdom, as all the old sayings tell us. Although I am confident I will shake this illness, I admit, it gives me pause. One thought consumes me above all. Why, after so many years, am I still writing in these damn books?

The day I decided to prove Ippolito d'Este wrong and mark my history for all the world to see, like Pliny's vast encyclopedia, changed me forever. That stinking goldsmith, Cellini, had the same idea to put his life into a book. He told me about it once, when he was in his cups in my kitchen hiding out after learning the pope had accused him of stealing jewels out of the papal tiara. I listened as he slurred his words, angry he had the same plans. He was my friend, but he was also a rabble-rouser, a boy lover, a cheat, and a liar. Why should he become famous for his life? I was a man who planned a life of accomplishments, after all. Now he is dead and where is his book? He will not be remembered. This is a lesson to me.

All I have done in the last sixty-nine years I did for two things: fame and love. I accomplished both, but at significant cost. And now, in the sunset of my life, do I truly think this legacy is one I want to leave behind?

Dante Alighieri tells us: "The day a man allows true love to appear, those things which are well made will fall into confusion and will overturn everything we believe to be right and true." Cupid's arrow nailed me in the heart the day my lover walked into my life. She is "the love that moves the

sun and the other stars." All that seems right to us is wrong to another. I
cannot bear the thought of any harm befalling her. We took such risks. I
do not want my age to cause a mistake that exposes everything.

I paused, releasing my held breath. Bartolomeo had a woman in his
life? It wasn't surprise I felt, but wonder. Bartolomeo loved women.
My uncle was one of the most charming men I knew, and while he
must have bedded more than one or two ladies in his life, never did
I imagine him to have a serious lover. I turned back to the journal.

I have come to believe I cannot leave the burden of my life to anyone. I cannot
unpack the lies of the years behind me and hand them over to those who know
me. And yet the habit of recording my life is so deep within me that the thought
of putting down this pen forever gives me considerable pain. Not because I
continue to believe these words matter, but because of the comfort such writing
has brought me through the years—especially when I cannot be near her.
 When I think about my journals and all they contain I do not feel
pride. I feel fear. Terrible fear.
 I used to think I would give my journals to Giovanni so he would know
SV IX OXLE FT SIT LX MRB FTF HEGE FTR HSOORXRQD B TS
DST DX HISMSGES ITFFTIRVS MRB DXD IXGLX BEX VPD RS
LXDX LX GXMLC CVC OTHIT FTR MRB LIBSSV C HE FTEID
GSG LVFHV DSSV MCRR EBVGA VPD TXXRTFS VAIX S FT DAG
Q TQAIS DBLLDX SX IXGLX

I read the passage twice but could not make sense of the jumbled
letters. I bent my head again, hoping to discover the meaning in the
rest of the entry.

Coding my words is tiring, but there is so much habit ingrained within me.
As I look back at that passage now, I wonder why I bothered. This is the last
time I will write in a journal. Tomorrow, when I am more up to it, I will take

these books to the gardeners' pits and burn my arrogant words, these attempts
to hold my love in my arms by keeping these memories on paper. I am lucky my
writing has never fallen into the wrong hands. But the years are no longer
so kind to me. I will not let senility or infirmity be my undoing. Everything
will burn. Everything. Tomorrow these final words will light up the heavens.

I turned the page, but the rest of the book was blank. I flipped
through the journal. To my chagrin, most of the pages were in code.
Why would Bartolomeo write his missives in cipher? If, as he seemed
to indicate, he began writing in his journals as a way of recording
his life for history, why use a method of communication that few, if
any, would ever be able to read?

My eyes fell on the dozen or so letters still in the strongbox. I
unfolded the first piece of parchment, revealing a woman's writing,
the letters curved and beautiful, written nearly two weeks ago.

April 3, 1577

My dear Barto, orso mio,

I woke this morning from a dream and thought I could still feel your hands
upon me. When I discovered it was but a fantasy, I had to stop myself from
tears, my longing for you is so strong.

Easter is nearly here. I picture you in a fervor, planning and plotting
another miraculous feast. My heart sings with joy that the pope has released
you for the day to work for the Colonna. I hate how Gregory's dreadful
ways leave your talent dark and cold. I long to taste your food once more.
Indulge me, my love, and bake a hundred marzipan tourtes dusted in sugar.
Then I will know you are thinking of me.

I am ever yours only,
S.

"Cristo!" I cursed, the sound barely audible above the howl of the wind outside. A memory from that month's Easter preparations came back to me. I had been confused why Bartolomeo wanted so many marzipan tourtes. "Let me make some prune or milk tourtes," I had argued. "We need a variety." But he was strangely insistent that the little shallow pies be only marzipan and decorated with orange blossoms. I had to poach one of Francesco's maids to help arrange the hundreds of flowers. At the time, I thought it was just more of the spectacle and excess for which my uncle was famous.

Over three hundred guests, none of whom I knew, had attended the Easter Monday feast held at the Palazzo Colonna. I racked my brain to think of who showed Bartolomeo favor, but came up with nothing. It was impossible to discern a single moment when Bartolomeo may have spoken to this woman who affectionately called him "my bear."

I near ransacked the room looking for the second strongbox when I recalled Francesco had mentioned something about the space behind my uncle's desk.

Sliding the heavy piece of furniture away from the wall was slow work, although the howling wind likely masked the scrape of the mahogany desk against the tiles. I did not want to take the chance the guards would come to check up on me. No wonder Bartolomeo hadn't hidden the last journal and letters, risking them in the locked box on his desk instead.

I found the second strongbox in a small hidden cupboard. Inside were dozens more of the small hand-bound leather journals. I decided it would be better to take everything back to the safety of my room, before the kitchen staff began to do their work, and before the cock crowed. I stuffed the journals into a burlap sack I found on a nearby peg, retrieved the additional papers in the desk, then pushed the desk back into place.

I lingered for a little while longer, not ready to leave the room where I still felt my uncle's presence.

Later, back in my room once more, I sat down at the small table in the corner. I lifted one of the journals from the bag and set it before me. As I stared at the first page, an amazing weariness overtook me. My eyes felt sticky and the words on the first page of the journal seemed to swim across the paper. I looked at my pocket watch and saw I had only two or three hours before Francesco sent someone to rouse me. Despite my desperation to know the contents of Bartolomeo's correspondence, I tucked the bag into the chest at the end of the bed and locked it. I fell asleep before I drew the blankets across my body.

CHAPTER 3

Giovanni

I woke to a loud and insistent banging on the door. I struggled to open my eyes against the blinding sun streaming through the windows. A crow cawed in the distance.

"Signor Brioschi, please wake. Please!" The young voice sounded frantic.

I opened the door to find Salvi, Bartolomeo's page. He could not be more than eight or nine years of age. His clothes were rumpled and the lines of sleep on his face looked like those of the stucco wall of the palazzo; I wondered if he had slept on the stones outside my room. His eyes were red and his auburn hair was tousled. Bartolomeo had been fond of the boy and treated him much like a son.

"Salvi, what are you doing out here?"

He paused for a moment before answering, perhaps considering which words would be best for me to hear. "*Signore*, I wanted to see you before they read the will."

I understood; Salvi no longer had a master.

"If they do not provide for me . . ." He trailed off and turned his face away, ashamed.

His fate was in the balance. Without Bartolomeo, he would be sent to an orphanage or, more likely, would wind up back on the streets.

"What would you like me to ask?" I probed. "Is there someone you want to work for?"

Salvi nodded, his thick auburn hair sweeping across his face. *"Per favore."*

I waited for an answer, but he only stood there, staring down at the colorful loggia tiles.

"Well, who?"

He didn't look up. "You, signore, per favore."

I groaned. I wasn't sure I wanted a page, but something about Salvi made me take pity. I found myself wondering what was in my uncle's will—what did it mean for me? I imagined my uncle would ask me to look after Salvi and I would, but I did not want to get the boy's hopes up in case Bartolomeo had other plans for him.

"We'll see what the will says, Salvi. I cannot promise you anything."

The boy nodded, but his mouth trembled, and he swallowed hard. "Grazie, Signor Brioschi. Grazie." He paused. "A messenger came a few moments ago. Signor Bossi is waiting for you in the piazza."

Across the loggia the sun was already poking up above the trees. *Dio!* It was far later than I expected. I planned to be present when they moved Bartolomeo, but Virgilio must have handled those preparations without me.

I waved at Salvi to be on his way. "Thank you. Please run and tell him I will be there presently."

I arrived wrapped in a black cloak, my stomach growling. It was quite late indeed. Throngs of people stood in the sunlight. Many dozens of clergymen, most of the kitchen staff, and hundreds of Romans, high- and lowborn alike, stood in the dirt of the sprawling piazza in front of Saint Peter's church. The sun was bright and warm in the spring sky, but the normally vivid dress of the people had been replaced by shades of mourning: black, slate, and the darkest browns. The only color came from the scarlet capes of the many cardinali milling about, waiting for the funeral procession to begin. The sound of carpenters and workmen on the half-built massive dome of Saint Peter's was absent, and in its stead the rhythm of the crowd blended into a mixture of conversation, crying, and the occasional peal of a child's misplaced laughter. Never had I imagined so many people would have turned out to accompany Bartolomeo to his final resting place.

"This way, Signor Brioschi." I felt a hand on my shoulder. It belonged to a man I recognized from the Company of Cooks but I could not recall his name.

"Did you manage to get any rest? Your mother asked us not to wake you until necessary."

"Thank you," I responded. It was something she would do. "Do you know if my brother and his family are here?"

"Yes. Cesare arrived a short while ago, but he left Maria and the children in Tivoli."

I did not look forward to seeing my brother. We shared the same slope of a nose and general build, but that was where our brotherly connection ended. Cesare was always sour, negative, and angry, and in recent years he had become unbearable.

I followed the slender man through the crowd. As we made our way toward the front of the piazza, people gave me their condolences. I barely heard them; my mind was on Cesare, hoping he would not mar our uncle's memory that day.

Six horses waited, adorned in the red and black of the Company of Cooks and harnessed to an open, canopied wagon festooned with ribbons. Upon it lay Bartolomeo's casket, draped with a cloth embroidered with the company's coat of arms. A bear was on the left side of the crest and a stag on the right. Below the central chevron and its two red stars were the tools of the company's trade, a crossed knife and a butcher's knife. The banner beneath bore a Latin phrase coined by Horace—*ab ovo usque ad mala*—embroidered in gold. From eggs to apples, beginning to end. Roman meals had always begun with eggs and ended with fruit.

"Giovanni!"

My mother rushed to me and buried her head in my shoulder. I could see little of her through the black veil covering her hair and face. She lifted her head to say something just as Virgilio arrived and threw his arms around us.

"*Amici miei*, my heart is with you both. But today we celebrate the life of the greatest cook who ever lived. We will bring him to the chiesa with a procession fit for a prince!"

Virgilio hugged us close, his bushy eyebrow scratching against my cheek. He was buoyant, clearly in his element, orchestrating this grand occasion. It was exactly how Bartolomeo would have been in such a situation. No wonder the two had become such fast friends. They both understood the power of a show, even one as grim as a funeral.

"Come now, we must be off. Giovanni, take your place with Caterina, there, behind your brother. He will lead the horse."

Virgilio led us to a spot directly behind the coffin. Seeing it made my heart constrict. Surely my uncle, the big man that he was, could not be inside that box?

I pulled my eyes from the casket, ignoring Cesare and turning my attention to the small group of people who also waited there, including Francesco, Valentino, and Cardinale Gambara. I inquired about Valentino's mother, Serafina, but he said she wasn't feeling well.

A tug on my cape captured my attention. I looked down, expecting to see Salvi or perhaps one of the Cardinali pages, but was instead pleasantly surprised.

"Dottor Boccia!" I fell to one knee and gave the old dwarf a hug. "Oh, I have missed you."

"And I you, *polpetto*!"

I smiled at the nickname. I met Boccia when I was nine, having just moved to Roma from Tivoli. One day I was helping Bartolomeo make meatballs when the court jester found us, and of course, the name polpetto stuck. Dottor Boccia (the name "Doctor Bowl" referred to his ever-round haircut) could make anyone laugh—that is, until Pius IV rose to the papal throne. Pius had no room for frivolity, and the first act of his reign was to remove the dwarf. Boccia moved to the other side of Roma to live with his sister and I rarely saw him.

"I came as soon as I heard the news. Your uncle, he was a good, good man. He never once made me feel small."

I nodded, unable to speak. I was spared from finding the right words by a loud neigh. Cesare approached, leading a black horse by the reins. The horse was adorned with a guild caparison of black and red with the crest on the side, all a symbol of an important man who would never ride again. I patted Dottor Boccia on the shoulder and stood to greet my brother.

Cesare wore all black from his cape down to his breeches; even his long beard and his eyes—so brown they were almost black—matched the occasion, the overall effect sinister.

"Brother. I hear you slept in." His voice was the same as ever, a thin, even whine.

I scowled, eager to change the subject.

"Your horse?"

Cesare adjusted the red feather affixed to his flat cap.

"Francesco Barberini owns her. A beauty, is she not? Bartolomeo would have loved her. A pity you are such a poor rider or perhaps you might better appreciate an animal so fine."

"No need to be rude, Cesare. You dishonor Bartolomeo's memory."

"Dishonor?" he scoffed. "He dishonored himself with every kindness he gave to you."

Although I knew it would not do me a bit of good, I could not hold my tongue. "Why are you so filled with hate, Cesare? Today, of all days, why can't we put this animosity aside? Our uncle is dead."

"Yes, the great Maestro Scappi is dead. And for you the best is yet to come, isn't it?" He sneered.

My chest constricted. The filthy dog. He was talking about the will.

Before I could retort, the whistle signaling the start of the procession rang out and I moved to my place beside Caterina. She wiped at her eyes with a handkerchief.

Rows of company men holding guild flags took their places on either side of the mourners. The horses began the slow parade from the Vaticano toward Roma to the sound of trumpets.

Santi Vincenzo e Anastasio alla Regola sat on the banks of the Tevere, on the outskirts of the Jewish ghetto, near the Isola Teverina. It was typically a twenty-five-minute walk from the Vaticano, but the funeral procession moved at a slower pace. With each step, I recalled my life with Bartolomeo. When he taught me to make pasta. The first sip of wine he let me taste. The sweets he brought when he visited us at Tivoli. With each heavy plod, a painful and new memory filled me.

At the bridge leading across the Tevere, I looked behind me to see almost a mile of river-hugging road filled with people who had come to mourn my uncle. I knew his fame was substantial, but to see it manifest made me draw in breath.

At the door to the chiesa, another hundred or so men and women waited. I recognized them as members of the company, cooks from the kitchens of the Farnese, stewards from the halls of the Colonna, scullery maids from the Chigi household, and servants from every important palazzo in the city.

The officers of the company lifted the coffin off the cart as the procession stopped. Together, with slow, metered steps, they brought Bartolomeo into the chiesa. Cesare gave the horse to one of the company men and put his arm around our mother before I could. My fists clenched around the edges of my cloak as I followed them up the stairs.

Cardinale Gambara led the Mass, delivered the eulogy, and invited others to speak. Many of Bartolomeo's friends mused at length about his effusive, boisterous style, his insistence on helping them when times were tough and caring for them when they were sick. I declined to speak. I could not endure standing in front of so many people.

When Valentino passed by my pew on the way to the podium, I was both surprised and grateful. For a wealthy patrician to stand and give a eulogy for a cook was more than unusual.

Valentino Pio da Carpi could always command a crowd. He stood at the pulpit with a confidence I envied. His clear voice rang out as he told of the time when he and I toppled a rack of wine playing in the cellar. Bartolomeo punished us by having us prepare the pork ears and cattle hooves for the gelatin that formed the base of his wine jelly. The stench was terrible and we were miserable as we strained the stinking pot over and over, but the result was sweet and delicious.

"I could have argued my way out of it," Valentino said, alluding to his station. "But Bartolomeo was the kind of man who I wanted to make proud. He taught me respect and how to respect others. I will never forget you, my friend."

I had been stoic until that moment, but could no longer contain myself. I put my head in my hands and wept. My mother wrapped her arm around me, and I sank against her, my shoulders quaking.

Afterward, the company laid Bartolomeo into the floor of the church. Cardinale Gambara blessed the grave, and several company men settled the ornate marble slab with a bronze inscription over the coffin with a thud that made me jump.

A woman I didn't recognize tapped my arm. She was elderly, but still stood tall, her dark eyes bright with sadness. She wore a black brocade gown edged with red. She held out a bouquet of red carnations and white narcissus. She stepped forward and placed the flowers on Bartolomeo's headstone, then stepped back and slipped into the crowd so fast I could not see where she went.

I stared down at the flowers. Narcissus was a common spring flower at funerals, but red carnations meant only love, deep abiding love. I had never seen her before. Who was she?

*   *   *

The day Bartolomeo was interred, a comet appeared in the western sky, visible even in the spring sunshine. After the funeral, I stood with Cesare and Caterina on the steps of the chiesa, gazing across the Tevere and past the half-constructed dome of Saint Peter's, wondering at the light in the sky, fresh and sparkling in the distance. Valentino appeared out of the darkness of the church and came to stand beside Caterina.

"What are you looking . . ." he began, then stopped as he spotted the comet, a blurred tail of red trailing behind. He smoothed his long dark locks back from his face and held up a hand to shade his eyes from the sun. *"Madonna!"*

Caterina crossed herself.

"It's a sign. He is watching over us." She pulled her shawl closer to her lithe frame.

I put an arm around her. She was sixty-six, yet her hair was as black as that of a young woman. I doubted she had slept, but if she was tired it was not evident.

A memory came to me, of Bartolomeo and Caterina on one of our visits to Roma when I was a child. That night we visited Bartolomeo in the kitchen of the magnificent palazzo of one of the cardinali who had fallen quite ill. Bartolomeo was cooking medicinal broths for the invalid. My uncle and Caterina talked while Cesare and I ate sweets and nuts. They drank bottle after bottle of dark wine. It was the first big kitchen I had ever seen, and I peppered Bartolomeo with questions. He answered them all, happy I cared so much about his trade. Eventually the wine caught up with them and Caterina and

Bartolomeo both broke out into song, heady ballads from Dumenza, the small municipality on the Swiss border where they had grown up. Some of the servants began to hum and Bartolomeo waved them over to join. Soon the whole kitchen was singing. It was then I decided I wanted to be just like my uncle—a chef. I wanted to bring the world as much joy as Bartolomeo Scappi did.

Caterina's voice took me out of my reverie.

"Oh, Barto, I wish you had died happy," she whispered.

I gazed down at her, a sudden understanding flooding through me. Caterina had known at least some of Bartolomeo's secrets. I did not press her further, seeing her tears.

We stared at the comet for some time. It did not make sense, why it hung in the sky without flickering like other falling stars. Where had it come from?

CHAPTER 4

Giovanni

After we watched the comet for the better part of a half hour, Cesare announced he would escort Caterina back to her house for food and a little rest. He stopped me with a glare when I fell into step behind them.

"We'll see you when the will is read this afternoon." He didn't wait for me to answer as he led Caterina down the stairs.

She nodded her assent. I had no desire to fight with Cesare on such a day. Instead I followed Valentino to the Inn and the Fig, a humble osteria across the Tevere from the Castel Sant'Angelo.

Over a flask of wine and a platter of chickpea fritters, I asked him what he thought of Caterina's earlier comment that Bartolomeo had been unhappy.

"It is strange to think of your uncle as anything other than jovial. He had more brightness and patience in his little finger than the angels," Valentino said.

I took a long sip, thinking back on times we spent with Bartolomeo. Valentino loved him nearly as much as I did. As the nephew of one of Bartolomeo's most important and long-standing employers, Cardinale Rodolfo Pio da Carpi, Valentino had seen Bartolomeo almost every day for much of his youth.

"Perhaps it was me—I did not live up to his expectation," I mused aloud.

Valentino snorted. "Don't be ridiculous. You were the apple of his eye. Everyone could see that."

I paused to think about the weight of his statement and took a drink before responding. "Perhaps she was misplacing her own feelings. My mother has often been unhappy. She still talks about how she misses my father." I never knew Nazeo Brioschi; he had died of the plague a month before I was born. The only memento she had of him was a small painting on the back of a locket she wore at her breast. Perhaps my uncle's funeral had brought back the sadness of losing my father.

"Your father has been dead thirty years. She still pines for him?"

"She must, or Bartolomeo would have arranged for her to marry again."

Valentino scrunched up his nose, puzzled. "You've never asked her?"

"No. It had never occurred to me until listening to the eulogy today. Bartolomeo took care of her, so I think she didn't have to remarry. But now, I'm not sure how I can provide for her in place of him."

Valentino drained his wine. "It's unlikely with her age you will find someone to marry her."

"I know. She must be worried about her livelihood."

I winked at Valentino, changing the subject. "Don't you have a courtesan's bed to warm tonight?"

"Sì, I'm trying to decide if it should be Pasqua or Tita. What do you think?"

"Tita," I said without hesitation. "Pasqua has a terrible Neapolitan accent."

A mischievous spark lit up his dark eyes. "I don't need her to talk, Gio."

"Come with me," he continued. "You need a diversion. I'll invite Tita to join us and you can listen to her sultry Firenze accent. She loves your brown eyes—she tells me every time we see you. She'll run her fingers through your hair and bring you closer to God than any of those priests in the stuffy Vaticano."

"I mustn't, Valentino. They are going to read the will soon."

Valentino shook his head. "Even more reason you should come with me—at least for an hour or two. It would do you good to relax a bit. Plus, a bit more wine would help. One of the best reasons to be hungover is when you have to deal with sour relatives and money."

He knew how strained my relationship was with Cesare. I clapped Valentino on the shoulder. "My heart is far too heavy. Besides, you are a much nicer drunk than I, Valentino. Too much wine turns me angry, and that won't do anyone any good."

Valentino covered my hand with his own. "You won't have any cause to be angry, my friend. I have a feeling Signor Scappi will leave you everything."

It was a sobering thought and one I knew was probably right. He had been grooming me in his stead for years and I was the closest thing he had to a son. "And yet, I want none of it. My uncle. That is all I want. My uncle, back in the kitchen, baking me a prosciutto pie."

*   *   *

I wandered the streets of Roma for a while. I needed the time alone. Slowly I made my way back to the Vaticano, where we would gather in Bartolomeo's studiolo to hear the will read. I arrived early and spent the time in the kitchen with Antonio, going over the week's upcoming meals for Pope Gregory. Even Bartolomeo's death had not halted the work that needed to be done. Everything was as it should be, rote and ever so simple. Gregory was a pope who liked no surprises.

Finally, Francesco passed through the kitchen toward the studiolo and motioned for me to join him. Cesare and Caterina arrived not long thereafter. A tingle ran down my spine when I crossed the threshold. My escapade to take the journals the night before was still fresh in my mind.

Besides my brother and mother, there were only a handful of clergy present, men Bartolomeo had known well. The servants brought in chairs from one of the chapels and Cesare sat in the front row, holding our mother's hand. I took my place on her other side. She patted my knee and smiled at me, her eyes red from hours of crying.

I didn't have to look at Cesare to know he was likely glaring at me from the corner of his eye. I could practically feel the anger and jealousy rolling off him like a foul tide. He expected Bartolomeo to give me whatever wealth there was to give, which was likely true. Not once in our lives had I ever seen my brother do anything to endear himself to our uncle. I closed my fingers on the arms of the chair and watched my knuckles turn white.

Francesco read the will slowly, with much difficulty, struggling not to be overcome by emotion.

The first part of the will was straightforward. To the Company of Cooks and Bakers he left one hundred *scudi*—the equivalent of two years of an average worker's salary. As any Roman with means was expected to do, he left a hundred scudi to the Ospedale della Trinita to help care for the city's sick. Then came the heart of the will. Bartolomeo requested that if approved by the pope, I would follow in his footsteps in the Vaticano kitchen. Although the pope had already appointed me cuoco segreto, I was glad Bartolomeo believed in me enough to put the request into his will.

To Francesco, Bartolomeo left his books and a small sum of money. To friends such as Cardinale Gambara, he left some prized possessions from his travels. Bartolomeo willed a gold necklace worth forty scudi to Caterina and a yearly pension of another fifty scudi for living expenses and upkeep for her house. He left fifty scudi for each of Cesare's daughters to add to their dowries.

Salvi was provided for as well. He was to serve me until the age of fourteen, then be sent to the guilds to earn a trade. There was a modest purse for the boy, to be given to him when he reached the age of twenty-five. Additionally, if Salvi desired, he could take on the Scappi surname. I was shocked at these provisions; I had no idea Salvi had meant so much to him. Nor did I know what I was going to do with Salvi.

"To my nephew, Giovanni Brioschi, I leave . . ." Francesco paused for a sip of wine. I resisted the urge to bite my fingernails. If Bartolomeo had given so much to others, what did that mean for his braccio destro? My heart pounded.

Caterina squeezed my arm, a kind, motherly gesture. I sucked in a deep breath.

"To Giovanni Brioschi, I leave nine hundred scudi. I also bequeath a sapphire and gold ring, worth fifty scudi, given to me by my late dear friend, Cardinale Rodolfo Pio da Carpi."

Nine hundred scudi! An average chef's annual salary was not usually more than thirty or so scudi—even a hundred scudi would have been staggering to receive. I had no idea my uncle had such savings. That would keep me comfortable for years to come.

"To him I also leave my best knife, which he must never sell, but will hand down to the apprentice he deems most fit to receive it."

I sat up a little straighter. Bartolomeo had never even let me touch his favorite knife. It was his most prized possession, given to him by the maestro at Palazzo Grimani where he once served in Venezia. I could not remember the last time my pulse raced so fast.

"I also name Giovanni the heir to all my goods, including my horses and my house in Roma. I will these with the provision they are not to be sold for at least four years, and Giovanni must promise to take the *cognome* Scappi and to name his firstborn male progeny

Bartolomeo. In God, his name I will these properties, on this day of May, in the Lord's year of 1576."

I was afraid to look at my mother or Cesare.

"Where did he get all that money?" Caterina said, not as much under her breath as she thought. None of us had any idea about Bartolomeo's fortune. How had he amassed it? Although Bartolomeo was well paid for his work, and the knighthood bestowed upon him as papal count palatine gave him scudi, as did the profits from his book, those alone were not enough to generate the inheritance he left behind.

As Francesco returned the will to the document folio, Cesare stood, knocking over his chair. He whirled on me.

"You set him against me." His voice was low but menacing. A collective gasp erupted from the small group of people, myself included.

Cesare waved his hands at me. "He barely gave me the time of day, but you, oh you, you were all that mattered. You underhanded *bastardo*, you coerced him."

Caterina tugged on his sleeve. "Cesare! Do not make a fool out of me," she said in a low, warning voice. Cesare shrugged her off.

Before I could stand to defend myself, Cardinale Gambara rose from his chair. He was a tall, imposing figure. He put out a hand to stop my brother from moving forward. "Cesare, Giovanni was your uncle's apprentice. They spent the last eleven years working side by side. It is only fitting Bartolomeo saw him as the primary beneficiary of his estate."

The clergyman caught Cesare off guard. His shoulders slumped. He opened his mouth to speak but no words came forth.

Cardinale Gambara reached out and took Cesare by the elbow, expertly propelling him away from me and toward the door. "Come now, let me accompany you and Caterina home. Perhaps we can pray together."

I flashed the cardinale a grateful look as they walked out the door, but then my eyes settled on Cesare, whose gaze was black. I turned away, my stomach churning.

The rest of the people filtered out afterward, their voices full of hushed words. Soon only Francesco and I were left. He presented me with a package containing a copy of the will, the deeds to Bartolomeo's property, and the key to his house.

"This is also yours," he said, handing me an old wooden box with brass hinges and clasp. I knew what the box contained, but still my pulse raced. With a deep breath, I opened it to find the ebony-handled knife, shorter than a traditional carving knife but still large enough for slicing meats. The metal showed a beautiful and delicate pattern resembling flowing water. I touched the flat of the blade and found it was smooth. And sharp. I nicked my finger with the slightest test. Satisfaction rippled through me. With this knife, everything I prepared would have a touch of Bartolomeo's magic.

After we finished going through the remaining details, Francesco asked me a question I had long wondered about.

"Why doesn't Cesare like you?"

I threw up my hands. "I know not. He has never liked me much, not even when we were children. Caterina told me when I was a baby she couldn't leave me alone with him because he would hit me and try to pull out my hair."

Francesco gave a heavy nod. "He is quite jealous of you, it seems."

"He is. But maybe he has a reason to be. Bartolomeo left me so much more."

"Your uncle loved you best," Francesco said simply.

I wasn't sure what to say. Instead I uncorked a bottle of wine I had asked one of the servants to bring up from the cellar earlier.

"How could he have loved me best?" I mused once the wine had been poured. "More than Caterina? I doubt it. He adored his sister."

Francesco looked thoughtful. "He must have seen something special in you. You were his apprentice. His legacy lies with you, Giovanni."

"He left me more money than I ever imagined having. Did you know he had all that money?"

Francesco shook his head. Dark rings rimmed his eyes. It was the first time I had ever seen him look his age. "Not until we wrote the will. He swore me to secrecy. I asked him how he had amassed such a fortune, but he only said he had been given the means to provide for you."

I grabbed his arm. My voice shook. "By whom?"

Francesco stared down into his cup. "He would not say."

*　　*　　*

When I left a short while later, Salvi was waiting for me at the door to the kitchen. I took in the state of his clothes, which were ragged from spending idle time in the streets. His jacket was torn at the sleeve and dirt was smeared across a cheek. His expression reminded me of a dog that had just been kicked.

"Signore, I am sorry to bother you." The boy's voice shook. He wouldn't meet my gaze. "Can you tell me about the will?"

I put my hand on his shoulder. "Let us go for a walk, Salvi."

The boy did not speak, nor did he look up as we walked down the length of the loggia toward the staircase leading to the recently finished Belvedere courtyard. It was empty save a few gardeners putting away the benches used the day before for the wedding of one of the cardinali's nieces.

"I've got good news for you, Salvi."

Salvi perked up. "I can stay?"

He sounded so hopeful I couldn't help but smile. "Yes, you can stay. For a while."

Salvi's brow knotted in disappointment. "For how long?"

I ruffled the boy's hair. "Until you are fourteen. Then you'll need to choose a guild."

Salvi skipped and danced ahead, giving little cries of delight. Becoming an apprentice meant he would escape life as a servant. "Is it true, Maestro Brioschi?"

We came to rest near the fountain in the lower courtyard. "Yes, Salvi, but you must make me a solemn oath."

Salvi nodded, a most earnest expression on his little round face. "Anything, Maestro Brioschi."

"First, you must start calling me Maestro *Scappi*. I am taking on my uncle's name."

"Yes, Maestro Scappi," he chirped.

I dipped my hand in the fountain and let the water rush through my fingers. It was cold—the spring sun was not yet strong enough to warm the liquid. I looked at the waiting boy, hoping Salvi would prove worthy of Bartolomeo's devotion. "I want you to swear to me you will be loyal and honorable to me. That you will never tell another of my secrets, my actions, or my work unless I specifically tell you to do so."

Salvi let loose a little breath. "Of course, Maestro Brioschi! I mean, Maestro Scappi! I promised the old Maestro Scappi the same. I swear, I swear!" He crossed himself several times.

"You promised Maestro Scappi to keep his secrets? What kind of secrets did he have?" I said.

Salvi turned away and gazed at the fountain, silent. I realized the hypocrisy of my words and touched the boy on the shoulder. "Do not worry, Salvi. You don't have to tell me. It's admirable you are keeping to your honor, even after Maestro Scappi is gone. But someday if you think you want to tell me, please know his secrets are as safe with me as mine are with you."

Salvi wiped at his eye with his hand. "Maestro Scappi was kind to me. Before he died he told me I had to be strong, and I was to help you. I promise you, Maestro Brioschi—Scappi—I will work hard, and I will be good."

I was moved by his earnestness. "I can see why Bartolomeo was so proud of you, Salvi. Thank you. Take your dinner in the kitchen tonight like you always do. I'll let the guard know you are still welcome. Tomorrow we will sort out what your new duties will be."

I reached into my pocket and pulled out a few *quattrini*. I placed them in Salvi's palm and the silver glittered in the bright sunlight. Salvi's eyes widened. "Get yourself some sweets from the market. And stay out of trouble."

He took the coins hesitantly. "Thank you, Maestro Brioschi. Ohhh . . ."

"It's all right, Salvi. It will take a lot of getting used to for both of us."

The boy scampered away. My uncle clearly had big ambitions for the child—and I would make sure to see them through.

*   *   *

I thought I would stay behind and help with the evening meal, but Antonio and Francesco ushered me out, demanding I take a few days off. Grateful, I retrieved the sack of journals and letters I had left in Bartolomeo's Vaticano apartment and shuffled off to my home in the nearby Rione di Borgo.

It was near dark when I reached my house and climbed the rickety stair to the second-floor *appartamento* I rented from a wealthy merchant who kept his shops on the ground level. The next day, I would tell the landlord I planned to move to Bartolomeo's house a few streets over. I envisioned the shock on the man's face when I paid him in full for the rest of the months I had promised to live there. It was a strange thing to think I now possessed the kind of money that would allow me to make such a payment.

I lit the candles and the fire, made a dinner of some bread and cheese, then finally sat down with a goblet of wine to go through the bulging bag on my kitchen table.

Bartolomeo's journals were all bound in simple brown leather, a date etched onto each cover. There were thirty-two books in all; the earliest was dated 1525, over fifty years past. Inside each book was Bartolomeo's unmistakable scrawl, tiny and purposeful. I put them into order.

I looked through the piles of letters. There were dozens of packets, grouped by date and gathered with twine. The oldest letters were yellowed and brittle. All of them, from the oldest to the newest, referred to a woman named Stella. I wondered at the name, but continued to organize the letters, wanting to understand it all before I gave the envelopes a closer eye.

After I sorted the packets, I picked up the pile of loose letters from the desk. These seemed recent, though they were undated. The script on the front still bore my uncle's nickname, Barto, but was less steady than when he was young.

I surveyed my findings. The number of words contained within all the books and penned missives was staggering. Fifty years of words. A woman named Stella. For fifty years, there had been a woman in my uncle's life—the same woman, it seemed, from the yellowed pages in front of me.

I decided to begin with the letters. I picked up the stack labeled *Venezia, 1525* and untied the ribbon. The letter was short. It was written on a small piece of vellum. The ink had begun to fade and it was hard to determine some of the words. If I hadn't been familiar with Bartolomeo's carved radishes, I might not have understood the phrase:

Your bouquet of radish roses was exquisite. And to your question, I say sì, sì, sì!

I picked up letter after letter, and though it was clear the relationship was progressing, I only had one side of the conversation. I gathered she was of noble birth, which made their correspondence a significant risk. Frustrated with the limited information, I turned to the first journal, the only book without any code, also dated *Venezia, 1525*.

I lit the candle near the table and began to read.

Venezia, August 12, 1525, Afternoon

I am Bartolomeo, born in the year 1508, of Albaro and Melina Scappi of Dumenza. Today I begin the story of my life, writing it here in this book to mark the ebb and flow of everything I do.

This morning, at the market near the Rialto bridge, I bought eggs for Maestro Claudio as part of the evening meal. When I made to return to the palazzo, someone pushed by me and knocked the basket of eggs out of my hands. It was Ippolito d'Este, the son of Duke Alfonso and Lucrezia Borgia. They have been visiting Bishop Grimani for a fortnight, and thank the Lord, they leave tomorrow. It's not soon enough for me.

The nobility says many bad things about Lucrezia, but they are in love with her beauty. She has been nice to me, but Ippolito, who is near my age, has been a devil. From the moment he saw me, he took it upon himself to ridicule me. He makes fun of my face. He sticks his foot out to trip me when I am walking by. He drops food on the floor when I go to take his plate so I am forced to bend down and he can strike me on the head. He is loathsome though I have done nothing to him.

I did not know it was Ippolito when the basket of eggs was torn from my hand. I watched them fall to the stones and I cried out after the lout. When he turned around, I understood my mistake.

He picked up one of the only unbroken eggs and brought it to me. His friends circled around me and I could do nothing but stand my ground.

He talked to me like I was a child. "This egg is like you. Remember, you are nothing. You will always be nothing. No one will ever remember you, and everyone will remember me. You will never amount to anything other than scrubbing kitchen pots. I am already archbishop of Milano. You have no legacy, nor will you ever. Every word you say will be lost to history. Every thought you think will be as dust in the grand scheme of the world. You are nothing, kitchen boy. Just like this egg."

He broke the egg in his hand, then flung the yolk and shell at my face. His friends laughed at me. I think I only escaped a beating because we were in public at the market. The widow Rizzo who sold me the eggs lent me a cloth to clean myself. She even, from the goodness of her heart, gave me more eggs to bring back to the kitchen so I would avoid punishment.

With this record of my legacy Ippolito will learn not all great men are born of money, born of princes, and born of property. I begin this journal today and will continue it throughout my life, as a record of my path toward greatness. I will prove Ippolito d'Este wrong. I AM NOT NOTHING. I will be remembered by history and my name will live on for centuries.

This passage helped me understand the one I had read the night before. How strange, I thought, that Bartolomeo's journals should begin and end with the name of Ippolito d'Este, a man I always believed to be a friend to my uncle.

The first journal, which covered a span of three years, primarily described Bartolomeo's work in the service of the bishop who eventually became Cardinale Grimani. It seemed my uncle would often skip weeks or months at a time, then go through a spurt of writing. There were long passages about the types of foods served and the steps taken to present the food with proper etiquette and flourish. He described the palace in intimate detail and shared tidbits of gossip about the staff. There was the occasional scuffle with noble boys, cutpurses in the market, and tales of elaborate pranks Bartolomeo and his friends played upon the other servants. It was in the second journal, dated 1527, that the accounts started to focus less on the mundane life of a servant and more on a woman.

I took a long sip of my wine and kept reading.

Today I saw the most beautiful girl in the world . . .

CHAPTER 5

Scappi

Venezia, 1527

She is the most beautiful girl in the world, Bartolomeo Scappi thought. *Never have I seen a woman so perfect, so angelic, so impossible for me to attain.*

"*Bella*," he breathed when air filled his lungs once again.

Even Ippolito d'Este's presence at the dining table could not mar his giddiness. The girl was so beautiful she glowed like a painting of the Madonna, making everyone around her seem colorless in comparison. She was clearly a principessa of a grand house, sitting between Ippolito's father, the Duke of Ferrara, on one side, and a woman most likely to be her mother on the right.

Bartolomeo sought to memorize every feature of this goddess with golden hair that shone with glints of red in the last rays of the day's sunlight. Her eyes were dark chestnut, rich and deep, while her lips were pink, like the inside of a seashell. Her hair was braided, but much of it flowed loose over her shoulders, teasing her pale skin. She wore a dress of red, with sleeves billowing white. Rubies and pearls spilled across her delicate collarbone toward her beautiful breasts. Scappi painted her picture in his mind and stored it deep within the frame of his heart.

That evening, while staring at the sky, his thoughts lost in the memory of the *signorina*, a shooting star passed across his vision. "Stella," he said under his breath. *I will call her Stella. My shining star.*

Two weeks after Stella's family had come to stay at the Grimani palazzo, Bartolomeo was carrying a platter of spiny lobsters when he noticed she was also staring at him. She smiled and his knees grew weak. He had to tear his eyes away and concentrate on the tiles of the palazzo floor, afraid his feet would not find the next step forward. He placed the dish on the table in front of her, hoping she would not notice his shaking hands.

His heart pounded so loud he worried the principessa would hear each excited thud. But she talked to him as though their conversation was the most natural in the world. This gesture shocked him, not just because of her beauty, but because of his station as a servant. Rarely did the nobles ever pay attention to the staff when they delivered the meals, much less with a sincere smile. There was something about her, something that made him think perhaps they had met in a life past.

"Thank you," she said, her voice reminding him of fruit and cinnamon. "It smells delicious! Is it?" she asked, glancing up at him. "Delicious?"

He didn't know what to say. His chin bobbed up and down in acknowledgment, but for all the charm he normally had with women, words would not flow from his lips.

He had to move around to her side of the table to serve the lobster, a prospect that filled Bartolomeo with both excitement and trepidation. He saw Ippolito as he rounded the corner of the table, but much to his relief, the young archbishop didn't even register his presence.

Then he was there, standing next to a Venus on earth. She glanced up at him, her eyebrow raised, her mouth curved in a smile.

Surely she knows the effect she has on me, he thought. He was close enough to smell her orange blossom perfume. Oh! What a glorious scent. He brought himself back into focus, leaned in, and with the large serving tongs carefully lifted the lobster from the tray.

Dear Lord, guide my hand. Do not let me make a fool of myself this day. Do not let me flip the spoon into her lap, please, please, guide my hand.

Not a crumb of the lobster's stuffing escaped as he laid it gently upon the exquisite maiolica plate decorated with scenes of pastoral life. Relief.

"Thank you," she said again. Her soft voice was a chorus of angels. She touched his arm in thanks and a thrill ran through him. When he left the table, it was only with deep reluctance. He wanted nothing more than to lean down and brush her white neck with his lips, but instead he departed before she could see the heat of embarrassment rising to his cheeks.

In the days to come he looked for the principessa everywhere in the palazzo, but only saw her at dinner. Every time he crossed the threshold of the dining room and glanced in her direction, her gaze was upon him. She would lock her eyes to his and dazzle him with a smile. His heart would fill up as though it might explode inside the cage of his ribs. Time and again he found he was extra thankful for the heavy apron he wore.

Bartolomeo was baffled by her stares. In fact, he was perplexed by everything about her. How could such a beautiful creature exist in this world? What compelled her to glance in his direction? He was confident about his attractiveness to the ladies, but by no means did he consider himself an equal. He was a mere apprentice. She was not a chambermaid for him to feel up in the darkness of the wine cellar. No, no. She was a gem among women, surely destined for the arm of some wart-faced prince with money beyond measure. She was young, perhaps five or six years younger than him. He gauged her to be perhaps fifteen at best.

Back in the kitchen, his new love interest cost him. During the first few days of her appearance, Maestro Claudio cuffed him on the side of his head regularly for his distraction. Bartolomeo flushed with shame when his master reprimanded him. He wanted to excel for the respected chef, a man who reminded Bartolomeo of his father so far away in Dumenza. But he could not tear his mind away from the creature he saw each night in the well-decorated *sala da pranzo*. He was bewitched. It was as though the devil himself drove his thoughts. He thought of nothing but her.

Bartolomeo was desperate to know the name of his beauty, but he did not dare voice his desire to other members of the kitchen. The kitchen maids were sure to know, but it would be folly to ask any of them. He had sown too many seeds among them and the dramatics that would ensue from their discovery of yet another rival would be more trouble than he could bear. Worse, if word got back to Maestro Claudio, he would be on the receiving end of a stern lecture about how far beyond his station she was. Bartolomeo could hear the old master now. *Do not tempt her! They will sink you with stones in the waters beyond the city. Do not be a fool, boy!*

Bartolomeo recalled his confrontation with Ippolito d'Este in the market, anger stirring within him.

I will amount to amazing things. I will be a self-made man, much like the famous Cicero!

But he knew in the depth of his soul his maestro and Ippolito were not completely wrong. To be with a woman like Stella was impossible; his longing would be for naught. He was doomed to gaze across the floor of the Grimani sala da pranzo, forever dreaming and wishing, and for that he vowed to curse the d'Este name.

In the little room he shared with the kitchen apprentices, sleep was slow to come. The other boys snored, but Bartolomeo's thoughts were of the sound of her voice and the smell of orange blossoms.

*   *   *

Each day, the principessa watched him again, tracking every move he made in the sala da pranzo. Bartolomeo experienced a strange sense of wonder every time he turned to find her peering at him from behind dark eyelashes.

One evening, not long after their first encounter, she wore a dress of blue velvet to dinner. He imagined her as a living incarnation of the sea. Breathtaking as a wave slamming against him. Stunning like the glint of sun across moving water. Impossible to take in all at once. He would never be able to do more than admire the girl from afar, but it did not stop him from dreaming of her each night.

Bartolomeo watched her bring a forkful of pheasant to her lips. She closed her eyes and savored the flavors. He himself had studded the birds with cloves and stuffed them with fennel, then wrapped them in pork fat and roasted them until crisp. He had spooned the pomegranate sauce over their wings, the little seeds falling onto the plate like tiny jewels.

He vowed if he could not have her, he would make her long for him and for the food he brought to her table. On the morrow, he would carve a rose from the biggest radish he could find and bring it to her with her evening meal. He wanted to unfetter the burden of love from his heart. If he could tell her, even if it came to naught, he might feel a little freer.

Bartolomeo endeavored to keep his desire for the signorina hidden and had worked extra hard to regain Maestro Claudio's favor. Fortunately, the maestro rewarded him with permission to assist his secondo, a wiry man with strong hands and eyebrows that knitted his face into a grimace. But his eyes were kind and he treated Bartolomeo as an equal, which surprised the apprentice, who helped the secondo stuff thick slabs of tuna with grated cheese, cinnamon, cloves, nutmeg, and saffron. They dusted them in fennel flour, then cooked them over the fire with a bit of garlic. Bartolomeo loved these crispy fish sticks and he hoped the little signorina would as well.

Maestro Claudio was pleased enough with his young apprentice's handiwork that he promised to teach Bartolomeo how to prepare fried duck tongues for the Sunday *cena*. It was another dish he could not wait to bring to his love.

His love. Oh, how he wished she could truly be his.

In those moments when he crossed the threshold of the sala every night and saw her beam a smile at him, he did feel like she was his. And when she ate his creations, he thought the same; with each bite she took, she took a little bite from his heart. He loved how she ate so happily, much to the admonishment of her mother, who always cautioned her to eat less, on the need to keep her humors balanced and other ridiculous things the quack physicians carried on about. Her mother spouted such words of wisdom with a stern tone, and it was everything Bartolomeo could do not to roll his eyes as he served the neighboring diners.

Despite her shrillness, the signorina's mother was right. Nevertheless, as someone who wanted to become a cook, Bartolomeo knew he should learn how to balance the dry and the wet, the blood and the bile. These things were in vogue, and he swore to himself he would learn, but a part of him could only rebel. His Stella needed none of that! She was a paragon of good health and didn't need to worry herself about the advice of doctors. She should instead worry about love. Love of the crumble of a lavender tourte against her tongue. Love of the delicate flavor of sole in a tarragon sauce. Love of the flaky crust of a prune and cherry crostata. Or love of the wine mingling with the taste of a pig freshly roasted on the spit. Those were the things she could concern herself with when it came to food. Leave the worry about humors to the sick. To the superstitious.

The evening Bartolomeo left her the radish rose, he also ignored the words of her gray-haired mother and gave Stella an extra serving of pappardelle, made fresh from ricotta, eggs, and goat milk, fried to perfection and dusted in sugar. They were called "gobble-ups" for a good reason, and the principessa was pleased to indulge, that is until her mother bade Bartolomeo to take the plate away. She glared at her mother and snatched one last fritter. Sugar coated the edge of her pretty lips and Bartolomeo thought he might swoon. He would give anything to kiss the sweetness away.

The rose was gone when he went to clear the plates. He could only hope she had secreted it away in the finely embroidered *saccoccia* hanging at her hip.

*   *   *

Forty-three days after he first laid eyes upon the most beautiful girl in the world, Bartolomeo had the good fortune to overhear the maids talking about a girl at the palazzo. Two of the serving maids huddled in the pantry near his post where he was prepping nightingales for the cena. When they mentioned the dress she had worn the night before, Bartolomeo realized the principessa was the object of their admiration.

One of the maids was a thin slip of a girl who served the cardinale's sister. The other was a young woman who had caught his fancy for a time the summer before, but soon bored Bartolomeo with her empty gossip.

"She's here from Roma," the first said, awe in her voice. They talked of the girl's extraordinarily wealthy family, of her famed dressmaker, and of how long it took to wrangle her curls each morning.

When they said her name, Bartolomeo had to put his knife down for fear of cutting himself. Oh, to know her true name! Happiness filled him like a carafe of fine wine. Her name, he thought, was like the taste of strawberries sprinkled with sugar. It was like the summer sun touching the petal of a freshly bloomed flower. That evening, when he gazed out his little garret window, he wished he could shout her name across the rooftops, but he could never say it aloud. To do so was too dangerous, for her and for him. He would take a thousand lashings for his Stella, but he could not bear to have her come to harm.

The next morning, Stella stopped Bartolomeo in the loggia. The sky was bright and the October air was still gentle and warm. He was readying to leave the palazzo to go to market when she approached. He was so startled to see her there he stopped in his tracks, mouth agape.

The princess was radiant in a red velvet gown, her hair piled high upon her head. Her beauty was staggering, her skin so clear, her cheeks ruddy and fresh. What a sight he must seem in comparison, with his own hair a tussle of wild waves, a grease stain adorning one sleeve. He hadn't bathed, and he was certain he smelled too much like onions and ham.

She recognized his discomfort and giggled, in a way that immediately eased his fear. She gently touched his arm with one hand, and with the other she pressed a piece of paper into his palm. "What is your name?"

He looked around to see who might be witnessing the exchange, but there were only a couple of gardeners in the vicinity, none of whom paid them any mind. "Bartolomeo," he said, gathering courage.

She released his hand and shared her own name. Bartolomeo's heart sang as she repeated the word he had been turning over and over in his mind since the day before.

"Please tell the cook how much I love his tourtes."

Bartolomeo nodded his head vigorously. "I will, *madonna*, I will."

She dazzled him with another smile. "I liked the radish flower the best, though." She winked and turned away. He stood there, staring at the curve of her departing body, wondering what had just happened.

He stared until she rounded the corner of the loggia. He was light-headed and it felt like he was spinning, like a little bird on a spit, fire rising all around it. The piece of paper in his hand was small and warm. He hurried out of the palazzo and down the cobbled street lining the adjoining Rio di San Luca canal.

When he was sure no one could see, he stopped and unfolded the little piece of paper.

If you are thinking of me, leave me another flower.

Nothing good would come of it, but he would do as she said and give her another carving, perfect, small, and tinged with red. He thought about tearing up the note and tossing it into the muddy water, but could not bear to part with it. He tucked it into the pouch at his belt, cursing Cupid for the arrow driving his desire.

*   *   *

That night's cena was a grand affair, celebrating the birthday of the cardinale's niece. To mark the occasion, the guests dined outdoors in the little piazza in the back of the palazzo, alongside the canal. Colorful lanterns were strung across the expanse, illuminating the diners below.

Bartolomeo had left not one radish but three exquisite roses with flourishes on the petals. Unfortunately, the maestro had caught wind of his talents with the knife and he had spent over an hour making flowers out of radishes, carrots, and beets to adorn the plates of all the guests. But only Stella had three in front of her.

Bartolomeo was serving a plate of braised and stuffed hermit crabs at the table next to hers when he saw her pick up the first rose, a smile teasing the edges of her lips. She beckoned to him with a tilt of her head.

He returned the nod, a tingle running along the length of his spine. As soon as he was able, he made his way to her seat. Her mother was chattering to Stella's father, a well-dressed man whose white beard was trimmed short. The resemblance to Stella was clear, particularly in his nose and eyes. He even looked powerful. He belonged to one of the wealthiest families in all of Italy and owned dozens of banks, endless acres of land, and many fleets of ships, with scores of merchants in his employ. His clothing was of the finest cut, studded with jewels. Snatches of conversation as Bartolomeo drew near revealed he had just arrived from Roma, after some business affair was completed. Her parents made no notice of Bartolomeo's presence.

But Stella did. She motioned to him, her eyes shining. "I'd like one of those crabs, please."

"Sì, madonna," he said, his confidence growing.

He lifted a crab by the serving spoon and deftly whisked it onto her plate. As he did so, her hand reached out to touch his.

"You are so kind and helpful," she said. Her fingers brushed his wrist as she slid a note into his sleeve.

As soon as he could duck into the pantry for a moment, he read the note.

Meet me in the rooftop garden in the morning an hour after the cock crows.
Bring me one more radish rose tonight if yes.

He slid the note into the pouch on his belt. He could not bear the thought of throwing it into the fire. He wanted to savor every word.

The rose he brought her was the smallest yet, carved with the finest petals, delicately edged and thin as paper. He delivered it when he refilled her wine, placing it next to her glass.

"Sì, madonna, I will," he said to her in a low voice as he leaned in to pour. When he looked up, a flush had risen to her cheeks. To see her vulnerable was like another whizzing arrow to his breast. He wanted to lean over the table and kiss her there and then, not caring who else might see. He refrained, knowing it would be the biggest folly of his life.

* * *

Sleep did not come to Bartolomeo that night. He rose long before the cock crowed, dressed in his cleanest shirt and trousers, and slunk out of the room he shared with the other apprentices. The palazzo was quiet and the only stirring to be heard was the cardinale's guards who said hello as he passed. Bartolomeo had learned long ago it was best to keep the guards on his good side. He often brought them sweetmeats or hand pies tucked into a napkin, which always garnered him favor and more than a few good words.

Bartolomeo's shifts tended to begin in the afternoon, and he often slept in as long as possible. But today a predawn walk seemed perfect. Venezia at this time of day was both mysterious and romantic. Even the ruffians were asleep, and the city was quiet save for the lapping of the sea against the stone walls.

He walked along the edge of the canal, watching the shimmer of soft waves. The first blush of the sun was on the horizon and the pink glow made him think of the color on Stella's cheeks when she smiled.

He could not decide what to do. If he met her in the garden, he put them both in jeopardy. Her father was not a man to cross. His unfathomable wealth meant his daughter's hand was meant for someone noble, and not for a kitchen boy.

The fishing boats started to head toward the lagoon, their sails bright against the rising sun. The caorlina and gondola drivers began their morning routes, their greetings carrying over the water. Bartolomeo sat with his feet hanging over the edge of the canal.

Could he do the right thing?

It was a familiar question for Bartolomeo. The devil on one shoulder taunted the angel on the other. He had to see her. If he didn't, he would always wonder what might have happened. What she would have said. If he would have been able to reach out and touch her hand. If she might have given him a lock of her hair. If she would have bestowed upon him a kiss.

Yes. He would see her. Just once.

*　　*　　*

The path to the palazzo's rooftop seemed endless. Bartolomeo took the back passages least used by anyone, including the servants, to reach the room on the fifth floor where one could access the garden. The space was used as a sitting room for the cardinale and his guests, primarily in the winter when the fireplace was stoked. That morning it was blissfully empty.

Bartolomeo did not give himself any time to think about the implications of what he was about to do. He slid through the window and shut it behind him. The balcony garden was small, facing the courtyard. Plants hung over the rail, bushes blossomed in pots, and baskets with the end-of-summer flowers finished their blooms.

Stella sat on a bench in the corner, away from the rail.

"May I sit with you, madonna?" He walked toward her and bowed slightly.

"I would like that," she said, her voice smooth, like velvet.

She turned toward him. Her jade gown made her eyes sparkle. "You are very brave to meet me here. You know who I am, do you not?"

Boldly, Bartolomeo took her hands in his. They were warm and soft.

"You are the brave one. I am but a commoner. You are a principessa."

She laughed. "Perhaps. I don't feel like one, though."

He ran his thumb along the smooth skin of her hand. "Your parents—"

"Want to rule my life," she finished. She squeezed his hands. "It is as though I already know you. Is it strange that from the moment I saw you, I thought I must meet you?"

Bartolomeo nodded. "Sì, I know what you mean." And he did. That moment, the touching of their hands, the exchange of words. It all seemed familiar to him. Not the feeling he had had the same moment before, but more of a sensation that he was born to be with this woman.

"I can't stop thinking about you," he said. "You are even in my dreams."

"And you are in mine," she admitted.

Then he was brave, leaning forward, his lips seeking hers. She did not pull away but met him, tentative at first, then giving way to her desire. He brought a hand to her beautiful face. She tasted like honey.

When they parted, it took every ounce of willpower he had not to take her in his arms and cover her with kisses.

"I liked that."

His thumb caressed her cheek and then ran across the bottom of her lip. "Me too."

"How long are you staying at the palazzo?" A part of him hoped she would say she was leaving on the morrow, as it would make everything so much easier—and safer—for them both. But then, the thought of her leaving was a pain upon his heart.

"I do not know. My father is acting as an ambassador to the doge and is doing some business in the region for at least the next few months. I heard he may sail to Greece, and if he does, my mother and I will remain here."

He dared to say the words aloud. "I hope that happens."

She grinned. "I do too." Her eyes flickered toward the window where they had entered. "Alas, as much as I enjoyed kissing you, we cannot dally here. It won't be long before my mother will expect me. We're going to visit the doge today. But I want very much to see you again."

Then Cupid's arrow nicked him anew and Bartolomeo bent to kiss her once more, his tongue seeking hers, his hands wrapping around her to pull her close. She melted into him.

"We cannot stay," she whispered as her lips broke from his.

"I know. I will write to you daily until we find our next opportunity," he said, though he never wanted her to leave. "In the music
room next to the loggia where we met, I know of a secret place
where we can exchange notes. I think it has been a hiding spot for
messages between lovers or spies in the past." Her eyes grew wide
at the idea. He described the drawer to her, carefully built into the
wall, out of sight in a corner of the room near a statue of Poseidon.
He had discovered it one day while moving chairs from one room to
another. Over the last year he had checked the drawer several times
and never found anything inside.

She agreed to put a message there when she could. She kissed him
again, then headed toward the window.

"Stella!" Bartolomeo called softly to her.

She turned to him, puzzled.

"It's my name for you. My code name, my secret name. You are
my sparkling stella."

Her face lit up. "I like it. For you I will always be Stella."

She blew him a kiss and disappeared inside the window.

*　　*　　*

Bartolomeo Scappi did not write in his journal again for seven months.
His soul was on fire, floating on the wisps of his passion. When he
finally removed the little leather-bound book from its hiding spot
under his mattress and snuck down to the wine cellar with a candle
to write, he was in anguish.

For months, he had known bliss—true, searing love. He and Stella
saw each other every day, but only in stolen moments. A passing
kiss in a hallway, the library, or tucked into the cramped *felze* of a
docked gondola. They had not consummated their love despite their
ever-pressing desire to do so. Bartolomeo wanted something better
for his little star than to deflower her in a dark corner.

But time had caught up with them. Bartolomeo had known his love for Stella could be nothing more than a passing fancy. Stella and her family were guests of the cardinale. Though they never spoke of it, they both knew her father would conclude his business with the doge and the family would return to Roma. But nothing had prepared either of them for what had happened.

Bartolomeo smoothed out the piece of paper he had angrily shoved into his belt pouch.

Caro Barto,

I fear I may not have time to see you tonight, so I must leave you this terrible news in a letter. I wish you were here with me now. I feel like I could die with what is to befall me.

I have just learned that one of the business arrangements my father made during his travels was to marry me to Giacomo Crispo, who is going to be the twentieth Duke of the Archipelago. I will become a duchess. For some time now, I have been afraid of something like this happening. I tried to appeal to my mother, to wait until I am a little older, but it was to no avail.

I will try to meet you soon. I must meet you soon! But the wedding planning has begun. My whole world is suddenly nothing but dress fittings and lectures on customs and manners.

Oh, Barto! I will not be able to bear a single day without you. Already Cupid is twisting his arrow inside my heart at the thought of our separation.

I know not what to do, my bear. I know not what to do.

In sorrow,
Stella

Bartolomeo fought back tears. He was not a man to cry, and he wiped them away with a rough swipe of his hand.

Determined to gather what details he could about the unsavory marriage arrangement, he sought out the aged kitchen hand, Furio, who was prone to gossip with anyone who would listen. As suspected, a general question about the wedding launched Furio into a detailed conversation, and Bartolomeo learned far more than he wanted to know as they shucked clams for the evening meal.

He learned the Archipelago was a dire, desolate place off the southern shores of Greece, more than a fortnight's journey by boat. Furio had been there as a youth and said the country was once lush farmland, well known for its academies and oratory schools, much in the style of the ancients. It had once been an important Venetian holding. But when the Crispo dynasty overturned the Venetian duchy and began its reign in 1383, that had ended. Despite their new noble status, the Crispos were known for one thing: pirating the Adriatic and Ionian seas. On the surface, it seemed strange a noble as wealthy as Stella's father would give his only daughter to a pirate, but Furio had an answer for that too.

"She's just a girl, Bartolomeo. A bargaining chip. Her father owns some of the most important fleets and trade routes in Italy, and Venezia is one of the most important ports. Crispo's fleets raid regularly up and down the sea between the Archipelago and Venezia. If he marries her to that Crispo fellow, he will be saving his sailors, his boats, and his millions of scudi."

There were many rumors about "that Crispo fellow." Reportedly, he was an older man, around forty, with a crooked nose and a penchant for eating snails. He needed an interpreter because he only spoke Greek. His left arm bore terrible scars from burns he received when one of his ships caught fire in a skirmish, and he narrowly escaped with his life. He drifted for two days until he reached the shore near his home in Naxos. Furio admired the man and, while Bartolomeo pretended to be equally impressed by his adventures, inside his skin a storm raged.

"That ugly duke is a lucky man, he is." The voice belonged to Piero, one of the kitchen boys chopping up carrots nearby. "The principessa is a beauty."

"Every night my brother's been masturbating to the thought of that girl," Bruno chimed in from his station where he was making pastry.

"What?" Bartolomeo asked, turning to the boy, hoping he had not heard correctly.

No one answered him. Piero glowered at his older sibling. "Bruno, you're a stinking donkey who talks out of the wrong end of his ass."

Bruno lobbed a piece of dough at Piero. "You think I don't hear your bed ropes creaking at night? And there ain't no maid helping you make all that racket. Just the one in your head."

Piero snatched another piece of dough from the table in front of Bruno and threw it back at him. "What of it? You'd bed her just as quick as any of us had you the chance. That's all a girl like her is for, putting babies inside."

He held his hands out and pumped his hips toward the imaginary woman he held.

Before Bartolomeo's ire could rise further, Furio spoke up. "Stop it!" He pointed at the pastry on the floor. "Pick that up, Bruno. If the maestro sees this mess, you're both in for it."

Bartolomeo felt tight, like a spit turned the wrong way. How dare Piero think of his Stella like that? He looked around the room at five dozen or so kitchen hands. How many others thought of the princess at night before they slept?

*   *   *

That same afternoon, the maestro sat down the kitchen staff to tell them the wedding, which would take place in three weeks, would be a sumptuous feast, with not a single scudo spared. The procession would start by gondola on the Grand Canal and would end with the bride emerging at Piazza San Marco by way of a monstrous arch of flowers. She would walk across the square to meet the crook-nose pirate, and together they would enter the magnificent basilica to exchange rings. A second grand procession would then wind through the streets of Venezia. The people would toss rose petals from their windows onto the couple below. The feast at the Grimani palazzo would span nearly a week, with 156 courses and lavish entertainment, including dancing and fireworks.

Bartolomeo's days from then until the wedding promised to be relentless, washing hundreds of tablecloths and arranging the elaborate place settings, preparing thousands of sugar sculptures and tourtes, baking bread, peeling onions, making sausages. If Dante had seen fit to put an eighth circle in his *Inferno*, Bartolomeo thought this would be it. Hell on earth was helping to prepare for the wedding of his lover to another.

*   *   *

The days until the wedding passed in a blur of sugar, herbs, and pasta dough. He met with Stella only once, in the tiny garden, and they were almost caught. They were tangled in each other's limbs when they heard one of Stella's maids toying with the latch on the window. Bartolomeo slid to the floor, pressing himself against the tiles in the farthest corner, while Stella went forth toward the window. He waited in the garden until he was certain most of the household had gone to sleep.

Before the maid had come, Bartolomeo learned Stella had not yet met her husband-to-be, who would not arrive until the day before the wedding. Stella was distraught, her tears dampening his tunic.

"Please, please, Barto, save me from this terrible sentence!"

They were to sail back to Naxos directly after the weeklong wedding feast.

He held her tight against him. "I promise you, my little star. He will not take you to Naxos. You will not be sailing away from me."

~ FDSMEAEMLDNGENPSGILAELDLI ~

CHAPTER 6

Giovanni

Roma, April 16, 1577

T he code stared back at me, taunting me.

~ FDSMEAEMLDNGENPSGILAELDLI ~

All night I had racked my brain thinking of who might be able to help me break his code. And then it occurred to me—Bishop Avito. He had given Bartolomeo his last rites. He had to know something. He usually began his day in the library. I resolved to go there as soon as it opened.

When the sun began to stream through the open window, I looked across the courtyard toward the brilliant star in the sky, which seemed a little brighter than the day before. I refused to think about its import and turned from the window. I knew I should be readying my belongings to make the move from my modest lodgings to Scappi's house, but instead began to rummage through the chest of journals, flipping through them at random.

January 10, 1551

Today I prepared a broth for Cardinale Andrea Cornaro. It was one my mother taught me before we moved from Dumenza. It is made from four capons and is full of healthy nourishment. It is not a thin broth, but one carefully gelled and flavored with verjuice, cinnamon, sugar, and salt. I colored it with pomegranate wine. The cardinale was greatly relieved by this broth, and although he is quite weakened by his illness, he told me eating it made him feel immediately improved.

I remembered when Cardinale Cornaro fell ill. I was still a child when he died, but he always talked to me like I was a man. He had been a kind soul, quite aged, with a soft face lined from years of smiles and laughter. Unfortunately, he died not long after my uncle made the entry, at the end of January that year. Cooking broth for sick cardinali was one of my first exercises in the kitchen. Bartolomeo took great pains to show me exactly how to make the broth, and even how to flavor it with quince in the fall or infuse it with saffron to give it a bright yellow appearance. It was one of the hundreds of recipes in his *L'Opera*.

I was interrupted by a call and a knock at the door. "Maestro Scappi! Maestro Scappi! Wake up! Are you there?"

When I ushered Salvi in he took position to the right of the door, folding his hands behind his back. He stood tall and watched me. "Maestro Scappi, how can I help prepare you for today?"

I could only smile at his earnestness.

"There is a lot to do today, so I'm glad for your help. I don't have to work, at least. Antonio is handling my duties for a little while. But I want to start moving to Bartolomeo's house. Can you go to Francesco and see if he will spare a couple of his boys to help us move? If he can, we can start this afternoon. We can borrow some of the carts from the kitchen garden."

"I will go right away."

"Good. Tell them to meet me here at noon. Have them bring the carts with them."

I washed my face and dressed. Before I left, I packed up my uncle's journals and letters and locked them in my chest at the foot of the bed. I planned to move the chest myself. I didn't want any of the journals to fall into the wrong hands.

Afterward I bought a sweet roll from a street vendor on the corner and headed to the Vaticano palazzo. I passed an old man sitting on a rickety chair outside a tenement.

"The devil wants to burn us all!" he shouted, pointing at the bright light in the sky.

I did not stop. I heard Scappi's voice in my head then, the sound of his voice when we would pass someone of such ilk in the street. *"Pazzo vecchio bastardo!"* I smiled with the memory.

I made my way through the halls of the Vaticano Palazzo Apostolico toward the new library. I knew it would not be likely the bishop would divulge any secrets to me, but I felt compelled to inquire.

I had been to the Biblioteca Apostolica Vaticana countless times, but the walk through the Vaticano never ceased to amaze me. The Apostolic Palace remained in a state of construction, as every pope sought to leave his own mark. Everywhere one turned there was something new, an unfinished fresco half coated in gold leaf, or freshly carved pews stacked in a corridor.

The library was one of the latest updates to the palazzo, rebuilt by Pius IV in 1564, just a year before he died. From the start, Bishop Avito was one of its most avid users. I found the old clergyman in his typical spot, on a long bench in the back of the library, asleep with a book on his chest. The bishop had taken a liking to the writings of Cicero, which made him one many scholars turned to when looking for sage advice. Bartolomeo often chided him for coming to dinner with ink-stained fingers.

I nudged Avito carefully, not wanting to scare him out of a dream. The bishop stirred and one eye opened.

"It's me, Your Excellency."

The old man shifted his spectacles and squinted. "Ahh, Giovanni. What brings you here?"

"I realize this is an unusual request, but I hope you will see it in your heart to help me, Your Excellency. I need you to tell me about my uncle. What he said when you gave him last rites. You spent a long time with him." I had planned for more decorum, but found that my impatience superseded my manners.

Avito eyed me, stroking his beard. He kept his voice low. "I cannot."

"It's important." It was difficult for me to keep my words to a whisper.

The bishop shook his head. "No, I will not break the sacred vow."

I tried again. "There are some things I have to understand. There is a secret of the utmost importance he kept from me. I know about Ste—"

Avito clapped a hand over my mouth.

"Not here," he hissed. "You foolish boy."

Shocked, I nodded my consent and the bishop let go. "I'm sorry," I began, "I just—"

"Hush," the bishop said, his voice still low, so low I strained to hear. "Speak quietly now and tell me what you know."

I dropped my eyes to my shoes. My hands were shaking. I couldn't meet the bishop's gaze. "Father, it's important. I know about the woman he loved . . ."

Avito waved his hand to silence me once more.

"He told me you were going to burn the journals," he whispered. "He planned to make you swear on it."

I caught my breath, surprised the bishop even knew about the journals at all. "I never swore. I never even spoke to him about them.

He thought Francesco was me. It was Francesco who gave me the keys to Bartolomeo's strongboxes."

Avito raised an eyebrow but did not ask any further questions. He picked up his book and slowly got to his feet. "If you knew what I do, you would not wonder why I have such caution. I don't know why you are here, though. You don't need me. I suspect Bartolomeo said everything you want to know inside those pages."

"Please, Father, you don't understand. I cannot read them. Most of the entries are in cipher. You are the only one who might know the truth."

The bishop frowned. "In cipher?"

"Yes. I know nothing about cracking code. Please, Bishop Avito, you must help me."

The bishop drew himself up, disapproval written across his face. "I cannot tell you what was told to me in extreme unction. I will not break my vow to God."

I could feel the energy draining from me. I tried a last, albeit weak, plea.

"Please, I cannot bear having this sliver of knowledge. It is an anvil upon my heart."

The bishop sighed. He reached for a piece of vellum and the ink pot sitting on the table next to the bench. He scribbled a few sentences, blew on the sheet to dry the ink, folded the note, and picked up a nearby candle to form a seal.

He handed the note to me. "Take this to the university and ask for Giovan Battista Bellaso. He is a friend of mine and he worked for Cardinale da Carpi when Bartolomeo did. Give him this and he will help you."

I glanced at the sealed note, unsure what to make of the bishop's gesture. Before I could thank Avito, the man had disappeared into the depths of the library rows.

*   *   *

The walk to the university took longer than I expected. Clouds had moved in, filling the sky, threatening to leave a torrent of raindrops. Still, the streets bustled with vegetable sellers, the rumble of carts being wheeled across the cobbles, and panhandlers begging for coin. I avoided them; years in the kitchen had made me nimble, a master at circumventing people in crowds.

As I crossed the little piazza in front of the ancient Pantheon, I heard my name called.

I stopped next to the beautiful new fountain designed by Giacomo Della Porta that Pope Gregory had recently installed in the center of the piazza. Water flowed in an upward plume from the giant urn that sat upon four cherubs, each spouting water into a clover-shaped basin. I craned my neck back to see who beckoned me. When I caught sight of the man, I gritted my teeth.

Domenico Romoli.

Anger rose within me. Romoli had once been one of my uncle's apprentices. He was also a thief. Several decades before, when I was quite young, he had stolen recipes meant for Bartolomeo's first cookbook and fled to Florence, where he changed his trade and quickly climbed to fame as a steward in the Medici court. In 1560, he published a book on the trade of the scalco with a chapter full of Bartolomeo's recipes sandwiched in between. He was the only man Bartolomeo ever spoke poorly of.

My first thought was to continue walking, but something made me pause. Curiosity or stupidity, I knew not which.

Romoli crossed the piazza to where I stood. He wheezed from the effort of the jog. He was a large man in all aspects. He wore his dark beard cropped close and his peppered hair cut short, and sported a white quilted doublet with pearl buttons and breeches of black velvet.

I reminded myself to be polite. "Signor Romoli."

68

Romoli clapped me on the shoulder as if we had been friends for decades. "Giovanni, I am so glad to see you. And so terribly saddened to hear of your uncle's passing."

I stepped back a pace at his touch. "I appreciate the sympathy."

"He was a good man. He taught me everything I know. I would be nothing if it weren't for Bartolomeo." His brow furrowed, as though he were remembering special times spent with his mentor.

"That's true." It was difficult to contain the anger I felt toward the man.

The feather in Romoli's green velvet hat fluttered in the breeze. He continued as though he had not heard me. "When Bartolomeo gifted me his recipes, it was the most important thing that ever happened to me. I could never thank him enough. Tell me, Giovanni, did they read the will yet? Barto told me when he passed he would leave more of his recipes to me."

The heat rose to my face and to the tips of my ears. I jabbed a finger at Romoli's chest. "You stole those recipes! How *dare* you ask if there are more for you."

Romoli brushed my hand away. "I don't understand this jealousy, Giovanni. I worked with him long before you did. I was called into service by the Medici and could not say no. It is because of that appointment you were even allowed into Bartolomeo's good graces. Why should you be so surprised he would promise his recipes to me?"

During the conversation, I slid my dagger from its belt sheath. I whipped it up to Romoli's chin. A bright bead of blood glinted against the blade. "Don't you ever ask for his recipes again. Don't come near me, don't talk to me, don't even say Bartolomeo's name aloud. You don't deserve a single crumb of your success. Thank your lucky stars and be content with what you have already stolen."

Once I was satisfied the dagger had instilled an adequate level of fear in him, I pushed the steward backward with the palm of my free hand. He tumbled down into the dirt and I strode off, ignoring the alarmed and curious looks of the pedestrians buying goods from the handful of stalls lining the little square.

"You wait, Giovanni Brioschi!" Romoli called after me. "You'll rue those words. I will have what is due to me. I will take what is mine."

I refused to give him a backward glance.

When I reached the university, I stopped at the central fountain to catch my breath and think about what had just happened. My forehead throbbed, and it took every bit of self-control not to break down with the sadness that filled me to the brim. What was he playing at? He would have no access to Bartolomeo's recipes and books, and I would be safe. As soon as I returned to the Vaticano, I would have them placed under lock and key.

*   *   *

The Sapienza University of Roma was one of the oldest in the world, founded in 1303 by Pope Boniface VIII. It had not fared well during the Sack of Roma in 1527, when many of the professors were killed and classes were closed. Pope Paolo III had revitalized the university several years later, and now a few hundred prominent scholars studied law, medicine, philosophy, and theology within its walls. I looked around, wondering how I would find Bellaso.

Inside the front doors of the university, a young clerk sat at a desk.

"Greetings!" he called out, motioning me over to him. "How may I serve you?"

"I'm looking for Giovan Battista Bellaso."

The clerk's eyes shone. He checked a sheath of vellum resting upon the desk.

"He is giving a talk now, but if you go down this corridor and wait in that chair there"—he pointed down the long hall to a lone chair at the end—"you can greet him after his lecture."

I waited almost an hour before the door opened and several men in university robes filed out of the lecture hall. I entered when the last of them had passed me by.

Bellaso looked like a professor. He wore black robes, spectacles, and a simple black flat cap on his extraordinarily large head.

The man barely glanced at me. "I can't tutor anyone today, please come back tomorrow."

I cleared my throat. "I'm not looking for a tutor. I need help breaking a code."

Bellaso continued to riffle through his papers. "Everyone wants me to break a code for them. I've not got time."

I placed the note from Bishop Avito in front of the professor.

Bellaso paused, then broke the seal.

"I see, you are Scappi's nephew. I am sorry for your loss," he said after a time. "Do you have the cipher?"

I pulled them out of my pouch. "This is only an example. I copied some of them for you. I tried to puzzle out what it said but it was no use." A part of me was afraid to turn over the scraps of paper to this man. I wasn't sure what they said. What if the paragraphs I had copied from the journals were damning? But if I did not share some of the code with this man, I might never know. I passed the papers to Bellaso.

He glanced at the papers for only a few minutes, then handed them back to me.

"There are two ciphers here. The first cipher is an extremely simple polyalphabetic substitution code. You'll need a cipher disk and a key to determine the second alphabet set. You will need to figure out what the key is—it's a secret word. The second code is more complex. It is a cipher I myself devised. You'll also need to know the countersign to decipher the code. Here, take this book. All the instructions are within."

Bellaso dug something out from a pile of books, scrolls, and papers and handed me a book entitled *The True Way to Write in Cipher.*

I took it. "How do I know what the key is? Or the countersign?"

The professor shrugged. "It's something only your uncle would have known. It's probably a special word or a phrase. If you are lucky, he may have hidden it within the cipher. If so, my book will tell you how to find it." He turned back to his papers.

"Can I pay you to help me?"

"No." His tone was matter-of-fact.

I took a breath, willing myself to be calm. Bellaso's indifference was maddening.

"How much do I owe you for the book?"

"Bishop Avito will take care of it for you. Now if you'll excuse me, I have work to do."

* * *

On the way home, I decided to stop in and see my mother. She was in the courtyard when I arrived, chatting amiably with two young women. As an herbalist, she was often sought out by her neighbors for simple health remedies, love potions, and powders for all manner of situations ranging from curing sadness to attracting luck. It didn't surprise me to see her back in the garden. It was where she always went in times of frustration or grief.

I recognized one of the women, a Colonna servant girl. She waved good-bye, then swept past me without a glance. I found myself transfixed by the other woman, whom I had not seen before. Her black hair was wild, without a hat or net to hold it down. She appeared in her late twenties, with eyes so clear and blue it took everything I had not to stare. She wore a brown dress with red cutouts in the sleeves. The dress was simple, but the material looked fine. She didn't seem to have a servant or a guard with her.

"Giovanni, my son! Your ears must be ringing. I was just telling Isabetta about you!" Caterina waved her hands wildly, as she always did when she was excited. "Giovanni, meet Isabetta Palone. Her father is a very successful silk and wool merchant."

I took Isabetta's hand to kiss it. I had kissed the hands of many women, but never had I felt my heart beat so fast as when my lips touched Isabetta's skin. She smelled like thyme and roses.

"I am pleased to make your acquaintance, Signorina Palone."

Isabetta gave me a lopsided but charming smile. A bloom of color glowed on her cheeks.

"And what were you telling her?" I asked my mother.

"Of your wondrous cooking. Of your humor."

In most situations like this, I would have found any way to change the subject. My mother had often attempted to play matchmaker for me, determined to improve the name of the family. There had been countless other arrangements for me to meet eligible women, but I had spurned them all.

Isabetta's eyes, however, burned through me. They left me with an ache in the tiny space above my heart.

Unnerved, I tore myself away from her gaze and looked to Caterina. "Is Cesare still here?"

She sobered. "No. He returned home to Maria and the girls. He will visit next week."

I felt as though a heavy pot had been taken from my arms. I didn't realize how much I had been dreading seeing Cesare until that moment. If Isabetta had not been there, I would have commented on it, but airing out family grievances in public was not something I wanted to do.

I gazed upon the dark beauty before me. "Isabetta, do you come to see my mother often?"

"Only one other time, when my brother was plagued with a terrible boil on his foot. Your mother's salves are legendary. He was cured in two days. I came today for some herbs to help me sleep better."

"I'm sorry you are not sleeping well. But you came to the right place." I motioned toward the little package in Isabetta's hands. "My mother's sleep remedies are the best you will find."

Caterina took the woman's hands in her own. She gave me a hopeful glance. "Perhaps Giovanni would like to call upon your father soon. Where do you live?"

Isabetta flashed a smile at me. "Our house is on the Via di Ripetta, number twenty-four." She gave a slight curtsy to Caterina, then she winked at me, her hand brushing my arm as she passed by.

"I will send a letter to your father soon," I called after her, a little more awkwardly than I would have liked—her wink had thrown me off guard. She looked over her shoulder and gave me a wave.

Dazzling was the word that came to my mind as she walked out of the courtyard and disappeared around the corner.

"It's about time a beautiful woman caught your fancy." My mother beamed at me. I rolled my eyes at her. "It's about time," she repeated, satisfied, before ushering me inside.

CHAPTER 7

Giovanni

Roma, April 19, 1577

I n the days after Bartolomeo's death, the comet grew larger. At night, it was as bright as the moon, lighting up the sky with a brilliant orange glow, and during the day it seemed like a smaller sun hanging in the heavens. Pope Gregory held a special Mass to ask the Lord for his protection from the comet. Word trickled into the city that pilgrims were making their way to Roma, hopeful their prayers at the city's basilicas would save them from the star they thought was surely going to crash into the earth. Some opportunists sold charms to ward off the comet's evil portents, shiny stones to be sewn into the hems of a doublet or worn about the neck as a safeguard.

I thought of my uncle every time I looked toward the horizon. The comet appeared to be moving with determination. It was a beacon, a sign, I believed, that Bartolomeo, now in the world beyond, had left for Stella.

Who was she?

Deciphering Bartolomeo's journals proved no easy feat. Bellaso's book was overwhelming, with its talk of symbols, countersigns, ciphertext. I wasn't a fast reader to begin with, and Bartolomeo's flowery script was sometimes code enough. When I wasn't reading

The True Way to Write in Cipher, I helped Francesco clean out Bartolomeo's rooms at the Vaticano and finalized some of the last details of my uncle's estate.

Doing so proved to be most fortunate. As I packed up a crate of items from Bartolomeo's desk, I noticed several copper disks scattered in the back of a drawer. I recognized their use only because I had been reading Bellaso's book. I brought them to Francesco's attention.

"Do you know why he had these?"

Francesco took one from my hand and examined it, nodding in recollection. "Ahh, cipher wheels. I remember he told me he had a friend who loved ciphers and taught him how to code. I'm surprised you did not know this about him. Barto could write ciphers with ease. He even helped other people to encode their letters. You remember how Michelangelo was always sure Pope Paul was spying on him when he was painting the altar wall for the Cappella Sistina? He often put his correspondence in code and Barto helped him with the ciphers."

Bartolomeo had often told me Michelangelo's tales of how he was poorly treated by previous popes. The old artist had been a friend to Bartolomeo and had often spent time with him in the kitchen. He was never interested in the food or drink my uncle prepared and only seemed to eat out of necessity. What he did love, however, was commiserating with Bartolomeo about the shortcomings of their papal employer.

I turned the copper piece over in my hands, examining how the letters spun around the wheel. Bellaso had said the cipher was a simple polyalphabetic cipher, which meant there was an alphabet with its letters rearranged that substituted for the real alphabet. Depending on certain parameters of the code and how the wheel turned, an *A* could represent an *R*, for example. Simple substitution had been around for centuries but was often easy to decipher. In recent years, a new sort of polyalphabetic code had been developed, one involving substituting different alphabet sets. While the letters of the alphabets might be the same, they were arranged in a different way within a set. This must be the type of code Bellaso had indicated Bartolomeo used for this first journal. The cipher wheel allowed the coder to alternate alphabet sets with ease.

I slipped one of the cipher wheels into the pouch at my belt, grateful I could abandon the awkward paper model I had started to make the night before.

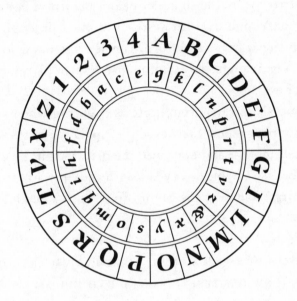

I couldn't return my attention to Bartolomeo's journals until after I had prepared the evening meal for Pope Gregory. I had not planned to go back to work so soon, but Antonio had fallen ill. Perhaps it was being away from the kitchen for so long, but I could not deny I loved to cook, to chop, to taste, to deliver nourishment that tasted divine. If only I did not cook for Gregory.

Before I sat down to read, Bartolomeo's housekeeper, Dea, who had agreed to stay on in my employ, brought me up some homemade mostaccioli cookies and spiced wine to dip them in.

"This is Bartolomeo's recipe, isn't it?" I asked.

She shook her head, a strand of gray hair pulling loose from the braid wrapped around her head. I estimated her to be about forty-five. She had worked for my uncle for as long as I had lived in Roma.

She grinned. "No, the recipe is mine. He asked me if he could use it for his cookbook. He loved them so."

"I had no idea." Bartolomeo had crumbled the biscotti on many dishes. "I love them too, Dea. Thank you."

She patted me on the shoulder before she left, a gesture I took to be as much comfort for her as it was for me. Although she never once complained, her sadness at my uncle's loss was evident. More than once, I had caught her examining an item of Bartolomeo's with tears in her eyes.

The journals did not seem quite as daunting when I sat down again to decipher them. I retrieved the cipher wheel from the desk where I had stored it and examined the disk. I spun the wheel.

With Bellaso's book by my side, I turned my attention to the journal entry I had read the night of my uncle's death and found the lines of code:

SV IX OXLE FT SIT LX MRB FTF HEGE FTR HSOORXRQD B TS
DST DX HISMSGES ITFFTIRVS MRB DXD IXGLX BEX VPD RS
LXDX LX GXMLC CVC OTHIT FTR MRB LIBSSV C HE FTEID
GSG LVFHV DSSV MCRR EBVGA VPD TXXRTFS VAIX S FT DAG
Q TQAIS DBLLDX SX IXGLX

No matter what I did, I couldn't figure out the code using the cipher wheel. After fiddling with it for the better part of an hour, I wondered if perhaps the passage was not written in the simple cipher Bellaso had described, but in the more complex code he himself had devised.

I thumbed through the journals, and it seemed that this type of code was used a bit more sparingly. I wondered if Bartolomeo had decided only to use it for the most important parts of the code. I attempted using the wheel to decipher one of the other, simpler-looking passages, which I was able to do without much issue. It was a few lines describing Bartolomeo's frustration working for Gregory—nothing of import, but I could see why he wouldn't want someone loyal to the pope stumbling across it.

I had to know what the other passage said. I turned to the book again and found the reciprocal table Bellaso insisted upon using. The table laid out different sets of letters to create alternative alphabets for use in the code. Bellaso also said I needed a "cipher key" to break the code. Based on what I had read in his journals, there was only one word I could think of that my uncle might have used: STELLA.

$$I\ D\ V\ Q \quad \begin{matrix} i & o & a & b & c & d & f & g & h & l \\ u & e & m & n & p & q & r & s & t & x \end{matrix}$$

$$O\ F\ E\ R \quad \begin{matrix} i & o & a & b & c & d & f & g & h & l \\ x & u & e & m & n & p & q & r & s & t \end{matrix}$$

$$A\ G\ M\ S \quad \begin{matrix} i & o & a & b & c & d & f & g & h & l \\ t & x & u & e & m & n & p & q & r & s \end{matrix}$$

$$B\ H\ N\ T \quad \begin{matrix} i & o & a & b & c & d & f & g & h & l \\ s & t & x & u & e & m & n & p & q & r \end{matrix}$$

$$C\ L\ P\ X \quad \begin{matrix} i & o & a & b & c & d & f & g & h & l \\ r & s & t & x & u & e & m & n & p & q \end{matrix}$$

The process of decoding was painstakingly slow. First, I wrote out a grid, with the key word repeated over and over on a straight line, followed by the coded words, which Bellaso referred to as "plaintext" under each letter.

S	T	E	L	L	A	S	T	E	L
SV	IX	OXLE	FT	SIT	LX	MRB	FTF	HEGE	FTR
LA	SA	VITA	MA	ORA	SO	CHE	NON	SARA	MAI

The letter of the key word specified which alphabet in the chart to use to decode the individual words. For the first word, I looked at the chart to see where the letter *S* fell and used the AGMS alphabet to decipher the word. *S* mapped to *L* and *V* mapped to *A*. Then I moved to the next word. The letter *T* in Stella corresponded to the BHNT alphabet. *I* became *S* and *X* became *A*. It took me a bit to figure out some of the letters were missing—likely to make the code more difficult, but soon the words became clear:

La sua vita. Ma ora so che non sarà mai possibile. È il mio più profondo rammarico che non saprà mai che io sono suo padre. Non saprà mai che Stella è sua madre. Non saprà nulla dell'amore che abbiamo avuto l'uno per l'altro.

Nessuno lo saprà.

I reread the words in disbelief.

I used to think I would give my journals to Giovanni so he would know the truth of . . . his life. But now I know it is not possible. It is my deepest regret that he will never know I am his father. He will never know Stella is his mother. He will know nothing of the love we had for each other.

No one will.

The room reeled, and I gripped the edge of the desk to steady myself. Bartolomeo Scappi was my father? No, no, that did not make sense. I read the lines again and again, certain I must have misinterpreted the code, but the words were the same.

The journal fell from my hands to my lap. My body suddenly felt heavy. I leaned my neck against the back of the chair and stared at the ceiling, trying to take in everything I had just read. Bartolomeo had doted on me like a son, not a nephew, but I always thought it was because I was his apprentice or because he did not have a son of his own. Who was Stella? And how could she be my mother? Which meant that Caterina was not. My stomach roiled at the thought. Had she lied to me for thirty years?

I turned away so I would not wet the paper in front of me. Questions bombarded my already raw senses. What did Caterina know about my mother? Why wasn't I supposed to know Bartolomeo was my father? And Cesare . . . he had taunted me throughout my childhood, claiming that I wasn't his real brother and cautioning me to sleep with one eye open lest my real parents steal me away in the dead of night. I had always assumed these were typical torments older brothers bestowed upon their younger siblings, but now I wondered, had he known the truth?

I pulled my copy of *L'Opera* down from my shelf. The entire first chapter was a discourse to me, his apprentice, on how to run a kitchen, on how to stock the shelves and whom to hire to make it all run smoothly. I reread the dedication, remembering the moment seven years past when Bartolomeo had given me the first bound volume. The first paragraph of the dedication contained the words I had always treasured. Now they took on new meaning.

I have always considered you like a son, having always set all my mind to making you a knowledgeable, astute expert in the art, so that after my death all my work and practical experience should remain in you.

My grief surfaced anew. This time I cried not for my uncle. I cried for my father. I cried because I had not grown up with the truth.

CHAPTER 8

Giovanni

Roma, April 20, 1577

The next morning, the comet winked at me as I headed to work at the Vaticano. I marveled at its presence—as strange and mysterious as the rest of my life. My whole world had changed overnight. Everything about who I thought I was—all different from what it had been the day before. I had slept poorly, too consumed with the truth of Bartolomeo and the lies he and Caterina had told me.

I didn't expect to spend much time at the Vaticano that day, as my services were little needed under Pope Gregory. Together, Antonio and I gave the kitchen staff the instructions for the afternoon and evening meals. We decided that the clergy would dine on wild boar, cooked in wine, rose vinegar, and sugar, with the snout and ears sliced thinly and served with a choice of mustard or onion sauce. It was one of Bartolomeo's favorite simple dishes.

In preparing the meal, I decided to use my new knife for the first time. I pulled it out of the box to slice up the boar, marveling at the feel of the ebony handle against my skin. A thrill rushed through me as the beautifully patterned blade sliced through the meat. It made me wonder—when had the blade been forged? I had the feeling that this knife had cut through the flesh of thousands of creatures and had

83

passed through the hands of many dozens of chefs, and yet it seemed as sharp and perfect as if it had been made yesterday. I lost all sense of time, and when I had finished carving the beast, I felt a profound disappointment; the task had been so pleasurable. I looked down at the carcass and was shocked at the precision of the cuts. No wonder Bartolomeo never let a soul near this knife. Reluctantly, I packed it up, slipping it into my bag to bring home. I determined to never leave it overnight at the Vaticano.

On my way out of the kitchen, preparing to head into Roma to visit Caterina, I saw Francesco pass in the hall.

"Wait!" I caught up with him and took the scalco by the arm.

"*Buon giorno*, Giovanni. Are you doing well?"

No matter how long we had known each other, Francesco always maintained a sense of protocol—manners and propriety were the backbone of his being.

"As well as I can be."

The scalco nodded. "Me too. As well as I can be."

"May I speak with you?"

When Francesco nodded his consent, I led him to Bartolomeo's studiolo, where we would not be overheard.

"Francesco, as my friend, you must be forthcoming with me. Did my uncle tell you why he left me so much money?"

Francesco ran a hand over his balding pate. "He did not."

I stared at him. Francesco was never one to lie, and yet there was something the man was not saying.

"Please, Francesco, it's important. Tell me."

The scalco's shoulders drooped, as though he was about to be relieved of a burden.

"*Dimmi*," I pressed.

"He never told me why he left you the money," he repeated. "But I think I know."

I wanted to shake the scalco, but instead I took a deep breath and waited. Patience might have been Bartolomeo's virtue, but it was not mine.

Francesco's eyes narrowed. "Are you his son?"

I hesitated, but it was enough to provide him with the answer.

Francesco placed a hand on my shoulder. "You look just like him," he said. "However, that could have been explained because you were Caterina's son. But when we worked on the will he said something that made me wonder."

"What?"

"I asked him if he thought Cesare might be upset at the disparity in the inheritance. He muttered something about Cesare only being a nephew and it was of no matter. I thought it odd, but he was in a mood and I did not think it prudent to mention that you too were only a nephew."

He must have seen how rattled I was.

"Rest easy," he said. "I will never speak of this again unless you desire it."

I fell into the hard Dante chair behind me, a relic from the old Vaticano kitchen before Pope Julius had everything rebuilt. I had sat in that chair hundreds of times when I talked with Bartolomeo, my hands rubbing the ebony wood of its arms, my feet tucked back against the X shape of its legs. I thought of the journals I had retrieved from this very room and then recalled the woman with the bouquet of carnations at the funeral. I described her to Francesco.

"It is hard to say who she might be, Giovanni. Bartolomeo had many ladies who fell at his feet. There are any number of women who have harbored love for him over the years."

"He knew how to charm everyone, it is true."

Francesco sat on a nearby bench. His eyes glistened. "I knew many, men and women alike, who would have followed him to the ends of the earth." He looked out the little studiolo window and I followed his gaze across the garden. Bartolomeo had loved that garden. When the world became too chaotic, he would sometimes disappear for a short while—never more than a quarter of an hour—and I often saw him walking among the green paths.

After many moments, Francesco broke the silence. "Do you need help in the kitchen?"

I snorted. "They don't need me. It's all the same with this pope." Francesco didn't say anything. It must have shocked him to hear those words as much as it did me to speak them. I know he probably felt as I did, but never had I voiced those words aloud to anyone other than Bartolomeo. I had never been one to shirk my duties. Aside from the time I took to nurse Bartolomeo, I had only missed two days of work in the last ten years of my life. To leave my post to another had always seemed impossible, but suddenly the idea of spending time in the kitchen—without Bartolomeo—turned my stomach.

"I am not sure I want to be cuoco segreto," I announced.

Francesco's eyes widened, but still he did not speak.

"Now, with the inheritance, I do not need to work. Barto—" I faltered at the sound of his name on my tongue, but continued. "Bartolomeo has seen to it. I never presided over as many banquets as he did or saw the grandeur of his most incredible feasts. I loved the times we cooked outside the Vaticano. I truly did. But while I love the look on the nobles' faces when they taste my food, and the sound of a prince or a cardinale clapping his hands at the beginning of a meal, I must admit, I do not love it enough to be a chef."

Francesco reached for the bottle. I handed it to him, and the scalco drank the last swallow. "That is where you and I differ, Giovanni. It is where you and your uncle differ. For he and I, the service has always been in our bones and our blood. There was nothing else for Barto and nothing else for me. Work is everything we are." He shook his head, as though he pitied himself.

It dawned on me what my friend was saying. "You do not need to work, do you?"

Francesco gave me a rueful smile. "No, I have never needed to work."

I was incredulous. "Then why?"

"Because I love what I do. I'm in a position of extraordinary power, Giovanni. I keep the Vaticano running! And I have no one to go home to. But that is of no matter. Do not decide yet, Gio. I think that the food is in your soul. To be away from the kitchens for long might be even worse for you. Take some time. I will help Antonio as needed. Do what you need to so your heart is unburdened."

*   *   *

Before I left the Vaticano, I went to the papal notary to see if he could help me arrange the change of my name, from Brioschi to Scappi. The world would believe it was to honor my uncle, not that I was taking on the name to which I should have been born.

My mother's—no, Caterina's—house was a twenty-minute walk from the Vaticano, passing over the Aelian Bridge and down into the crowded district of homes, workshops, and markets surrounding the Pantheon. It was a beautiful day, and ordinarily I welcomed the walk, relishing the sight of vendors hawking their wares in the streets, the sound of their carts scraping along the cobbles, and even the smell of manure left behind by flocks of sheep shepherded through the city on their way to the market to be sheared. On this day, however, I was surprised at the anger welling up inside of me. My whole life had been a lie, and the woman I had always called Mother had helped to preserve that lie.

Not far from her house I slowed. A crowd of fifty or sixty people had gathered in the *piazzetta* a short distance from her front door. A portly Dominican friar, his bald pate shining, held them in his thrall, his voice commanding.

He reached his hands up to the sky. "The scourge is nearly upon us! God willed the fiery comet above to warn us all. God has prepared a great dinner for all Italy, but all the dishes are bitter. I have given only the salad, which was a bit of bitter lettuce. Understand me well, Romans: all the other dishes are yet to come, and they are all bitter and plentiful, for it is a grand dinner. Italy is now on the verge of her tribulations. Oh, Italy, and princes of Italy, and prelates of the church, the wrath of God is upon you, and you have no remedy but to be converted! And it will come about not because you do not know how things have been ordered. Oh princes of Italy, do penance while the sword is not yet out of its sheath, and while it is not yet bloodied, flee from Roma! Flee from Roma, that is, flee from sin through penitence and flee from the wicked! If you do not, God will burn us all!"

The priest pointed to the sky, and all eyes turned to the bright comet streaking across their vision. It burned with a stunning white blue nucleus and a shimmering tail of silver and red. It was still small, but larger than the day I first saw it, the day of Bartolomeo's funeral. The crowd murmured exclamations of fear.

I did not feel afraid when I gazed at the comet. I felt only the warmth of Bartolomeo's light. I could not think of the orb as anything other than his presence shining into our world from the one above. I thought of the type of salad he might have served—it might have been bitter chicory, true, but sweetened with fennel and pea shoots, drizzled with a bit of oil and vinegar, mixed with some sugar and spices, and topped with a little pepper or cheese.

"Heed my words! It will burn through you, tearing everything you know apart!" I turned away from the priest, chuckling at his fearmongering.

My amusement soured quickly as Caterina's house—my own childhood home—came into view. I was still unsure about the conversation I intended to have with her. The notion that she was my aunt was still foreign and I knew not how it would color my words.

When she opened the door and attempted to hug and kiss me, I stepped backward to avoid the embrace.

She knitted her brow. "You have something to say to me." She wiped her hands on her apron. "Come inside."

I followed her to the sitting room, my stomach sour as I thought of the confrontation ahead of me.

Caterina poured wine into a pair of carved glass goblets and handed one to me. She sat down and took a long draft.

I put the goblet down without drinking. I walked to the window and stared through the pane. The pale blue glass distorted what I could see, but I wasn't focused on the view.

"Talk to me, son."

"I'm not your son." I heard her intake of breath, but didn't turn around. I couldn't bear to look at her.

After a moment, she replied. "No, Giovanni, you are not a son by blood. But in my heart, you are my true son."

I stared blankly out the window.

The silence was thick. Finally, she spoke again. "How did you find out?"

I thought about the journals and letters hidden in the chest in my room.

"In some of the paperwork Barto left behind," I replied.

She sighed again, and much to my relief, she didn't ask more. Instead she rose and came to me, putting her hands on my shoulder. I shrugged them off and spun away.

"You want to find your mother." Her eyes were rimmed with tears.

"Yes. And I want to know why Bartolomeo lied. Why did you lie?" I could not help the level of my voice or the anger lacing my words, which flowed too fast, like a sack of grain accidentally slashed open, spilling across the floor.

"Oh, oh, Gio!" Caterina gathered me in her arms, ignoring my halfhearted struggle. She held me and together we cried, my head buried in the tangle of her hair.

She pulled away. "Come, Giovanni. Sit and I will tell you all I know."

She led me to the little table where she and Bartolomeo would often play cards. I sat down across from her and she reached over to hold my hands. Her fingers were warm and her touch, despite all my mixed emotion, was comforting.

"I always feared this day would come, Gio. When Barto died, I thought, finally, I would not have to worry. His secret would go with him to the grave. I never thought he would have a change of heart at the end."

I took a deep breath. I could not tell Caterina that Bartolomeo had never intended to tell me. It was clear that she had never intended to tell me either.

"It was a month after I lost Nazeo. Cesare was not quite four years old. We had only recently moved from Firenze to our little house in Monterotondo, and I wasn't acquainted with a soul save for a couple of neighbors and the midwife who had helped me give birth to a stillborn. Bartolomeo came to make sure I was all right, but then left abruptly, saying he had to be somewhere, that it was an emergency. Between his swift departure and losing Nazeo and my baby, my heart was utterly broken. So broken I thought of taking Cesare to an orphanage and hanging myself in the woods."

I couldn't believe my ears. Caterina had always been devout. Suicide was an invitation directly to the devil's side.

"Fortunately for us all, Barto showed up before I could muster the courage to carry out my miserable plan. He arrived in the first hours of morning. You were swaddled and strapped to his chest, not more than a couple of days old.

"He had ridden from Lord knows where to deliver you to me. He refused to tell me anything except that you were his son and that your life was in jeopardy.

"I remember his words clear as yesterday. *'You can never tell this boy that I am his father. We may all lose our lives if anyone suspects the truth.'*"

I pulled my hands away. None of this made sense. "What about my mother?"

Caterina shook her head. "I know nothing of her. I tried many times over the years to get Barto to tell me, but he would not say a word. Not her name, not her address, nor her station. I couldn't even get him to tell me the story of how he came to bring you to me. *'You are his mother now,'* is all he would tell me.

"You saved my life, Gio. You gave me purpose at a time when I thought I would be overwhelmed by loss. I threw myself into being your mother. Nursing you was second nature. Barto provided for you and Cesare. He was very paranoid about anyone finding out and he moved us to Tivoli within the week so the few people I knew would not wonder how my stillborn became a kicking child."

I squirmed in my chair, trying to take in this new information. "Cesare knew I wasn't his brother."

Caterina nodded. "Barto and I immediately began planting an elaborate web of untrue memories for him, telling him you were his brother, that the other baby had not died. We gave you the birthday of my stillborn son, not your own. I hated myself for lying to him. Still, I think he always knew. After you arrived, he became an angry, impossible child."

"At least I know why he despises me so. He suspects I'm not your real son. I never truly belonged."

Caterina clasped his hands again. "Never say that, Gio! You are my son in every way except by my womb. In every way."

She meant what she said. Yet things had changed, perhaps irrevocably.

"I love you, my dear Gio. My sweet Gio."

I stood to leave, unable to hear more. I pecked Caterina on the cheek and refrained from saying what I really wanted to, that I still needed time to understand the injustice—they had hidden the truth from me for thirty years.

Instead I said, "I love you too, Mamma."

CHAPTER 9

Giovanni

I had almost reached home when Salvi came racing up to me. "Maestro, Maestro!" He flapped a letter in the air. "It's from Signor Palone. He made me wait while he wrote out his reply to you."

My heart did a somersault. A note from Isabetta's father! "Thank you, Salvi." I took the letter, not wanting him to see how excited I was to open it. "Were there any other messages?"

The boy nodded his head. "Aye. Madonna Farnese wants you to come for dinner this week. Valentino told me that you must come; he will not accept no for an answer. I saw them at the big palazzo Chigi while I was delivering something for Francesco."

The Chigi family had two palazzi in Roma, and if it was the biggest one, not far from the Pantheon, they must have been visiting her family. Serafina and Valentino lived in a smaller palazzo on the opposite side of the Tevere, just south of the Vaticano.

"Please tell Madonna Farnese I would be happy to join them on the morrow."

Salvi agreed and sped off through the crowd. I watched the blue of his coat as it weaved in and among the passersby, marveling that he was now my charge.

I peered at the note, at the careful folds and the white wax seal with a solid circle in the center, a ball, the symbol of the family. I ran my thumb across the seal, then slid a finger between the folds to break the wax.

To the most excellent Signor Brioschi,

My daughter, Isabetta, says you are interested in visiting, which I take to mean you might want to court her. She tells me you are well mannered and of good stock. This is appropriate, as I will not marry her to someone who does not know how to conduct himself.

I must be candid and tell you that while my daughter possesses the best qualities a wife can have, she cannot bear you children. Her womb is as dry as a desert. Her previous husband divorced her for this.

If children are not important to you and you are looking purely for a wifely companion, I will entertain your request to meet. Break bread with us in four days hence.

May the great and good God preserve you,
Rolando Palone

Only a few days ago this note would have meant something different. I would have been considering how to continue the Brioschi name. A wife who could bear me children was something I always assumed was in my future. Now it mattered not that Isabetta was barren. If Salvi took the Scappi name as I did, and he had children, it would live on.

*   *   *

I was readying myself to sleep when I remembered the line of code in the first journal. It was the line that had prompted me to seek out help from first Avito, then Bellaso. I dug into the chest where I kept the journals, looking for the correct volume.

I found it and flipped it open to the page.

~ FDSMEAEMLDNGENPSGILAELDLI ~

The lines after it were considerably longer, many letters strung together in one long block. I picked up the cipher wheel and returned to the book for instructions.

As before, I needed a key to know how to best align the cipher disk. It must be Stella.

To begin, I placed the letter *A* of the small ring on the cipher disk below the *S* of the larger ring to designate the alphabet to be used. Sure enough, my suspicion proved right, as I was able to make out the first word: *Giacomo*. I painstakingly copied each letter.

When I finally looked to see what the decoded line spelled, I froze.

Giacomo Crispo is about to die.

I could not believe the words before me. What did these words mean? Did he know of someone who planned to kill the man? Or did my father intend to kill the Duke of the Archipelago? No, that couldn't be it. The idea of my big, jolly uncle—no, my father—killing anything other than an animal for the kitchen was unthinkable. He adored people, even down to the lowliest servant on his staff. I had a very hard time believing such a notion. My father wanted to take the Duke's life?

Regardless, I was equally baffled that Bartolomeo had committed these words to paper, even in code. If anyone at the Grimani palazzo had found the journal, they, like me, would have read enough of the undeciphered part of the journal to easily surmise that his cipher key—his words, his world—revolved around Stella.

I could only think that when Bartolomeo wrote those words he was young and did not think these things through. At this point in his journal writing, he was twenty years old. Diaries had been in vogue in the last few decades, but this type of confession was the kind that would leave a man hanging by a rope if found.

I tried to imagine him then. He must have thought all his deeds would be lauded in some later life. But Bartolomeo had been right: his journals were dangerous. Before I took the decoded pages to the flame, I read them through once again, committing every piece of the story to memory.

*　　*　　*

The next day I followed the road along the winding Tevere to see Serafina and Valentino. They, along with Serafina's second husband, Carlo Farnese, lived in the sprawling Chigi palazzo a short distance across the river from the bustling Campo dei Fiori where the tailors, hatters, crossbow sellers, and key makers all plied their trade. After the death of her previous husband, Ludovico Pio da Carpi, in 1547, Serafina moved into her late uncle Agostino Chigi's luxurious summer villa, decorated with frescoes by the famous Raffaello. Agostino's brother and Serafina's cousin, Lorenzo, had burned through the family fortune, and it was rumored that without her assistance, the beautiful villa would have been sold long before. Carlo had joined Serafina there when they married. Carlo's nephew, the esteemed Cardinale Alessandro Farnese, had been pestering Serafina to let him buy the villa. He intended to build a bridge from his monstrous Palazzo Farnese near the Campo Fiori to the beautiful house, where he wanted to entertain guests in the summer. Serafina refused to sell.

I was grateful she held firm. I loved visiting the beautiful palazzo where they lived. And I was especially glad at the timing of their invitation. Reading the journals and going through Bartolomeo's belongings had taken an emotional toll, and until I arrived on their doorstep I had not realized just how much I needed the company of friends.

The sun was low in the sky, shining bright over the terra-cotta rooftops when I arrived. "Madonna Farnese is readying herself for dinner," the scalco told me as he led me across the courtyard and through a tall wooden door opening to the garden, a long expanse of land sloping toward the Tevere river. "I will take you to Signor Carpi now."

Valentino reclined on one of several cushioned chairs under a tree overlooking the river, staring at the blazing comet in the sky. He rose when the scalco announced me.

"Come, Gio, have a seat! Have some wine and tell me how you fare." I did as he asked, and the scalco poured me a glass of wine from the pitcher sitting on a small table nearby.

When he was gone, Valentino lifted his glass toward mine. "To Bartolomeo," he said, his face solemn and his brown eyes dark. "May the Lord watch over his soul."

I raised my glass, my heart still full of pain.

"He was a good man, Giovanni. I was not prepared to lose him. I wish I had an uncle half as good as Bartolomeo. No . . ." He paused and gazed toward the river. His voice quieted. "I wish I had had a father half as good as he was."

A father half as good. I willed myself to remain impassive. Valentino had been an infant when his father, Ludovico Pio da Carpi, had died.

"I thought you got on well with Signor Farnese."

He stared in the direction of the Tevere. The water upon which he gazed was aglow with the shimmer of sunset. To the north the shining star appeared bigger and redder than it had even a day ago.

"He has always been kind to me, but there is a distance between us, and always has been. I envied the relationship you had with your uncle. He was like a father to you. I never felt like I had that with anyone."

Like a father.

"Well, perhaps in some way I thought of him as the closest thing I had to a father. He was always kinder to me than any other man in my life. He gave me advice the way a father would give a son," he continued.

"You are right. He was a good man," I replied, unsure how to react. Valentino was not one to show sadness or regret.

I took a deep breath. "I learned something important about Bartolomeo."

Valentino took a sip of wine. "What?"

"He had boxes of journals he wanted me to burn." My face grew hot.

"Did you?"

"I-I couldn't . . ."

I buried my face in my hands, empty at the loss of my father, my mentor. Would this hole in my heart ever mend?

After a moment, I felt Valentino's hand on my shoulder. He had pulled his chair close. I sat up and wiped my face on my sleeve.

"You did what I would have done. And what Bartolomeo would have done. Do you think for a moment he could resist such a temptation were it placed in his own hands?"

The thought gave me comfort. Bartolomeo was never one to follow the rules. He was always the one making them.

"I take it you found something in them, or you would have burned them by now."

"I did."

I paused. I desperately wanted to tell my friend, but at the same time I wasn't sure I should surrender such a secret.

"Dimmi, Gio. We have never kept things from each other."

He was right, we had not.

I sighed. "Bartolomeo Scappi is my father."

"*Madonna!*" Valentino exclaimed, then checked to see if any of the servants had heard. It was the kind of loud exclamation that would send a scalco to try to make a situation right. When no one appeared, he lowered his voice. "Barto is your father? Dio mio! That explains so much."

"What do you mean?" I asked.

Valentino stood and went to stand next to the tree. He shook his head, incredulous.

"Val, what do you mean, that explains so much?"

He began to pace, a habit that had always helped him think. "Looking back, I can see all those moments more clearly: how he doted on you, how he bragged about you to others, how he dedicated his cookbook to you."

He stopped and stared at me, concern darkening his eyes. "Who else knows?"

"Francesco guessed, but we have not discussed it. And Caterina."

"If Caterina is not your mother, who is?"

I shook my head.

Val poured himself another glass of wine and downed half of it. He offered me the pitcher and watched me pour.

"Did he write about your mother?"

I drank my wine. "I think the woman he writes about is my mother, but I am not sure. Most of the important details are in code. It is slow work to decipher them."

"Dio mio. Dio mio."

Panic seized me. "Val, you can't tell anyone. Not a soul. There is a woman, of high nobility, that Bartolomeo describes in his journals that I think might be my mother. I think she may still be alive. But Bartolomeo told Francesco that if others found out the truth it would be dangerous. Please promise me, Val, no one will know."

Valentino pulled an item from a small slit in the edge of his doublet. "We will swear on this. I have always carried it for luck."

It was a little wooden pig no bigger than the tip of a finger. I recognized it immediately. Bartolomeo had carved one for each of us when we were boys. I had lost mine long ago. I was shocked to see my friend still had his. He held it in his left hand and raised his right.

"I swear, Giovanni, on the name of Bartolomeo Scappi, I will keep your secret safe until you release me from this oath or until I am in the grave, whichever may come first."

We gripped hands and hugged. I had always been grateful for our friendship, and now I was even more sure of the trust I had placed in him.

"She was a principessa?" he asked when we had settled back into our chairs and taken up our goblets once more. While there were no kings and queens in Italy, the sons and daughters of nobility were referred to by princely titles.

"Sì."

He shook his head. "Barto was right. It must be kept quiet. If this woman made her husband a cuckold by bedding someone so far below her station . . . *Madonna!* Whoever your mother is, Giovanni, this information would end in her ruin."

Ruin was a mild word to describe the revenge for the offense. Even decades after the fact, bringing such shame upon the family could lead to death—it would be her husband's right to decide such punishment. At the very least, she would be cast out and dispatched to a nunnery where she would have little contact with her family and loved ones. The convents were full of such unfortunate women.

"And danger for me if there is vengeance to be paid . . ." The family might come for me, and for Caterina, for Cesare and his family. People often took justice into their own hands when it came to protecting their family's reputation. If that family was influential, the powers of authority turned the other cheek.

Val understood.

"Are you going to look for her?" he asked.

I drained my glass. "I must."

I knew this as certainly as I knew the proper way to carve a capon.

"And if you find her?"

I had no idea what I would do, what I would say, or how I would relate to the woman who birthed me. "I know not. But I have to find out who she is."

A woman's melodious voice caught us off guard, causing us both to jump.

"There you are!"

Serafina appeared, her maid following a few paces behind. She wore a gown the color of the sky, adorned with gold and silver embroidery. Her gray hair was braided with ribbons and pinned up in the crowning style popular among women.

She hugged me tight. When she pulled away, she appeared moved but shed no tears.

"Come now, up to the loggia. Let us drink to the memory of Bartolomeo Scappi. Let us dine and remember all the times he made us smile." She held out her hand in the direction of the house where a long table had been set.

Valentino clapped his hand down on my back. "*Mia madre* is right, Gio. Let us celebrate the life of your uncle. What a man he was!"

*   *   *

I had always loved dining with Valentino and Serafina. The grand loggia of Cupid and Psyche that welcomed visitors into the house exhibited a view of the sprawling gardens. The famous Raffaello had painted the loggia ceiling with frescoes of the mythological figures shortly before Serafina's uncle Agostino Chigi died, nearly sixty years before. Raffaello had also decorated the magnificent lodge deep in the garden. The lodge had an ornately painted pavilion covering a natural basin of water that flowed in from the Tevere, where guests could once bathe among the fish. The lodge, now in disrepair, was rumored to have been the place of many exorbitant banquets. Bartolomeo told me the famous story of a dinner in which Agostino, an eccentric who reveled in luxury, showed off his enormous wealth by serving the meal on gold plates with gold utensils and then throwing them all into the Tevere. Later, and unbeknownst to the guests, he had the servants gather up the nets set out to catch the tableware that would have been lost to the river.

As I sat in the loggia, beneath the beautiful paintings of the great master, looking out toward the darkening garden, the sunset waning and that errant star in the sky bright with its sparkling tail, I felt a sense of wonder. How many people had ever seen such beauty?

The arrival of the food snapped me out of my reverie. Like many chefs in Roma, the Farnese chef had taken much inspiration from Bartolomeo over the years. The first course included slices of Parmesan; olives from Tivoli; cherries in little gilded cups; a salad of sliced citron with sugar and rosewater; veal rolls dredged in coriander, spit-roasted, then topped with raisins soaked in wine; peas in the pod served with pepper and vinegar; salted buffalo tongue, cooked, then sliced and served cold with lemon; a delicate soup of cheese and egg yolks poured over roasted pigeon; blancmange white as snow and sprinkled with sugar; roasted artichokes and pine nut tourtes.

I found both comfort and sadness in every dish. The conversation filled me with much of the same.

"I think that our cook is trying to impress you, now that you are cuoco segreto for Pope Gregory." Serafina waved her hand at the bounty before us.

I was surprised at the idea that I was worth impressing. But I was impressed. "Every bite is exquisite. Please convey that to him."

"I'll let him know," Valentino confirmed.

"Your uncle was an inspiration to me," Serafina said, raising a spoonful of blancmange to her lips.

"How so?"

She swallowed. "Bartolomeo was an artist, a magician. His genius was boundless. He deserves to be celebrated as much as the artists my uncle surrounded himself with when he was alive." She gestured to the frescoes adorning the ceiling above us. "Every time I ate one of his meals I was transported. He understood flavor and color and emotion."

"There will never be another like him," Valentino said, his voice quiet.

"No," Serafina agreed. "There will not."

The conversation turned to Roma and the problems of the papacy.

"I hear Pope Gregory wants to change the calendar, to help it match the stars more accurately," Valentino said.

"Yes. We can't have Easter falling later and later every year," I joked. "Christ might get confused on what day to return."

It was blasphemous, but they laughed, and we raised a glass in toast to the church.

"What is this world coming to?" Serafina asked, shaking her head.

I observed the bright star ablaze in the sky and wondered that myself.

CHAPTER 10

Scappi

Venezia, August 1528

M y *stellina, I swear, he will not take you to Naxos.* Bartolomeo repeated the phrase as he hurried over the bridges of Venezia to his uncle Romeo's apothecary at the far end of the Cannaregio. It had been two days since he'd seen Stella. When they had last parted, a plan had formed in his mind. He lied to the maestro, claiming an imaginary aunt was ill and needed help, which bought him an afternoon away from the kitchen.

It was a fair walk to the little shop, so Bartolomeo did not often see his father's younger brother. All the Scappi children had trained in the herbal arts, a long family tradition. A short time after Bartolomeo was born, it became evident that there wasn't enough room in Dumenza for two apothecaries, so his uncle, Romeo, made his way to Venezia while Bartolomeo's father remained in Dumenza to head the family business. When Bartolomeo had declared he wanted to become a chef, it was Romeo who had helped him secure his apprenticeship with the maestro of the Palazzo Grimani.

Romeo's shop sat in the heart of a vibrant neighborhood and sold a variety of remedies and herbs, cosmetics, exotic spices and sugars, wine and liqueurs, even ink and paper. But his specialty was pigments.

The shop was well known as the place where Tiziano Vicellio came to purchase the colors that graced masterpieces all over Venezia.

Romeo greeted Bartolomeo with a bearlike hug, then ushered him in and offered him a glass of wine. He had always doted on his nephew and took great delight in showing him his latest acquisitions, especially the poisons. Bartolomeo had hoped for such a reception.

Romeo opened a small box and held up one of the vials contained within. "I acquired something special this week, Barto. This, my boy, is liquid death. Of this substance, you must tell no one."

Bartolomeo's ears perked up. He had come for poison, but he wasn't sure what type would best suit his purpose—arsenic might do the trick, or perhaps belladonna—and he couldn't easily ask his uncle what he thought of the matter. "What is it? How is it different from arsenic?"

Romeo was gleeful, his eyes shining with excitement. "It comes from leaves the natives smoke in the New World. It's called *tabaco*. It was brought to me by one of my contacts from Spain. An herbalist there discovered how to press the oils from the leaves of the plant. I purchased it at a heavy cost. Those damned pirates know how to bleed a man!"

"What does it do?"

"That's just it, Barto! What makes it unusual is that not only is it colorless and odorless, it's absorbed through the skin. With just a small quantity, fifteen or twenty minutes of contact with the flesh is enough to kill a man."

Bartolomeo's heart beat a little bit faster. He had been trying to figure out how to administer a general poison such as arsenic to the Duke of the Archipelago. If poison appeared in a dish, it would be easy to discern who might have tainted the food or wine—the person who cooked the dish, the server, or a person sitting on either side of the victim. Bartolomeo could not afford to have any fingers pointed at him. He thought he would have to be creative with how the poison found its way into the duke's food or wine, but this presented a new, better opportunity.

He stared at the vial.

"What are the symptoms?" he asked, hoping his voice did not quaver.

"I tested it on one of my rats. I put a little cloth in the bottom of its cage, and before long it was vomiting, convulsing, and panting, then it died."

Romeo had always kept a half dozen or so rats in the cellar for his experimentation. Bartolomeo had never liked to visit them.

The door to the apothecary creaked and one of the little bells tied to its doorknob rang out. "Romeo, Romeo!" It was a woman with a thin, high-pitched voice.

"Forgive me, boy, I must attend to my shop. It should not be long. Signora Bertelli needs a new tincture for love, I suspect." Romeo put the cover on the box, tucked it away on a bottom shelf, and walked to the front of the store.

Bartolomeo could not believe his luck. The vials of poison from the New World were the same as those that held his uncle's arsenic. And they even looked the same. Bartolomeo suspected the viscosity might vary a little, but with the brown tint of the bottles it would be a while before the difference would be discovered. And with that thought, he took one of the many bottles of arsenic off the shelf and swapped it with one in the box. He placed the vial of tabaco gently into the little leather pouch he had brought with him, knotting the closure tight before slipping it into his purse and tucking it into his pants. He had a fleeting vision of tripping and breaking the vial, the fluid seeping out into his clothing and skin. Or what might happen if his uncle touched the tabaco, thinking it was arsenic? Or one of his clients? No, no, that wouldn't happen, he rationalized. His uncle was always extremely careful with his poisons. He rubbed his palms against his breeches, imagining the direst of consequences. He almost replaced the vial, then thought again of the pirate who was going to marry Stella. He pushed the thought away.

When his uncle returned, Bartolomeo was sipping his wine and tracing the whorls of the wood table at which he sat. He hoped his hands did not shake when he picked up his glass.

*　　*　　*

The night before the wedding, Bartolomeo went to bed at an hour long past midnight. As soon as dawn broke, the staff would be up to finish the feast preparations. Bartolomeo lay awake, waiting until the other kitchen servants were all snoring or breathing heavily. Then he stole down to the cellar where he wrote. Except this time, he did not write. He put the candle on the table and found the pouch with the poison vial. Then he extracted several napkins he had tucked away inside the folds of his shirt and spread one of them on the floor. Using a stone, he made a thin mark that would not be noticed by anyone in the corner to help him identify the tainted napkin. He poured the poison generously over the cloth. He was careful not to splash any drops on his fingers or hands, but had brought a pouch of water in his bag in case he needed to wash up. He was not going to take any risk of prolonged contact with the liquid death.

In the morning, before the cock crowed, Bartolomeo stole into the dining hall and replaced the groom's napkin. The table had been set the night before, so nothing appeared out of place. He then discarded both the poison vial and the gloves he used to fold and set the napkin by slipping them into a pouch, weighting them down with a stone, then dropping them into the waters of a side canal. By the time the maestro arrived an hour later to direct the kitchen, Bartolomeo was already making the peacock sauce, grinding up the Milanese almonds with currants, hard-boiled egg yolks, and chicken livers.

Late that morning, Bartolomeo heard the wedding bells chime across Venezia, but he did not look up from his work. He tried not to think of the kiss the grizzled pirate would place upon his lover's lips to seal the vows. He continued to stuff the guinea pigs on the tray before him, readying them for the pies.

At long last, the wedding party arrived for the Grimani feast. Bartolomeo could hear their laughter ringing through the halls, hundreds of tittering women and their posturing highborn husbands. Having worked hard for many hours, he knew the maestro would allow him to shift to the lighter work of serving foods from the *credenza* inside the ballroom. The monstrous sideboard held all the cold foods and the many elaborate maiolica plates used to serve the dishes.

Bartolomeo stole a glance at the high table where Stella and Giacomo Crispo sat. A lump formed in his throat. Stella was radiant in a rose-colored gown embroidered with hundreds of pearls. She wore a surcoat of dark red velvet, also lined with pearls, and woven with gold thread into elaborate patterns across the fabric. A veil of gold had been pulled back to reveal her face. She was breathtaking, although she did not smile. When she caught Bartolomeo's eye he nodded to her. And there, to her left, lay the napkin, a silent invitation to the afterlife. Bartolomeo swallowed. He had never believed much in God, but what if he was wrong? What if God did strike him down? What if he sent a bolt of lightning down to burn him on the spot? Then, the horrible thought—what if Stella picked up the napkin? She knew that he had a plan, but not the mechanism. Bartolomeo's stomach lurched at the thought of her expiring before his eyes. Was it too late to retrieve the poisonous cloth?

He took a step in that direction but stopped when Crispo turned his face toward Bartolomeo, his attention focused on a servant asking about his choice of wine. Crispo had harsh features, including a long scar crossing his hooked nose and one cheek, and tiny eyes set too close together, so that he squinted when he smiled, giving him a look of malice. His hair and beard were salt and peppered, making him look more like a man that could be Stella's grandfather than her husband. Bartolomeo imagined the duke kissing Stella and anger overtook the fear within him. Even if God was real, he decided, he would court hell before he let Giacomo Crispo lay another finger on the woman he loved.

Stella looked miserable. She stared at her plate of food, her face devoid of any joy.

Soon, he wanted to tell her. *Fear not, stellina, he will not take you to Naxos. Soon.*

It was soon. A few moments later, the groom tucked his napkin into his collar so it rested against the skin of his neck and throat. He cut into the elaborate pie in front of him and ate with relish. On occasion, he wiped his lips with the edge of the napkin, and with each swipe Bartolomeo's heart leapt inside him. It would not be long. He readied himself for the chaos about to ensue.

Fifteen minutes into the banquet Crispo paled. Bartolomeo noticed the change and moved to be farther away from the table, earnestly taking up several sideboard dishes and delivering them to the tables of other diners.

From the back of the room, he saw Crispo remove the napkin from around his neck and begin to wipe the sweat from his brow. It was not five minutes later when Crispo began clutching his napkin in what appeared to be discomfort. Scappi quickly turned his gaze away and busied himself serving. He only looked up again when he heard the thud as the duke fell out of his chair, and he turned just in time to hear Stella scream. Another man yelled that the duke was having a fit and to find a doctor, but within a quarter of an hour, before one could be found, he was declared dead.

"It was the guinea pig pie!" Madonna Grimani screeched. "I know it! The pie! Something was wrong with the pie!"

Bartolomeo's mouth went dry. The pie had been deemed safe by

Cardinale Grimani's tester before it was served—but what if they decided it didn't matter? He had made the pies; he could hang. He returned to the kitchen in terror.

When he arrived, the maestro instructed him to go back out to gather up all the servants and send them to the kitchen. He wandered through the hysterical throngs of courtiers and gave the order to the servants to check in with the maestro, his heart beating louder and louder as he got close to the table where the wedding party had sat. He was surprised to see that they had already moved Crispo's body and all the food and wine—likely to test it. No one stood nearby. He gathered his courage and drew close, picking up napkins to give the impression of tidying as he went. Then he saw it, the napkin on the arm of the chair where Crispo had sat. He willed himself to keep his eyes on his task, to make it look like he was doing his job, not looking around to see if anyone was watching. Holding another napkin in his hand, he plucked the poison napkin off the chair and tucked it into the folds of another, then kept moving, picking up other napkins as he made his way back to the kitchen. Then, he did check to see if anyone was looking before hastily stashing the cloth on the bottom shelf of a bench. After that, his heart pounding and a sweat on his brow, he went to wait with the rest of the staff to find out what their fate might be.

In short time, he was whisked away to a room on the second floor of the palazzo where a squat *capo dei sèstiere* interrogated him for almost two hours. "You made the guinea pig pies?"

"I made the stuffing for the pies, but Bruno made the pastry, Stagio cleaned the pigs, and Piero assembled them." Bartolomeo knew his voice trembled, but hoped it would be seen as nervousness in the situation rather than a sign of his guilt.

The captain was nose to nose with Bartolomeo, his breath stinking of last night's drink. "Where did you get the poison you put into the pie?"

"Puh-poison?" Bartolomeo asked. He dove deep down inside himself to conjure up the semblance of innocence. "I would never! I don't even know the people I made the pies for!"

"Who paid you? Was it wolfbane? Was it arsenic? Did the house of Mocenigo put you up to this? The Foscari?"

The questions came at him as fast as pepper from a mill.

"Tell me, boy, or I'll have your fingernails ripped out."

"I don't know anything!"

"I think you do," the captain said, shoving a finger into Bartolomeo's chest. "Which would you prefer? No fingernails? Or perhaps we remove your thumbs?"

Terror drained the breath out of him and he found himself gasping for air.

"Puh . . . lease," he breathed. "Puh . . . lease . . . let . . . me . . . go. I know nothing!" He pursed his lips, trying the trick his father once taught him to regain his breath. "I . . . need . . . my . . . thumbs. I . . . want . . . to . . . be . . . a . . . cook, puh . . . lease!"

He did not need to fake his terror. He only had to keep his story straight. In the direst moments of the questioning, he pictured Stella's face and it gave him strength.

When he was finally released, he overheard the captain telling the maestro he believed in Bartolomeo's innocence. He did not know when his heart would ever slow down.

The doge ordered prisoners to be brought from his dungeons to test the rest of the food, but they uncovered nothing. Guests and servants were questioned. The capi dei sèstiere searched every inch of the servants' quarters, even discovering the hiding place where Scappi had once stashed his diary. They found only a few scudi and a lock of hair that could have belonged to any girl. They could not know it was Stella's.

When evening came, Bartolomeo filled the napkin and gloves with rocks and, like the vial, threw them into the sea.

*   *   *

When prisoners are executed in Venezia, they hang them from a platform erected in the piazzetta in front of the Palazzo di Doge between two columns, one topped with a winged lion, the symbol of the city, and the other topped with a statue of Saint Teodoro, the first patron saint of the city. The last thing a condemned man sees is the glittering canal before him.

Bartolomeo stood in the piazzetta, watching the throngs of people who gathered to see the murderer of Giacomo Crispo hang. His stomach churned. He wondered if the nightmare of the last week would end once the man's feet dangled and twisted in the air above the platform.

After the capi dei sèstiere let him go he had not dared return to the kitchen. He didn't want to know whom they might decide to condemn in his stead. But avoiding the kitchen did not stop the gossip, and it wasn't long before the whispers reached him. His guilt had kept him from sleep at night.

The crowd erupted into cheers and Bartolomeo turned to see the object of their attention. His heart jumped.

Stella.

The principessa stood on the upper balcony of the palazzo, alongside the doge and dogaressa, Signor Grimani and his wife, and her parents. A small contingent of men in the colors of the Archipelago stood with them. The people shouted to Stella that she would be avenged. *Oh, Stella, they know not what they say,* Bartolomeo thought.

You are safe, Stella. I promised you, you would not go to Naxos. You are mine, Stella. And you are safe.

Stella wore a dress and veil of black, and in her hands, she held a bouquet of white roses. She remained very still as she observed the crowd. She did not wipe her eyes as her mother and the dogaressa did.

He had not dared to try to contact the principessa. What did she think of him? Was she glad she did not have to marry the duke? Or did she hate him for what he had done? He shivered with the thought. No, he could not think that. She had begged him to save her, and he had.

The doge waved a hand and the crowd's attention turned to the platform. Four of the doge's men brought the prisoner forward. It was Piero. Seeing his former colleague barefoot and clad only in sackcloth made Bartolomeo's stomach lurch. He knew not how they concluded Piero was the murderer. The authorities had marched him from the kitchen three days prior, and no one had seen him since. Bruno had been distraught and angry, accusing everyone in the kitchen of turning against his brother. Finally, the maestro had to remove him from the kitchen. Time to cool off, he said to Bruno, telling him not to come back until he could treat the rest of us with respect. Twice during the week Bartolomeo almost told them it was he who had done the deed, but then he remembered Piero's pumping hips and kept his mouth shut.

Now Bartolomeo struggled to keep the bile down.

"I didn't do it!" Piero screamed, struggling. The crowd hurled epithets and pieces of fruit, spitting upon him when he passed.

The executioner read the sentence, then asked the prisoner if he had any last words. Piero repeated his claims of innocence. The executioner drew the sack down over his head and tightened the noose, muffling him.

Bartolomeo considered what would happen if he were to come forward, to yell to the executioner to stop, that it was he who killed Giacomo Crispo. What would it feel like to be the one in the noose? Then he caught a glimpse of Stella.

Nothing mattered but her, not even the innocent man sentenced to hang before him.

When the doge gave the signal, the executioner pulled on the lever releasing the trap door. The crowd's response was almost deafening.

Bartolomeo thought his heart might drown him with the weight he felt as the door released. He wanted to turn away. But he didn't. He thought it penance to watch.

*   *   *

It was two agonizing weeks before he and Stella could arrange another meeting. They came together in the garden in the early morning before most of the household was awake. The summer sun was hot, and the air hung heavy like a blanket over the quiet waterways of the city.

Stella looked haggard.

"I haven't slept in days," she confessed, breaking down into tears. He held her until she could speak.

"Barto, it was terrible," she continued. "They thought I had been the one to poison the duke! But I gave nothing away. They asked me hundreds of questions. They tried to scare me into confessing, and just when I thought I could no longer endure they brought forth that man from the kitchen."

His heart wrenched with guilt. That he had put her through such anguish made his stomach turn.

"Did you know the man?" she asked. "Please tell me he was not kind. Tell me he deserved it."

He shook his head. Bartolomeo did not want to talk about Piero. "I am so sorry. I did not want to bring you pain. My stellina, my little star, you are safe. You do not have to go to Naxos."

"Barto, orso mio, I know how much you love me. You risked everything for me. But it was all for naught! I may not be going to Naxos, but now I am to marry another, a cardinale's brother. I leave for Roma at the beginning of March." Her tears began anew.

Bartolomeo could not believe his ears. Panic rose within him and his right eye began to twitch.

"No," he managed to say. "No, you are mine. I will keep you safe. You will not marry him. I took care of the pirate. I can take care of a cardinale's brother."

Stella ran her hand through his hair. "No, Barto. You must not think of it. It will be the death of us. I cannot endure another interrogation or bear to have you tortured and hanged if you are caught. No, Barto. I must marry this man, if only to save you and me. Take heart, my bear. We have six months. We should treasure them."

They held each other, their tears mingling with the sweat from the summer sun.

When he pulled away he was determined. "I will follow you. I will find work in Roma and you and I . . . we will find a way to be together. If you must have a husband, so be it. If you have his children, so be it. But I know he will never have your heart. I claim that, Stella. Your heart belongs to me."

She smiled, a broad grin that lit up the features of her face. "If you come to Roma, I will find my way to you. Always, Barto. You are my *cuore*—my heart."

*　　*　　*

When night fell, after most of the other servants had fallen asleep, Bartolomeo snuck into the wine cellar. He was relieved to find the satchel he kept under one of the barrels. He had not been down to the cellar since the day of the duke's death and he had bitten his nails to nubs in the worry it might be discovered in the search for the killer. But nothing had been moved. Inside the satchel was ink, quills, drying sand, more candles, a spare notebook, and a little wooden cipher wheel.

He opened the journal and pressed the pages apart. He turned to the page where he had last written:

~ FDSMEAEMLDNGENPSGILAELDLI ~

He began to spin the cipher wheel, copying down the letters on the wheel as he turned it. It was time-consuming, but he felt he had to capture the details of the last few days.

Someday, he reasoned, people would publish the story of his life as a history. It would be the talk of every city in Italy, he assumed, once they read the truth of his dangerous, secret, and outrageous life. The life of the most famous chef that Italy had ever seen.

He thought of the napkin, now at the bottom of the Canal Grande, and felt a small, guilty stab of pride that he managed to pull it off. If he did not write the story, how would anyone else know of his genius once he was gone? He dipped the pen into the ink.

CHAPTER 11

Giovanni

Roma, April 24, 1577

When I set down my quill and read the shocking entry I had just decoded, it was well after midnight. The fire in the grate had died, and the candles on my desk were almost stubs. Dio mio. My father really was a murderer. Despite all of his words to the contrary, I could hardly picture it. Bartolomeo was such a kind man, someone who would often move spiders from the house to the garden rather than kill them. When he was slaughtering animals, he made sure they died in the least amount of pain. He would give leftover food to beggars and street children. He had kind words for nearly everyone. He exuded love and charm from his very pores.

It seemed he loved one person more than all the rest. More enough that he would kill for her. Who was she?

With a dying candle, I lit the decoded pages alight over the grate and mulled these questions over and over as I watched each burning ember flare to life, then slowly wink into blackness.

* * *

I began the day I was to dine at casa di Palone in the Vaticano kitchen, helping Antonio prepare the pope's meals. For noonday, we made barley soup, apples, and a little cheese and bread. For the evening meal, we prepared the same soup with bits of roasted capons, and I made a *zabaglione* egg dish with a little malmsey wine. I suspected the pope would not touch the custardy dessert, but I felt compelled to take a chance. The worst that might happen was that he would order me to go back to his regular menu. And at best, perhaps he would recognize the joy of food God gifted to us.

Once we had finished the general preparations, Antonio helped me bake a *crostata* to take to the Palone house that evening. He set to work making the pastry as I cleaned the visciola cherries—fresh from the market—and coated them with sugar, cinnamon, and Neapolitan mostaccioli crumbs. I nestled the biscotti among several layers of dough that Antonio had pressed into thin sheets to line the pan. Atop the cherries, I laid another sheet of pastry cut into a rose petal pattern. Antonio brushed it with egg whites and rosewater, sugared it, and set the pie into the oven to bake.

Francesco joined us just as I placed the finished crostata on the counter to cool. The cherries bubbled red through the cracks of the rose petals and the scalco gave a low whistle. *"Madonna!"*

Antonio and I stared at him, shocked at the use of the word as a curse. Francesco laughed. "That pie is so beautiful I think even our Lord might swear." He clapped me on the shoulder. "It is good to see you cooking something besides barley soup, Gio. It's been too long since this kitchen has seen such a beautiful dessert."

The fragrance was magnificent. I hoped the *famiglia* Palone would find the pie tasted as good as it looked.

I waited outside the house on the Via Ripetta for many minutes, gathering my courage. I stared at the comet, the giant moving star in the sky, thinking of the love my father had for Stella. What was it like to have a love that ran so deep? I had only just met the woman.

But while this visit was to secure my ability to make Isabetta's acquaintance more formally, without commitment, I knew in my heart I was already smitten.

When I knocked on the door to the *casa*, an aged servant greeted me. He led me through the courtyard where two large black hounds lazed in the sun. Isabetta stood on the rail of the second-floor loggia, and when she saw me, she gave a little wave and a broad smile. I felt my hand shake as I returned the wave.

Rolando Palone stood in the main salon. He was an imposing figure, towering over the desk. His cloak, adorned with a collar of leopard fur, was simple but well tailored. He was perhaps seventy, with a long beard and head of silver hair. Several documents lay scattered atop the desk, weighted down with colorful stones. He ushered me in. I stopped the servant before he left, indicating the pie.

"A gift? What is it, pray tell?" Signor Palone made his way out from behind the desk and strode over to where I stood. I lifted the lid on the basket.

"*Magnifico!* When I heard Bartolomeo Scappi's apprentice would be joining us for dinner, I wondered if you had any tricks up your sleeve." His grin said it all. I hoped I was winning him over.

The servant took the pie from me. Isabetta passed him as he was leaving the room and her eyes wandered across the basket, curious. I could not wait to see her expression when she tasted the pastry.

"Daughter." Rolando affectionately wrapped an arm around Isabetta. She was dressed in a cobalt velvet gown that darkened her deep blue eyes.

"Thank you for coming," Isabetta said to me, bowing her head a little. When she lifted her face up, she winked at me, just as she had in the courtyard of my mother's house. I gasped.

Rolando indicated we should move to the next room. A long dining table ran its length, but only part of the table was set for guests. Tall windows let in the last vestiges of the late afternoon light.

"Come, let us talk. I want to know you better," he said as he took his seat at the end of the long dining table and gave me the seat of honor to his right. Isabetta sat on my other side. Her knee brushed against mine and a thrill ran along my spine.

"I am sorry about your uncle." Rolando lifted the goblet of wine before him. "Everyone has been talking about his magnificent funeral. We were not acquainted, but I was fortunate enough to have had his food once, at one of Pope Julius's *feste*. I have traveled a lot, and his banquets were spoken of across the country."

My heart constricted. "Thank you, Signor Palone. He was a good man and I learned everything I know from him. The world is darker without his light."

Rolando raised his goblet. "To Bartolomeo Scappi, the greatest chef of his age!"

Isabetta and I lifted our glasses. I was touched by the respect Rolando Palone had just given to me by honoring Bartolomeo.

"Drinking without us, I see." The voice was cutting. A man appeared in the far doorway. He appeared to be nearing fifty, with a mantle of graying hair that curled under in the popular style, draping across his broad shoulders. He removed his cap and handed it to the servant, then came forward to sit in the chair opposite me.

"My elder son, Richo," Rolando said by way of introduction.

"And the other son, Tomaso." Another man closed the gap between the door and table, taking the seat adjacent to Richo. He was slender, with dark locks not quite as long as those of his brother, and a strawberry birthmark marring the skin around his left eye.

"I am pleased to dine with you all."

The servant poured their wine.

Richo downed half of his in one swig, then leaned in toward me. "So, this is the man who wants to court my sister. Tell me, what sort of mettle are you made of?"

His stare was like the cut of a knife. My mouth opened, but Tomaso interrupted before I could say a word.

"Pay him no attention," he reassured me. He gestured to his sister. "Isabetta, what do you call this man?"

Isabetta's hand reached over to pat mine. "Giovanni Brioschi. He's the cuoco to Pope Gregory."

"The pope? *Cazzo!* May he get dog worm and die." Richo took another drink.

My jaw dropped open. I was used to such vulgarity in the taverns, but never in what I considered polite company.

"Richo, you insult our guest," Tomaso said, giving me a sympathetic look.

"Pope Gregory is a rotten devil!"

The pope wasn't popular with the common people, but it was shocking to hear such disapproval expressed aloud.

Rolando put a hand on Richo's shoulder. "Enough." He turned to me, his face unreadable. "Tell me, Signor Brioschi, how did you become acquainted with my daughter?"

I took a breath, trying to keep my voice even. "Scappi, Giovanni Scappi, if you will. My uncle bequeathed his name to me when he passed."

"Signor Scappi, then. How did you meet Isabetta?"

Isabetta had likely told her father the story. This was just a means of moving into further conversation. "My mother is an herbalist, and I met Isabetta one afternoon when she came to call on her."

"The herbs to help me sleep," Isabetta added as a handful of servants swept into the room, carrying with them the first dishes of our meal. They laid before us plates of marzipan biscuits, sugared ricotta, and candied fruits and nuts to help us aid our digestion.

The centerpiece to these dishes was my cherry crostata. The Palones' chef had warmed it up and a delicious aroma wafted through the cuts of the rose petals in the crust. The scalco walked it around the table so we could admire the artistry before he sliced it.

"*Bellisima!*" Isabetta exclaimed.

"It smells delicious," Rolando agreed. "Your uncle taught you well, it seems."

"Those cherries are going to a festa in my belly," Richo joked, a gleam in his eye.

We all laughed. I was pleased the pie, at least, had made a favorable impression.

The crostata had barely been placed in front of us when Richo devoured his slice. He asked for a second piece even before the rest of us had made a mark in the first.

*   *   *

"This crostata . . ." Rolando began, stopping to savor another bite. He closed his eyes as his lips closed around his fork. He swallowed, then opened his eyes, which were glistening. "I have not tasted something so marvelous since my wife, Sandra, passed."

"I am sorry, signore. May she rest in peace," I said to be polite. With the depth of emotion he expressed, I assumed her death must be recent.

"Peace? There is no peace for my mother's soul!" exclaimed Richo.

Rolando grasped his son by the shoulder once more. "Richo, stop. Now. Or I will ask you to leave."

He stabbed his fork into a cherry, the sound screeching against the maiolica plate. Isabetta put her hand on mine again. "Our mother was a midwife," she explained. "She died a few months after I was born."

"She was *murdered*!" Richo pushed back his chair and stood up. "I will kill the bastards if I ever find them. I will tear them limb from limb and I will seek out every member of their families and do the same." He slammed his silver goblet down on the table, turned on his heel, and left.

Rolando reached for a biscotti. "Mind him not, Giovanni. My sons are full of passion."

And drink, I thought.

"I never knew her," Isabetta said, "but I am told she was the best midwife in all of Italy."

"She was." Rolando's voice was wistful.

"She was the light in our family," Tomaso said to me. "Richo was right about the vendetta. We would all carry it forth if we find who killed her."

"How did it happen?" I asked.

Rolando gazed off toward the windows when he answered. "We lived in the little town of Toffia north of Roma. She had an urgent summons in the night. A company of guards came to escort her, so I assumed it was one of the Orsini—they control the region north of Roma. Two days later, Captain Ottavio arrived at our doorstep with Sandra, dead on the back of a cart. Her body had been dumped on the side of the road to Farfa. The captain claimed it was bandits, but she was still in possession of all her jewelry and even the pouch with her money tied to her belt."

"I'm surprised the *shirri* did not take it," I mused, almost to myself. The local authorities were never to be trusted.

"I grew up with the captain of that region. He would never cheat me," Rolando said bitterly.

"What about the woman who gave birth?"

"We don't know who she was."

Isabetta waved the servants forward with the next course. They moved through the room, replacing the sweet plates with spit-roasted pheasants, pork belly dumplings, chicory soup, and a platter of wild asparagus.

The conversation turned to other matters, the Vaticano kitchen, the pope's Reformation, the wool and silk trade in which Rolando had made his money. Eventually, the last course of salads, fruits, vegetables, and fried fish arrived.

"I approve." Rolando sat back and pushed his plate away.

"A delightful meal, thank you." I was stuffed.

He laughed. "Of course, it was, but you misunderstand."

Isabetta rubbed her leg up against mine. "He approves of you courting me."

Tomaso guffawed. "She will eat you alive, dear cuoco."

Isabetta threw a piece of bread at her brother.

"Thank you, signore." I hoped the heat I felt did not manifest itself on my face.

"If you break my sister's heart, cuoco, I will string you up and leave you hanging on the platform on the Capitolino." Richo had rejoined us. He sat down and began picking at the leftover *calamari fritti*.

Isabetta rose before I could respond. She touched me on the elbow. "Come now, Giovanni, let us retire to the salon, away from the foolishness of my brothers."

I looked to Rolando, who nodded his consent. Gratefully I followed Isabetta to a little receiving salon at the front of the palazzo.

"Are your brothers always like that?" I asked when we were alone. She sat down next to me on a long chaise longue.

"No, they were on their best behavior today. But they look out for me."

"Do they not have wives?"

She moved a little closer and wrapped her arm in mine. "Richo's wife ran off a few months ago with a traveling minstrel. You've seen how well he's taking her departure. And Tomaso's wife died of fever two years past."

"It's been a very long time since your mother died. They are still burning brightly with vendetta," I said, more as an observation than a question.

"It's true. I do not always understand it as I never really knew her. But they remember her well, and we all know how much her death hurt my father. Woe to the person who brought her death. Every year they renew the vendetta on *Pasquino*, and whosoever might have killed her would be so lucky to read it and to flee so as not to be torn limb from limb."

That morning I had walked by *Pasquino*, an ancient Greek statue missing its arms and legs, which held a prominent place in the city as a "talking" statue. When people had a grievance against the pope, a bad merchant, or some other injustice, they would post poems on the base of the statue as an anonymous way of sharing their dissatisfaction with the rest of Roma. Every week or so the city would clean off the layers of paper, and just as fast new posts would go up. These missives formed the heart of much gossip in the city. There were several other talking statues and they often "talked" to one another, responding to what was said on a statue in another part of the city.

"Are you sad that you never knew her?" I asked.

"Every day." She smiled, but it was not a sad smile.

I thought of the letter Rolando had sent me, about Isabetta being unable to have children. "And why are you not married?" I asked, unsure if I would upset her.

She gave me a rueful smile. "You are being polite. I know my father told you I was barren. It's why my husband left me three years ago. Does it bother you?"

I smiled down on her. "It does not. I have a fosterling who will carry on the Scappi name—that's all that matters to me. A boy who was in my uncle's care."

"Good," she said, pressing herself even closer to me. Her eyes sparkled. She tilted her face toward mine and there was nothing else I could do but kiss her. She tasted like sweet cherries. Her lips were soft, like pillows of whipped cream.

Richo's warning jolted us apart. "Remember what I said about broken hearts, cuoco."

He was gone by the time I turned back to the doorway.

"He's like a yappy dog," Isabetta said, her voice bright. "All bark but with no bite."

I wasn't sure I believed her.

CHAPTER 12

Giovanni

Roma, May 1577

In the following weeks, I saw more and more of Isabetta. As was customary, we met every few days. We sat in the courtyard or the loggia at her home, drinking wine and talking about the world beyond. We stared at the comet and shared endless theories about what made it move, or what might happen if it grazed the earth. We stole kisses, and sometimes my hand found its way into her dress but never much farther. Her brothers were always around. They delighted in tormenting me with veiled threats or attempts to embarrass me in some manner or other. Sometimes Rolando joined in, regaling us with stories of his youth. He told his tales with true panache, leaving us with a sense of wonder at all that he had seen. On occasion, I brought Salvi with me; no one loved Rolando's stories more than he did.

If it was all true, Rolando had lived an extraordinary life. In the years before he settled in Roma as a merchant, he spent time on the trade routes and had been to cities so distant they were practically imaginary in my mind—Lisbon, Tripoli, Budapest, Constantinople, Antioch, Cracow, London. He had loved his life of adventure, but when he met his wife, Sandra, he decided to settle in Fara in Sabina and start a family.

Between my time courting Isabetta and my work at the Vaticano, I continued to decode my father's journals. It was fascinating to discover another side of Bartolomeo. Often, in reading about his experiences, I could picture him as a young, handsome, and reckless man. Other times I could hardly believe the person in the journals was the same as the person I knew and loved.

October 1, 1528, Venezia

Today we were discovered. Truly! Stella's youngest brother, A., found us in my employer's caverna where the gondolas are housed. He came upon us with such stealth that we did not hear him. He watched us long enough to realize who we were and to see we were entangled in something more than a simple kiss. He pulled me off Stella and tried to drag her away. She scolded him and told him to be quiet or she would tell their father about the girl he had been sleeping with. He did not care, he said. Her honor to her betrothed was more important than his. He was going to inform their father at first light.

Stella panicked and bade me to run after him and convince him not to tell their father. I ran through the calle *and was ready to give up when I heard a commotion near Palazzo Rossini. It was A., beset upon by thieves. I yanked one of the pilferers away from him and punched the man, hard. He reeled and fell backward into the canal. Then the second thief was upon me. I always carry a knife in my belt and I don't even remember removing it, but I slashed him across the face and along his neck. He screamed and ran off, leaving a trail of blood behind him.*

When three of the Officiali di Notte appeared, having heard the noise while they were on patrol, they thought I was the one who had beaten A. They pulled me away from him, but A. cried out to leave me alone, that I had saved his life. Two of the Officiali di Note followed the trail of blood through the dark calli *and the other helped me carry A. back to Palazzo Grimani.*

The next day, both Signor Grimani and Stella and A.'s father praised my bravery. Stella's father gave me a purse that will keep me solvent for a long while to come.

For saving his life, A. swore loyalty and secrecy to Stella and to me, and he promised to aid us in any way to keep our love from the world. He seems sincere, but only time will tell. Whatever fates have given me this gift, I thank them.

It seemed I had an uncle as well! I scanned the journals and A. was mentioned many times, mostly as an escort for the lovers.

I found the journals to be an endless source of fascination. In the years after Giacomo Crispo's death, Stella was true to her word, helping Bartolomeo land a job as an apprentice in the kitchen for Francesco Coronaro, the cardinale priest of Santa Cecilia in the Trastevere, south of the Vaticano. Bartolomeo worked for Cardinale Coronaro for a few years, and then, seemingly on his own merit and without help from Stella, moved to the kitchen of Cardinale Campeggio, who became famous for his part in excommunicating England's King Henry VIII. Campeggio was often absent, but when he was there, the feasts were magnificent.

* * *

It was late in the morning and I was in my room decoding a journal when I heard footsteps on the stairs. Salvi was talking to someone, but I could not register the other voice. I rushed to hide the journal and my notes, but before I could reach Bartolomeo's chest, Isabetta opened the door and poked her head in.

"Giovanni, *caro cuore*, my dear heart, I thought it was high time I come to visit you. If I had to sit in my father's courtyard one more time, my legs crossed, desperate for you, I think I might burst."

She entered the room and shut the door, sliding the bolt to

lock it behind her. She grinned and strode toward me, her blue dress caressing her legs with every step. I was stunned to find her before me. Aside from that time in Caterina's courtyard, I had yet to see her beyond the walls of her home. I had been to her house at least a dozen times and had, just the day before, resolved to ask her father if we could start taking walks on Sunday after the midday meal.

I set the journal on the nearby table. She hiked up her skirts and straddled my legs, her faint jasmine perfume intoxicating my senses. Her hands wound into my hair and then we were kissing, deep, in a way that wasn't stolen like all our other kisses. For a moment, I thought I might drown with pleasure.

Her hand ran down my chest and settled on the bulge between my legs. "You are happy I decided to visit," she said, her breath hot against my ear.

"But how . . ." I began. I didn't understand how she could be in my house.

Her hand rubbed slowly against the fabric of my breeches. "I'm not a principessa in a gilded cage, Gio, who needs a chaperone to go where she desires. I remembered you told me your housekeeper always visits her mother on Tuesdays. Salvi let me in. I gave him some coin to spend at the market if he gave us some time alone . . ."

I thought of all the afternoons in the Palone salon. "But, why haven't you come before now? Why didn't you tell me that you could visit me? I thought your father was protective."

"He is, but he doesn't need to marry me off for gain. I choose who I want to be with and I wanted to be sure of you. To be sure of your intentions. It's been long enough. I have decided on you, caro Giovanni. Do not fret, *amore mio*. It's just you and me. I have been waiting far too long for this moment."

So had I. Desire rose within me and I stood, holding her, knocking the chair out of the way. I carried her to the bed and fell with her against it, our limbs wrapping around each other. Our caresses were fevered, a fire rising between us. It was everything I could do to keep from tearing her dress off her body. Together we unlaced her bodice, a deep kiss accompanying each ribbon undone. Once unclothed, our bodies moved together as one, our skin slipping on skin in the mid-May heat.

"At night, when I go to sleep, I think of you," she breathed in my ear as I teased her nipple with my tongue.

I lifted my head. "What do you think about, *dolcezza* mia?"

"This. What it would feel like to be with you, to have you touching me."

I ran my hand along her thigh and let my fingers explore her sex, rubbing the little spot before her opening. She moaned. "Does it feel like you imagined?" I asked.

"Better than I—oh!"

My fingers slid inside her folds, teasing with gentle movement. She pushed her body against me. I moved my mouth to cover hers.

She tasted like cucumbers and salt. I wanted to devour her. I explored every part of her with my mouth, my teeth grazing her skin, the flavor of her exploding against my tongue.

When I pushed myself inside her, I thought I would lose myself. She was hot and smooth, my knife to her butter. I wanted to feel this moment, to know this pleasure of the body forever. I moved inside her, the rhythm a stirring of our souls. When her soft exclamations of pleasure grew louder and louder and finally climaxed in one long sensuous moan, I could no longer contain my own enjoyment and I lost myself. For a moment, I thought the sky had opened up and all the stars fell down around me.

Afterward, I rubbed her shoulders and we lazed about in the morning sunlight streaming through the windows. Before I knew it, I had drifted off to sleep, Isabetta purring in my arms.

When I awoke, she had donned her dress once more and it hung loosely off her lithe frame without the bodice, which she likely needed my help to lace. She sat in the chair, with her feet upon the window-sill, and to my horror, she was reading Bartolomeo's journal.

"What are you doing?" I asked, sitting up.

She didn't look up. "This is your uncle's journal, isn't it?" She thumbed through the pages. "Or at least that which I can read. Why is so much of it in code?"

I swung my legs out of bed and pulled on my breeches. I was sweating, but not from the heat. I plucked the journal from her hands and turned away.

I considered returning it to the chest, but then she would know about all the others. I went to the mantel and put it on top. I stood there, looking at it, not sure what to say.

"Giovanni, what's wrong?" I heard the rustle of her dress. "Why can't I read it? He is not here to object." She put her hand on my shoulder, turning me toward her.

"I, um, it's complicated," I said, knowing it was a weak answer. "It would not be safe for you to know the contents." I turned around to face her.

Her brow furrowed in confusion.

She put her hand against my cheek and closed the gap between us, her body pressing up against me. I felt my desire rising once more. I pushed a hand softly against her, in a halfhearted attempt to push her away. "Isabetta, I want to tell you, honestly, I do. But I can't."

Isabetta leaned in, her lips brushing my ear. "Gio, if there is to be a you and me, then you cannot keep secrets from me." She pushed her fingers into the curls of my hair.

My tongue would not work. Her eyes were like the blue ocean. I could drown in those depths.

"We feel something special between us, Gio. You took me there, on the bed, and I will let you take me again, and again." Her fingers brushed my mouth, pulling softly at my lip. "But, caro, I do so because I believe we are forging something new, something that will, I hope, take us through our lives to the very end."

A surge of passion pushed through me, overflowing like wine in a too-small goblet. I pressed my lips against hers and tasted her sweetness once more. One hand entwined in her hair, the other against her back. "You are right, cuore mio. *Ti amo, ti amo.*"

She held off my kisses, her hand against my cheek. "And I you, Gio. Your face has haunted my dreams since I first saw you. But if you love me, if you want me to stand by your side and to warm your bed . . ." Her hand squeezed my backside and I drew in a deep breath. "Just as we are one, now, when we kiss, when we touch, we must be one in the way we speak behind closed doors," she continued. "I will give you everything and tell you everything. And, Gio, you must promise me the same." Her hand had found its way to the front of me.

"Yes, dolcezza mia," I breathed, unable to say anything else, unable to think of anything other than her fingers against my sex, her voice hot in my ear.

She fell to her knees and took me in her mouth. My hands clutched her head, feeling the motion of her against me. When I thought I could take no more, I pushed her back, to the floor, pulled up her skirts, and drove myself between her thighs.

"I promise, Isabetta," I whispered in her ear as I melted into her.

CHAPTER 13

Scappi

Roma, 1536

Bartolomeo had been living in Roma for nearly seven years when he
knew he was destined for greatness. It was the day his oft-absent
employer, Cardinale Campeggio, told him he would be responsible
for a Lenten banquet for the Holy Roman Emperor, Charles V. He
had only been cuoco for the cardinale for two years, and never had
he been asked to do anything so grand.

Cardinale Campeggio had summoned him to the library for the
news. Bartolomeo stood in front of the fire, one of the last of the
season. Early spring sun filtered through the cloudy glass windows.
The cardinale paced the floor as he spoke.

"You have eight weeks, Bartolomeo. Can you do it?"

He nodded.

"It will be the most memorable feast the emperor has ever had,"
he assured the cardinale, his heart swelling with pride.

"Good. Money will be no object, so let your genius run wild, boy.
It is the least I can do for the emperor."

"He backed you for pope, did he not?"

"Yes, for all the good it did me. That damned Farnese pope will
accomplish nothing with his ridiculous council."

Bartolomeo said nothing. Pope Paul III had always been kind enough to him. But he had heard the gossip and knew there was unrest among the clergy. Martin Luther's preaching had deeply damaged the church, but no one seemed to know how to counteract his message. They were loath to set aside the life of luxury and nepotism that Luther condemned.

Cardinale Campeggio was one of the worst offenders, having given his illegitimate sons and his nephews precious Roman bishoprics, governorships, and positions as legates to the English Crown. He owned numerous palazzi in Bologna and Roma. He rewarded those who were loyal to him—and Bartolomeo was one of those men.

The cardinale had stopped pacing and leaned against his desk, wincing in pain.

"Is your gout acting up again, Your Eminence?"

Campeggio nodded, his long gray beard bouncing against the red of his robes. "Will you make me your veal with garlic tonight? Lots of garlic?"

"Of course. I have heard the emperor suffers as well. Is it true?"

The cardinale waved at an elaborate chair in the corner where four Moorish slaves waited for his command. "He does. He is the one who told me how beneficial having a sedan chair can be."

For the past few years, Campeggio's slaves carried him forth through the streets of Roma and the hallways of the Vaticano alike. Even when his feet were not bothersome he kept to the chair, citing a need for "prevention." Bartolomeo suspected a combination of ego and laziness.

"How many courses do you think we should have?" the cardinale asked.

"Thirteen should be elaborate enough," Bartolomeo said, looking skyward as he did a bit of math in his head, considering how many stewards and carvers he would need. "Three *scalchi* and three *trincianti*.

About two hundred dishes or so. That should keep twelve people fat and full for a few hours."

Campeggio chuckled. "I should say it will."

*　　*　　*

Preparing for the banquet was one of the most exhilarating experiences of Bartolomeo's life thus far. While he had made many a feast for the cardinale, he had never cooked for a king, much less an emperor. He hired new scalchi and several new servants. He sent missives to dozens of merchants, arranging for the delivery of the choicest ingredients including crustaceans and fish. He ordered new dishes for the credenza, huge platters of maiolica, and goblets made from silver and gold. New tapestries were hung in the vast hall where the meal was to take place. And then there were the sugar sculptures.

Before his apprenticeship, Bartolomeo was fortunate he had learned the trade of an apothecary from his father and knew the formula for making sugar paste. He wouldn't have to hire an apothecary to make the many varieties of paste that would be needed. But just two days before the cardinale asked him to create the meal, Bartolomeo's most prized sugar sculptor died, his head bashed in by robbers in a dark Roman alley as he staggered home after a night in the osteria. The death left Bartolomeo at a loss.

"You must know some sculptors," Stella said one afternoon as they lingered in a hidden grove in the Vaticano gardens, a favorite spot for them to meet. Whenever her brother visited, the siblings would go for long walks—or at least that's what Stella's husband believed. In actuality, Stella's brother would accompany her to whatever clandestine location Bartolomeo had secured before joining one of his favorite wenches at the nearest brothel, a pastime subsidized by the lovers. It was an arrangement that suited all of them.

"Of course I do. Except all the men I can think of are employed by other cardinali or princes."

"No, my silly beast, I'm not talking about sugar sculptors. I'm talking about regular sculptors. Someone who works in bronze, perhaps?"

Bartolomeo's hand stopped its movement and lay on her head as he turned over her words in his mind. "Benvenuto Cellini would be ideal, but I heard he's in Padua doing Cardinale Bembo's medal portrait."

"What about Michelangelo?"

Bartolomeo shook his head. "He sculpts in marble. I need someone who can understand how to make molds."

Stella sat up and took his face in one hand. She pulled him close and kissed him. It was a long, slow kiss. He wrapped his arms around her and they stayed locked in an embrace for several moments, lost in the feel and taste of each other's mouths, lips, and tongues.

When they pulled away, Stella winked at him. "You're wrong."

Bartolomeo gave her a cockeyed glance. "Wrong about what?"

"Michelangelo. I know for a fact he can sculpt in bronze. Haven't you heard about the huge statue of Pope Julius II that he cast in Bologna? When Julius died, when was it, hmm . . ." She lifted her eyes in thought. "I think in 1511? They had to tear it down and they scrapped it. And," she added, "a few years ago, I bought a set of his bronze panthers with beautiful men riding them for the long table in our entryway. They are magnificent. I assure you, orso mio, that man understands how to make a mold."

Bartolomeo stood and pulled her up with him. He lifted her and swung her in a circle. She giggled.

"Oh, Stella! If he will agree to help me make the sugar molds, I will make you a hundred sugar stars! You'll be counting them all night at the banquet."

"I'll take a thousand kisses," she murmured. "You had better start now. I cannot linger much longer."

"One," Bartolomeo whispered, placing his lips on the flesh of her upper right breast.

She smiled and closed her eyes.

*   *   *

Late that afternoon, Bartolomeo went to Michelangelo's studio a stone's throw from Saint Peter's in the Borgo Nuovo neighborhood. He brought with him a bottle of brandy milk, a strong liqueur made with brandy, orange, vanilla, and cream. It was a drink once created for Lorenzo the Magnificent. Bartolomeo had bribed one of the Medici cooks for the recipe when he visited Firenze. He had made it often for Michelangelo when he was at the Vaticano and he hoped it would open the sculptor's ears to hearing his proposal.

A young student met Bartolomeo at the door and waved him in. The sculptor stood on a ladder in the big room, chipping away at a piece of marble. Bartolomeo could make out the shape of a shoulder and an arm, but the rest of the body remained a massive piece of marble.

"What do you want?" Michelangelo asked, not bothering to look away from his work.

"It's me, Bartolomeo." He waved the bottle at Michelangelo. "I brought you something you might like."

The sculptor stopped his chiseling and glared down at the cook. "Humph. I suppose you want something if you are bringing me gifts." Despite his gruff response, he rested his chisel on the piece of scaffolding next to him and climbed down the ladder. He was nearing sixty and his descent was not as fast as Bartolomeo remembered it in the past.

"I'm wondering if you might accept a commission."

Michelangelo took the bottle from him and twisted out the cork. He took a swig, then gave a satisfied sigh. He looked at Bartolomeo.

"A commission?" He began to laugh. It was a hearty, rueful sound that made Bartolomeo wonder why he had bothered to make the visit.

Michelangelo clapped him on the back and waved him over to a long bench lining the side of the studio. "Tell me, what could a cuoco like you want me to sculpt?"

No sense holding back, Bartolomeo thought. "Sugar."

The sculptor had started to lift the bottle to his lips once more, but at this word he paused. "You want me to make sugar sculptures? Ha!" The bottle continued the path to his mouth.

"I want you to make the molds. I'll pour the sugar and unset them. Any design you want."

The old artist snorted. "I don't work in sugar."

Bartolomeo took a gamble and stood. "I am sorry, my friend, I should not have asked. Sugar is a hard beast. I should not have assumed it would be something you could do. I'll find someone else to cast molds for the emperor's feast." He tipped his hat and began to head toward the door.

"No, wait, wait. For the emperor, you say?"

Bartolomeo grinned and turned back.

*   *   *

"Our Lord imbued some measure of talent upon you, it seems." Charles V waved a knife at Bartolomeo. It was the seventh course, and the young cook had been asked to present himself at the table. He bowed his head, humbled to be in front of the most important man in the world. Even Pope Paul did not cross this emperor.

"I hear you coerced Michelangelo into helping you." The pendant on the chain around his neck flashed in the candlelight—a golden fleece, the symbol of the highest knighthood one could achieve. He thrust his bearded chin toward the sculptures.

"Yes, Your Majesty." The word felt unfamiliar in his mouth.

Charles was the first royal personage to insist upon something other than "Your Highness." "We worked together on the vision. We wanted to create something that exalted you to the heavens itself."

The table before the emperor was spread with an entire city of sugar, a city so resplendent it was as though a door had opened into heaven itself. Groves of trees dotted the table's landscape with beautiful painted castles nestled among hills of pale green. Stars hung from the trees and graced the castle flags. From the ceiling, many dozens of gold and silver stars hung by ribbons over the table, creating a fantastical sky. Amid this wondrous landscape there were sculptures of ancient Roman gods in various scenes: Jupiter on a mountain, lightning bolt in hand; Venus born from a sea of blue; Bacchus in drunken debauchery in a grove of delicate green vines. Ever one to be in control, Michelangelo had insisted he not only develop the many dozen molds but that he also be the one to pour the sugar and finalize the details with sugar paste.

"We are fortunate to have had his help," Cardinale Campeggio chimed in. "He's been readying La Cappella Sistina to paint the altar and was waiting for the plaster to dry. I heard that he just began painting today."

Bartolomeo's eyes flickered to Stella, who sat four seats down from Cardinale Campeggio, next to her husband, who sat on the emperor's right. She flashed Bartolomeo a grin to melt his heart and made him more nervous than standing in front of any king ever could. Then he caught the eye of Stella's husband, who had clearly witnessed their exchange.

The emperor followed his gaze and raised an eyebrow. Bartolomeo's elation turned to fear, but Charles only asked him what the next course would bring.

"Your Majesty, the next course will be cold dishes. An *insalata* of fennel and one of thistles with salt and pepper; fresh split almonds; muscatel pears; stuffed dates; pear and pistachio pastries; a prune and visciola cherry tourte; wine-soaked cherries in sugar; and finally, ricotta and almond fritters."

Bartolomeo hoped his voice did not waver. He cursed himself for daring to look at Stella among such company. What a fool he had been!

"Very good. Now come close." The emperor waggled a finger at him. "I have some advice for you."

A bead of sweat broke out on Bartolomeo's forehead. He wiped it away, gathered his courage, and stood across from the emperor's table. Charles beckoned him to lean in. His breath smelled like fish.

"I see not only do you have fine taste in food, but also in women." His eyes glanced down the table toward Stella. "Do not set your sights so high, young cuoco. If you do, you may find all the glory you have today will slip right out of your fingers." The emperor sat back and looked away, a clear gesture of dismissal.

Once the guests had gone, Cardinale Campeggio summoned Bartolomeo to the library. He still had crumbs stuck in his long beard. Bartolomeo averted his eyes so he wouldn't have to see the particles bobbing up and down in the gray curls.

"I heard the emperor's warning to you. He is a man who knows how to see into another man's heart. Tell me, maestro, tell me, do you know the principessa? Have you ever talked to her before? Don't you dare lie to me."

Bartolomeo sifted through his memories of that moment, to the shining smile on Stella's lips. A surge of determination rose within him. He was not going to jeopardize any of what they had. He would not, could not.

"We have never spoken before, Your Eminence. I looked at the diners when I stood before the emperor and the princess was smiling. I was nervous in front of His Majesty and I could not help but smile back. I have never had such an opportunity before. I meant nothing by it, Your Eminence." Bartolomeo tipped his head to appear contrite.

The cardinale seemed placated. "Very well. But I will also warn you not to think beyond your station. Your career will come to an end if you make the prince a cuckold. I already have enough problems with managing that damned English king, Henry. I do not need to worry about things here at home. You will not step out of line when you work for me, Maestro Scappi." He waved his hand toward the door. "Now go. You did well tonight. I will see to it your salary reflects tonight's success."

Bartolomeo was light-headed with relief. He managed to murmur his thanks, bow, and leave the room.

When he was finished for the evening, he penned a letter to Stella. *We have caught attention, my love. I know my employer well, and he will watch me like a hawk. Silently, but surely. We must cease our meetings for now. Have patience. You are my light, and I will be yours. Ti amo, stella mia.*

While they saw each other at public events—at which they barely acknowledged each other—they exchanged furtive letters and they did not meet in private for several years.

*   *   *

When they saw each other again almost four years later, it was an early afternoon on one of Bartolomeo's rare days off working for his new employer, Cardinale Du Bellay. Stella's brother had escorted her to the private garden adjacent to the house that Bartolomeo had purchased not far from the Vaticano. The brother emerged alone from the other side of the garden, into the streets, to return three hours hence as they had previously agreed.

"Oh, how I've missed you, stellina mia." They had collapsed together amid the blankets after a second bout of lovemaking.

"Never again," she said. "I cannot bear to be apart from you for so long. Whenever I would see you at a banquet I was sure my heart was going to break in two. I was inconsolable for days afterward. I think people were starting to assume I was *pazza.*"

"You are pazza, stellina."

She nuzzled closer, laying her head on his shoulder. "It was too long," she reiterated.

"It will be easier now. I dared not make a move while Cardinale Campeggio was alive. He was a remarkable man, but he was ruthless if you crossed him. The cardinale loved your husband like a brother. I could not take the chance."

She sighed. "I am sure my husband does not remember that event. He's dined with the emperor more than once and you aren't the only man to smile at me, you know."

"I have something for you," he said. He leaned over to the bedside table and closed his hand over an object. "Something to keep you, or maybe us, safe."

"What is it?" she breathed, just loud enough for him to hear.

He took her right hand and slid the ring onto her middle finger. It was a good size ring for a lady, raised with a round top with a golden star framing a cluster of rubies.

She started to touch it but he stopped her with his hand.

"Careful with this ring," he whispered. He took her hand and with a squeeze to the edges, he popped the lid open. Inside was a white powdered substance.

"*Cantarella*. I know the poisoner who used to make it for the Borgias."

She nodded her understanding. Memento rings were common and usually held a lock of hair or sometimes a cameo of a loved one.

"Thank you, Barto. I hope I will not ever have use of it." Her eyes were moist. "I know the story I will tell if asked about the ring. It will be a gift from my new friend."

He knitted his brow. "Your new friend?"

"Yes, I have a new friend to tell you about! It's perfect, the timing of this gift!"

He ran his hand down her shoulder and across the fullness of her left breast. "Do tell, but hurry, I am getting hungry for you again. You are like honey for this big beast."

She laughed and pulled back so she could look at him. She stroked his hair and kissed his nose playfully. "I have a new friend, a confidant. Someone who understands me, and you."

Bartolomeo stopped his caresses and sat up. "What? Who have you told?"

Stella only laughed. She pulled herself up to sit next to him, her back against the ornate headboard. "Relax, orso mio. I have become fast friends with Laura della Rovere."

"The bastarda daughter of Giulia Farnese and Pope Alessandro? Stella, you cannot put us in danger."

"There is no danger. She is the daughter of the 'bride of Christ,' remember? She grew up in love, but a love borne of sin. She understands our plight well. And her husband leaves her alone. Her children are grown and she is her own woman in many ways. I was away from you for so long, Barto, and she became my confidant. There is nothing to fear, I swear to you. She has offered her home to us. We can visit whenever we like."

Bartolomeo turned to Stella. He took her in his arms and stared into her brown eyes. "You told her about us? Do you trust her that much?"

Her chin bobbed up and down. Her lips reminded him of the statue of an angel he saw on one of the churches he passed daily on his way to the Vaticano. Full. Perfect.

"I would trust her with my life."

Bartolomeo kissed her, his tongue seeking hers, filling him with the taste of strawberries. He ran his hands into her hair and then they were folding themselves back into the pillows, their bodies warming against each other.

He rolled her over and lifted his mouth away from hers.

"Then I will trust her too," he breathed as he thrust himself inside of her.

CHAPTER 14

Giovanni

Roma, June 1577

I sabetta was a quick study. She learned to tackle the code faster than I had, and soon became an expert with the cipher wheel. Now that she had set a new precedent for our courtship, we began to alternate between my visits to the Palone household and her trips to my home. I would often stop by in the evenings after my main duties at the Vaticano were finished, and on my days off we would take little walks around Roma, picnicking in the ruins of the Forum, spending time at the markets, or wandering the magnificent Musei Capitolini.

Rolando Palone adored and trusted his daughter. He placed few rules on Isabetta other than demanding she be home by sunset, and though we'd been courting for two months, he did not press me to ask for her hand in marriage. I suspected it was so he wouldn't have to provide her dowry before he had to. Fortunately, we were not nobility and there was nothing for either family to gain through the marriage, so for the most part, we were free to pursue our new love in the way we best saw fit.

When Isabetta visited me at my home, it became a habit for us to spend our spare time decoding the journals. We would often read passages aloud to each other in between our lovemaking. Talking to Isabetta about Bartolomeo was hard for me at first. She had never known him, and her questions brought me sadness, but they eventually drew us closer together as I invited her into the memories of the man I had held so dear.

"Reading about these meals is making me hungry," Isabetta declared one afternoon. Her finger ran down the page. "There is so much food. Even on a Lenten day these cardinali knew how to eat! Listen to this menu: pieces of gilded marzipan; radish and fennel salad; braised lampreys from the Tevere; fried trout with vinegar, pepper, and wine; white tourtes; razor clams; grilled oysters; pizza Neapolitan with almonds, dates, and figs; octopus and fish in the shape of chickens; fried sea turtle; prune crostatas; stuffed pears with sugar; elderflower fritters; candied almonds . . . Oh, the list goes on and on!"

"Bartolomeo was a masterful cuoco. He taught me everything I know. Say the word, *cara*, and I'll cook you any one of those dishes. I know all the recipes you named."

She smiled and bent her head back down to the journal. I watched her for a few minutes, marveling at the way her ink-black hair caught the afternoon sunlight. My heart full, I turned back to the passage I had been reading.

Bartolomeo and Stella continued to see each other over the passing years. They met often in the Vaticano gardens, or slipped into unoccupied rooms at parties, away from other guests, taking great risk with every stolen moment. When it came to meeting each other in clandestine places, there was no limit to their ingenuity. When Stella began to bear her husband's children and could not so easily slip away, they corresponded by letter through Stella's brother A., who had followed her to Roma and spent his time living the life of a rich, bored bachelor. Over the course of several journals, I worked out she had six children: A., a boy, came first in 1531, followed by a girl, V., in 1535. Another baby girl, L., born in 1537, died after only a few months. Two more children followed in 1540 and 1541, a boy and a girl, both of whom died of plague before they were two years old. Another boy, referred to by the pet name "my *cipollino*," was born in 1546. I had been told that I was born in 1547, but was that true? Everything else I had known about my birth was a lie.

Was I Barto's little onion?

February 1546

My cipollino was born last week. I have never felt such worry as I have in the last few days waiting for word about Stella. But today, her brother was able to meet me in the garden. My stellina, my beautiful little star, she is safe and so is my tiny little boy. Her brother says he is a babe with a wisp of dark hair and a strong grip. I can only pray he looks more like his mother than he does me. I know not if her other children are mine, but this one, I know he is. Stella's husband is too dull to pay attention to the dates, so when she discovered she was pregnant, thankfully early on, she immediately went to her husband and seduced him. Idiota! He is none the wiser.

But I am. She gave him a name that I chose, a name of valor and bravery. I know not when I will see this babe, but to know he and his mother are healthy makes my heart swell with pride.

I am desperate to look down upon my son, my dear dark secret son, my little onion, my cipollino. He may not live with me, but I will find a way to be a father to him.

Isabetta furrowed her brow, puzzled. "Is he talking about you?"

"I'm not sure. I was born in 1547, not 1546, but if everything I know about my past is a lie, it wouldn't surprise me. I don't remember him ever calling me his little onion, though."

"It's a common enough endearment for a child. Does the journal say how you ended up with Caterina?"

I shrugged. "It might, but there is still a lot of decoding to do. The next few months aren't in code and are devoted to more banquets and working for Cardinale Du Bellay. After that, Bartolomeo went to work for Cardinale Marino Grimani."

"Was he from the same family as the one in Venezia?"

I popped a grape into my mouth and swallowed it. "I think he was the nephew of Doge Antonio Grimani, who was the cousin of the Grimani that Bartolomeo worked with when he lived in Venezia. So, yes. I'm sure he landed the job because of that connection."

Salvi appeared in the loggia. He presented himself in front of the table, standing up straight, his eyes fixed ahead. I suspected Francesco had been giving him pointers. His formality was new but in earnest, and it was hard for me not to chuckle.

"Simona Bossi brought this for you." The boy stepped forward and placed a wooden box in my hand. It was tied carefully with a blue ribbon.

"Who is Simona?" Isabetta asked, her voice holding something more than a note of curiosity.

I patted her hand and gave her a smile. "Worry not. The wife of the guild master of the Company of Cooks and Bakers. She had a fondness for Bartolomeo."

I untied the ribbon and Isabetta scavenged it, tying it to her wrist. "For new purse strings," she explained when I raised my eyebrow at her.

I opened the latch and lifted a jar from its confines. It was about one and a half *palmi* high and made from the finest maiolica. Upon it was painted an array of kitchen instruments including molds for pasta and candies, mortars for grinding spices, knives, and other accoutrements of my trade. Across the center of the jar was a white band upon which was painted the word *Mostarda*.

Isabetta peered into the box and found a small piece of parchment that had accompanied the jar. She handed it to me.

I read it aloud.

Caro Giovanni,

My heart aches for you and for the loss of your uncle. Bartolomeo was a man greater than all men and the world is a darker place without him. He once told me he loved Venetian mostarda the best. A few months ago, I asked my brother to acquire me a jar on his travels and he has returned. I cannot give it to Bartolomeo as I had intended, so I give it to you. I hope you will enjoy it as much as he once did.

> *In Bartolomeo's memory, I give this to you,*
> *Simona Bossi*

"What a sweet gesture," Isabetta said. "She must have thought highly of Bartolomeo."

"Yes, she and her husband were good friends to him." The thought of Simona possibly being my mother tugged at the corner of my mind, but I pushed it away. It couldn't be her. She wasn't from a noble family. I thought back to the woman at the funeral with the bouquet of flowers. I wished I knew who she was.

Isabetta picked up the jar and turned it over in her hands. "What makes Venetian mostarda so different?"

"The mostarda you probably know is made with all sorts of fruits, such as figs, raisins, and pears, but in Venezia the mostarda is made with quince, which you can't always find in Roma. Bartolomeo would always lament how much better the mostarda was in Venezia."

Isabetta rubbed my arm, knowing instinctively how hard remembering my father sometimes was for me. I took the jar from her and ran my fingers over the painted letters.

"I will make you a feast soon, Isabetta, and we will have this mostarda."

"I know Bartolomeo will be with us in spirit."

"Signor Scappi!" Salvi raced through the loggia toward us, his face flushed from his run back up the stairs. "Um, signore, your brother is here." Salvi's voice trembled. "He wants a word with you."

"Stay here," I commanded them both. Isabetta had risen to follow me. "Please," I added. She relented and sat down, fingering the blue ribbon on her wrist, a sullen look upon her face. I did not want Cesare to see Isabetta. The Lord knew what type of trouble he might make for our relationship. Nor did I want him to come across the journals.

As I descended the stairs, I wondered at his sudden arrival. It had been two months since I'd seen him last at Bartolomeo's funeral. He had never been one for casual visits, especially since Tivoli was a half-day ride.

Cesare was pacing the *sala* when I arrived. He wore black as he customarily did, lending more weight to the sinister look that pinched his face.

"I didn't know you were going to be in Roma or I would have arranged for dinner. What is wrong?"

He thrust a finger toward me. "You! You are what is wrong. I am tired of the lie, I am tired of pretending."

Could Caterina have told him the truth? I cursed myself for not strapping on my rapier before coming downstairs. I surveyed the room in the event I needed a weapon. Cesare had always been violent and unpredictable. There was little nearby save a vase of roses.

I tried to keep my voice even. "*Fratello mio*, what has happened to turn you so against me?"

A vein pulsed on his forehead. "I have never been for you."

"I know," I said, sad and weary of Cesare's melodrama. I had seen him in moods like this before.

"I have been thinking much about you since Bartolomeo died. About how your life is a sham, a lie."

"Why are you here? What do you want?"

"I want what is due to me. What you have stolen. I am the eldest male in this family. If you are Bartolomeo's son, then you are a bastardo. Your life is a lie. What you have now should have been mine as his closest heir. You are a fraud, a rogue, the thief of my mother's affections, the stealer of my inheritance. I know you are lying in your throat—every word you say. I remember the day you were dropped into Caterina's lap. You are not my brother."

He started toward me and I backed up, but he only breezed past me.

"Cesare," I began.

He spun on a heel and cut me off.

"Beware, false brother. I will see you dragged through the streets. Your time has come now and another who is worthier than you will take on the legacy you believe should be yours. You deserve nothing less, you filthy mouth-stinking goat. If you were wise, you would go hang yourself before worse befalls you."

Then he was gone.

"Your brother sounded angry." Isabetta's voice flowed over me, the calm after the storm.

I held my fingers to my temples to calm the pounding in my head. "Yes. I am sorry for his cursing. He and I, well, I think you could gather we do not get along."

She laid a hand on my shoulder. "You should take him to court for this slander. For his curses against you. I would be your witness, as would Salvi."

"I will help, Maestro Scappi!" Salvi chimed in from his perch on the stairwell.

"No, no." I shook my head. "That would only make matters worse."

I turned over his words in my mind, particularly the part about someone else taking on the Scappi legacy. Who? What could Cesare mean?

Isabetta laid her head on my shoulder. "Do you fear your brother?"

Truth be told, I did, but that was a fear to which I refused to give voice. "He's all bluster and nonsense. He has always been somewhat terrible."

"I hope you are right. He sounded like he would see the end of you."

I turned her to face me. "My Isabetta, dolcezza mia, you cannot be rid of me so easily."

She smiled and let me lean in. I kissed her, hard, pouring every bit of my feeling into the moment, hoping it would make all the unpleasantness of my brother's visit disappear.

CHAPTER 15

Giovanni

That night I found myself wide awake in the dark. After what I thought must have been an hour or more, I decided to tackle decoding another journal. It was too hot indoors, so I went to my table in the loggia, grateful for the slight breeze that broke the summer heat. I found that I didn't need to light a candle—the light of the massive comet paired with that of the moon was more than enough to illuminate my father's words.

In one of the passages, dated only a few months past, Romoli's name jumped off the page at me.

December 27, 1576, Night

I cannot sleep. I finally gave up and now I sit here, in the cold deep dark, and I am angry.

I have not thought of that whoreson Domenico Romoli in many years, but today his name lit into me like a raging fire.

I delivered a gift to Stella today—sweet buns with my note tucked in the bottom—and when I was leaving, I ran into that damned old Farnese carver, Vincenzo Cervio, who had visited Stella's cuoco. I haven't seen him since we did that dinner in Bormazo years ago. He tells me he was "inspired by me" to write his own book about being a trinciante, about carving and stewardship.

That rotten prattler, he thinks that he can puff me up with flattery and still steal my idea. And then he tells me I was far too kind when I gifted recipes to Romoli—that the devil deserves no help. I agree with Cervio there, but hearing how that bastardo Romoli is telling others that I gave those recipes to him made me want to punch something. I set Cervio straight and told him Romoli had stolen the recipes decades ago when he fled Roma to work for the Medici, and if I ever see him I will slash his throat. Perhaps Cervio was shocked by my threat of violence. He cut our conversation short and departed, for which I was glad. My ire was such that it was better I walked home alone.

I wondered at Romoli's desperation to have more of my father's recipes. Bartolomeo's cookbook had been selling well for the last seven years and it had already been reprinted many times. I could only think he wanted to steal more of his success.

I flipped the pages. There was one other very short entry I had not yet read. It was dated January 2 of this year. I decoded it, and when I finished, I thought I might not be able to slow my heart, given what I read:

Today I went to the market in Piazza Navona first thing this morning. My path took me by Pasquino. *I was stunned to see this poem pasted to him:*

> *Gone from us nearly three times ten*
> *Sandra Palone, our mother hen.*
> *She gave life to babies far and wide*
> *But she is dead and her murderer alive.*
> *From Toffia to Roma, from Farfa to Firenze,*
> *We will take this hunt to the world's end.*
> *This vendetta we declare each year anew,*
> *With our rapiers we will run him through.*

I memorized it. I felt that I should. Mi dispiace, Signora Palone.

Oh, *Pasquino*! The ever-changing words pasted on the base of that statue brought many a bout of indigestion to the people of Roma.

I felt like a bird caught in a storm, the wind ripping it from its path and dashing it into the bricks of the closest building.

Sandra Palone was Isabetta's mother.

But I did not know why Bartolomeo was sorry. There was no other explanation in this section of the journals, just the poem.

I remembered the first time I met Isabetta's father and brothers. The pain of their loss, even decades later, had been evident. The vendetta they held in their hearts for Sandra's death was real.

I thought of Bartolomeo and I recalled the lessons of my youth, of the priests and scribes who taught me the lessons of Exodus and Deuteronomy and that all sons may be judged by the sins of their fathers. The Bible contradicted itself in this regard in several places, but few Italians would swerve from the centuries old belief. No, the tradition of vendetta ran deep, very deep.

I had to hide the journal. I could not let Isabetta find it.

I briefly thought of burning it, but in the end, I decided it might be better to keep it as I puzzled out the situation.

I made my way to the kitchen, careful to make as little noise as possible so as not to wake Dea or Salvi. On a shelf near the back door was a wooden document box, painted simply in black and red. It had been Bartolomeo's; the very one from which Romoli had stolen his recipes, removing one or two of them at a time over the course of many weeks, until Bartolomeo had noticed. I had added a lock when I acquired the box. I took the key I kept at my belt and opened it. Inside were all of Bartolomeo's most important documents and hundreds of recipes—the ones that did not make it into his cookbook, the ones he developed after its publication and the ones he wanted to keep secret. I placed the journal on top and shut the lid, locking it once more. It was perfect. Isabetta would not consider looking there—she never stepped foot in the kitchen.

I sat down at the long table in the center of the room, poured myself some wine, and watered it down. I sipped it and listened to the sounds of the early morning streets, hoping to calm my churning stomach. How did my father know Isabetta's mother? Why did he feel it his duty to memorize *Pasquino*'s poem? Question after question tumbled through my mind, all culminating in one big question: What cruel fate had befallen me? My world was not at all what I thought it was. Each word I read from those journals made me question everything about myself.

"Maestro Scappi, why are you up?" It was Dea, dressed and ready to prepare for the day. She shuffled over to the table and poured herself some wine and water. She squinted at me. "I never see you awake before the bakers begin their calls."

I had to smile. When Bartolomeo was alive I was always up before the crack of dawn, preparing the papal kitchen for the day ahead. Now that I was the maestro, however, I didn't have to work on the early schedule. While I liked sleeping in a little, I would trade that luxury in a second if I could have my father back.

"I couldn't sleep," I said.

"You poor soul." She moved around the table until she could pat my back in a motherly way. "Next time ring the kitchen bell and I'll bring you my best sleep remedy."

I gave her a grateful smile. "Grazie."

She crossed the kitchen to stoke the fire for the morning. "Will we see you for the evening meal tonight or will you be dining with Signora Palone?"

Isabetta.

"If the pope doesn't need me, I'll dine at home tonight," I said. I would send a note to Isabetta that Pope Gregory required my services that evening—a lie, but only a small untruth. I needed time to understand the import of what I had found. Could I keep the secret from Isabetta? Or would it eat me up inside?

"Excellent. I think I'll make rabbit. Salvi said he saw some nice ones at the market yesterday and it got me thinking." She rubbed her hands together as if anticipating the taste.

"I am already looking forward to it," I told her as I rose from the table.

*   *   *

The Vaticano kitchen was bustling when I arrived. Pope Gregory's needs were meager, so much of the day was spent preparing meals for the clergy who lived on the grounds. While the pope was perfectly happy with bread, gruel, and perhaps an apple or two, the cardinali would riot if their food was so restricted. Gregory seemed to realize that, so while he had eliminated the big feasts and the more luxurious ingredients, he left the bulk of the clergy meals alone.

I had drawn up the week's menus a few days past, so the kitchen servants were already at work when I began to make my rounds of the cooking stations.

"Don't set that pot down there!" I yelled at a lanky boy with hair the color of fresh wheat. I didn't recognize him and surmised he must be one of Antonio's new boys. Everyone knew the blancmange station must be kept as clean as possible. Nothing was to contaminate the part of the kitchen where the white foods were made.

I was directing the bakers making the rose tourtes when I heard my name. I looked toward the door where one of the Swiss Guards waved a sealed piece of paper at me. I wiped my hands on my apron and made my way to him.

"A special summons from the governor's court of Roma," the guard said, handing me the paper.

I frowned. What could the governor's court of Roma want with me?

I broke the seal and unfolded the page. The script was bold and official with a stamp of the gubernatorial judge adjacent to the flowery signature.

> *You are hereby alerted to your required participation in a hearing. Signor Domenico Romoli is requesting rightful possession of the recipes of the now deceased Bartolomeo Scappi. Please report to Capitano Ventura, at the Palazzo Senatorio, at noon three days hence, on the 25th day of June in the year of our Lord, 1577.*

I gasped. Servants standing nearby stopped and turned in my direction at the sound. Heat rose to my face and I folded up the paper. "Get back to work!" I snapped. When their heads bent to their tasks once more, I went to find Francesco.

Sometime later, after being redirected many times by servants and clergy alike, I found him in the laundry, where he was instructing a new woman to oversee the washing of the papal vestments. When he saw me he paused, his eyebrow raising in alarm. I rarely sought him out beyond the kitchen, so he knew immediately something was wrong.

He put his hand on my shoulder and propelled me away from the bustle of the laundry to the quiet courtyard in the center of the Apostolic Palace.

"What is wrong, Gio, that you had to come to find me?"

I passed Francesco the summons. His eyes narrowed in disgust as he scanned it.

"That man is a disgrace. After everything Bartolomeo did for him!" He folded the summons neatly and handed it back.

"Do you think he stands a chance?" I asked.

"Absolutely not. The *bargello* won't dare cross Pope Gregory. The pope may have many faults, but he does not abide by lying and cheating. He will see Romoli as a man trying to profit from Bartolomeo's death, and worse, from recipes that were created in service to the church."

I hoped he was right and the captain in charge of the city's justice would not stand for Romoli's deception. "Do you think Pope Gregory will help me?" I asked.

Francesco nodded. "Without a doubt. I have an audience with him this afternoon. Give me the summons. I'll show it to him."

*   *   *

Later that afternoon, I informed the serving boy I would take the pope's supper to him directly. I climbed the stairs with a mixture of hope and fear.

I knocked on the door to his chambers and he called for me to enter. He sat at his desk near the window. "Ahh, Maestro Giovanni," he said as I set down the tray on the table where he usually took his meals. "Francesco told me you need a bit of help."

"If it pleases you, Your Holiness, I would greatly appreciate a kind word from you in this matter."

Gregory slid the big papal ring off his finger, took the nearby candle in hand, and dribbled wax onto a spot on the folded piece of paper before him. He pressed the ring into the hot wax to mark the seal. He came over to the table where I waited. He handed me the letter.

"Capitano Ventura has been the Roman bargello for the last twenty years and he owes me more than one favor. Just give this to him when he asks you for witnesses."

"Thank you, Your Holiness." I tucked the letter into my jacket.

"May the Lord bless you, Giovanni." He sat down and took up his fork in a gesture of clear dismissal. I backed out of the room and shut the door.

I ran into Francesco as I was leaving the kitchen to return home. I waved the letter at him.

"That should do the trick," he said, giving me a broad smile.

"I hope so. Otherwise I'll be sitting in a jail cell waiting for the trial to take place. You might be too." If a hearing went to trial, all the parties involved usually wound up in holding cells to prevent them from leaving before court was held.

"Do not fear, Gio. Romoli will never get his hands on those recipes."

* * *

The next morning, my day off, I woke to the sound of laughter downstairs—Dea, Salvi, and Isabetta. I cursed as I dragged myself out of bed and pulled my hose and doublet on. I wasn't ready to face Isabetta. I did not know how I could hide what I knew from her. I was sure she would read it on my face, see it in my eyes, taste it on my lips.

It wouldn't be long before Isabetta found her way up the stairs to come wake me. She would be hungry for my kisses and for my body. While I too felt the same hunger, I knew it would be my undoing. I needed time to find comfort with her once more—and that would be better in the company of others.

The three of them were all in the salon playing frussi, a bluffing game that was popular in salons across Europe. Pope Gregory and Pope Pius had forbidden the clergy from playing—gambling was immoral—but under previous popes the frussi parties were said to be grand.

The brightly painted cards were spread across the table and Dea was scooping several quattrini into her apron.

"It looks like you are the lucky one today," I remarked to her. She jumped at the sound of my voice.

"Maestro Scappi! Please forgive me. Let me go fetch you some wine to break your bread."

"It's my fault," Isabetta said. "Salvi wanted to learn how to play. Dea and I gave him coins to learn."

"I almost won!" Salvi jumped in, holding up his final hand, a flush of four cards ranging from four to seven.

"Hard to trump my hand, Salvi, dear," Dea said, patting the boy on the head. Salvi nodded, a pout on his face, and pointed to the hand on the table, a chorus of four aces.

"Did you put on your bluffing face?" I asked the boy.

"He's quite good," Isabetta said. "Better than you might be, I suspect."

I looked down at the cards before me.

"I'll show you how good I am, Maestro Scappi!" Salvi jumped up and came to me. He took me by the arm and led me over to the empty seat at the table.

"Now we'll see who the best at bluffing is!" Isabetta giggled.

Dea gave her quattrini to Salvi. "Take these, boy. I'm going to fetch the maestro a bit to eat. Win big!"

Isabetta shuffled the cards and dealt them to the three of us. My hand was dreadful, with not a single *fluxus* or *supremus*, only a pair of twos. To win this hand, my bluffing skills would need to be the best they ever had been.

I glanced up at Isabetta, watching the way the sunlight played across her features. She deftly organized her cards, reorganizing them to better see the suits. Her tongue was between her lips as she concentrated, and it made my heart constrict.

Salvi tossed two quattrini into the pile. He looked at me, his brown eyes bright with pride. Isabetta also added two quattrini to the pile. I dipped into my pouch and added six.

Salvi cried aloud. "Six?"

I smiled.

Isabetta tossed her cards in and Salvi looked at her, then back to his cards before following suit.

"You are too easy," I chuckled as I lay my hand down.

"Giovanni!" Isabetta smacked me on the arm.

Salvi sat there stunned. "You tricked us!" He flipped over his cards. He had a *primero*, a card for each suit. He flipped over Isabetta's cards. She had a *supremus*, a three flush and would have won.

"You could have kept going," I said as I scraped the quattrini off the table and into my hand.

Isabetta was grinning in disbelief. "Maestro Scappi, who knew you had such a face for bluffing?"

I swiped Salvi's cap off his head and deposited my quattrini into it before handing it back. "Don't spend it all on sweets," I warned.

We played a half dozen hands, and while I didn't win every one, when I did, there wasn't a moment when Isabetta or Salvi knew I was truly bluffing.

*   *   *

That day was warm, and after our game Isabetta wanted to take a stroll along the Tevere. I obliged her, glad to be out and about rather than inside with the journals. It didn't, however, stop the conversation about them.

"Bartolomeo's stories are just marvelous. In the one I'm reading now, your father tells an incredible tale about how Cardinale Campeggio threw a big banquet for Cardinale Ippolito. Your father was so angry that he was going to have to make food for Ippolito that he decided to show him up. The entire meal had a bird and egg theme, including magnificent castles with birds that flew out when the tower tops were cut off, roasted peacocks that still looked alive, swans made out of sugar paste, and hundreds of eggs dyed black in the water of walnut hulls. I would have loved to have seen such a sight!"

I wondered why Bartolomeo never spoke of that feast. He liked to boast, so it was curious that in all the time I had known him he chose not to mention that particular meal.

"It sounds magnificent," I agreed.

166

"It does," she said, grabbing me for support as she stumbled on a rock. I held her steady. "Bartolomeo did not linger to find out if Ippolito recognized the symbolism of the black eggs. At the end of the meal when he would normally have presented himself to the guests, he refused to show his face to Ippolito, telling Cardinale Campeggio he was ill and retiring for the night. He couldn't face him. After all that, he couldn't do it."

I was surprised to hear my father could not let the rivalry with Ippolito d'Este go by the wayside after so long. "Barto was never one to let someone get the better of him. It seems so counter to the person I knew."

We found a rock on an outcropping not far from Castel Sant'Angelo and perched ourselves upon it to survey the Tevere. Boats traversed the muddy water under the bridge that led from the *castello* to Roma.

"It's so big today." Isabetta jutted her chin at the comet above.

Big was an understatement. I had never seen anything like it. It shone brighter than the morning star, Venus, and it had a massive, silvery, curved, bowlike tail, resembling bright lightning, the brilliancy of which illuminated the earth below when darkness fell each night.

"Pope Gregory is planning a big sermon about it for the next Mass." The Vaticano had been abuzz about the comet. Every clergyman, it seemed, had been expounding on the meaning of the appearance of this bright heavenly body.

"The breath of Jehovah, like a stream of brimstone," she quoted from the Bible.

"Exactly. All hellfire, death of us all, repent, repent. Ad nauseum."

She laughed, but then turned serious. "Do you believe it? That the star will doom us?"

"No," I said, although I wasn't sure anymore. If it was the spirit of my father shining above, it was a spark of his dangerous genius. Everything I had learned about Bartolomeo's life since the comet had appeared was something unexpected, often something terrible. How close must the burning ball of light come before it would burn up me—and everyone I knew?

"And is it a star or a comet?" she asked. Everyone seemed to use the words interchangeably.

"A comet. Stars don't fly through the sky. One of the bishops once told me the word means 'long-haired star' in Latin."

"Bella," she said.

She ran her fingers along the nape of my neck and changed the subject. "What about the journal you are reading? What juicy details does it contain?"

My stomach tightened, but I had been rehearsing what I would say if this moment arrived and my words did not fail me. I calmed myself by thinking of how good I had been bluffing at cards.

"I didn't want to tell you," I said, letting my voice grow quiet and trail off. "I feared you would worry."

She turned to me, her face full of concern. "What happened, Gio?"

I looked away, as if in shame. "It happened a few days ago. I shouldn't have taken it with me, but I thought to decode some in my office at the Vaticano. I never had the chance, and when I was on my way home late, just there, crossing"—I pointed to the bridge—"I was set upon by two scoundrels who took my money pouch and tore through the bag I carried. When they found the journal, they tossed it into the river."

Isabetta sucked in a breath, her hands flying to her mouth in horror. "Oh, my Gio! Did they hurt you?"

"No, but only because I did not give fight. I had a stiletto at my throat the entire time. It would have been easy for them to slice me open and toss me into the Tevere like they did the journal." I told myself to stop embellishing, to stop making the event bigger than it already was. I worried the news of this "attack" would wind its way back to Caterina.

Isabetta flung her arms around me and held me close. I could feel wetness against my neck. I had not been prepared for tears; in fact, I had never seen her cry before. Guilt coated my stomach.

"Gio, oh my Gio. You must be more careful! What if they had hurt you? What if I lost you?" She pulled back and looked at me, her blue eyes glistening. Her vulnerability weakened me. I hated myself for the lie.

"I could not bear to lose you," she said, burying her face in my shoulder once more.

I held her like that for a while, my heart aching over the deception. But, oh, to tell her the truth? I did not believe we could survive that—if not her, then her brothers would be the ones to put a stiletto against my neck.

CHAPTER 16

Giovanni

Roma, June 25, 1577

The new facade of the Palazzo Senatorio glowed in the late morning sunlight, forcing me to shade my eyes as Francesco and I crossed the Campidoglio. The palazzo sat upon the ancient ruins of the Tabularium on the edge of the Forum. It had been Roma's center of government for the last fifteen hundred years. Michelangelo's grand design for the space was not yet complete, which meant the courtyard between the three buildings on the top of the Capitoline Hill had not been cobbled, and by the time we reached the new steps of the palazzo our shoes were covered in dirt.

I was grateful for Francesco's presence. I needed someone stable to temper the anger I felt for having to go before the court to defend Bartolomeo's legacy. The scalco had even forced me to down one of my own milk potions to calm my nerves.

"You cannot take your ire into the courtroom, Giovanni," he counseled me as we walked. "You want to be the calm in the storm, the one with the answers."

"I have no answers!" I told my friend. "I have only frustration. And dare I say it, hatred."

He put his arm around my shoulder and leaned in as we talked so others climbing the stairs would not overhear. "Hatred is a dark seed that has no place in a man's heart. If you are full of fury when you stand before the bargello he will turn against you. No, no, Gio. You must appeal to his sense of righteousness, of justice. You have done no wrong; Bartolomeo did no wrong."

I winced but did not tell my friend that he was wrong—that Bartolomeo had killed a man. I also did not voice my other concern, that I worried the actions of my father's past might come to weigh upon my own fortune.

"It is with that confidence you will win over Capitano Ventura."

Francesco was the one who was always calm in a storm, not I. I was a chef, with fire burning deep beneath my breast, smoke curling from my ears, knife and burn scars upon my fingers.

"I am not sure I can be that person," I admitted. "Romoli does me the greatest dishonor. I cannot let him get away with this."

Francesco's grip upon my shoulder tightened. "You must. Bartolomeo would agree. He was a man who knew how to win hearts, all hearts. He would twist the bargello right around his little finger. And how would he have done so? Not by cursing. Not by violence."

I met his eyes and was surprised by the intensity I saw within. I could not refute his logic, despite knowing my father was, in fact, someone who had used violence to protect his secrets. But if Bartolomeo were in the courtroom? Francesco was right. Bartolomeo had a certain charm that bent nearly everyone to his will. I needed to find a way to emulate him.

The bells in the palazzo tower began to ring the noon hour. I nodded my assent to Francesco and together we rushed up the stairs.

An elderly clerk at the entrance examined my summons and pointed us down a long hallway toward the stairs. We made our way through the bustle of people flowing through the halls and found the long central room on the second floor. The room was lined with statues from the ancient ruins. At the far end were a tall judicial podium and rows of benches full of people. Several uniformed *sbirri* stood near the front, ready to take the people in hand if needed. An older man with a creased brow and a mouth permanently curled into a frown presided over the crowd in long robes in red, with a black and red cap upon his head.

"That's Capitano Ventura," Francesco confirmed.

We took our seats in the middle of the benches and to the side of the crowd. I scanned the room looking for Romoli, hoping he wouldn't show. To my chagrin, I spotted him on the front-row bench. He cut a sharp figure in a white silk doublet with red breeches and hose. I glanced down at my dark wool jerkin and wished I had worn something better. With my inheritance, I could afford finer clothes, but I had never felt comfortable in silks and velvets. They might have served me well in court.

The bargello heard several cases, ranging from disputes over courtesans to accusations of theft before he called our names. In situations where he decided to move the case to trial, the sbirri shackled all parties involved—the accusers and accused—and sent them off to the jail to await the trial. It was a dreadful practice I hoped I would not have to endure. Sitting in confinement for a week while I waited for the case to continue would be maddening. They could place Romoli in a cell near mine and, if I had to listen to his prattle, I would want to slash my wrists before the end of the first day.

It was an hour before the court official announced our hearing. "The bargello of the Governor's Court of Roma will now open the hearing for Signor Domenico Romoli, who is requesting rightful possession of the recipes of the now deceased Bartolomeo Scappi. Will Domenico Romoli and Giovanni Scappi come before the judge."

I stood and followed Francesco to the front of the room. I was grateful my friend took a place next to Romoli, for I did not want to stand next to that scoundrel.

The court official brought a Bible forward. We placed our hands upon it, swore to tell the truth, then kissed the rough leather of the book's cover. It was a small, petty thing, but I watched to see where Romoli placed his lips and chose another part of the book for my kiss. I had made a vow to myself to be civil, but I refused to dirty myself with his touch.

"Domenico Romoli! Speak your case to Capitano Ventura."

It irritated me that Romoli was to speak first. I had hoped to give the capitano the letter from the pope, but propriety demanded I wait my turn.

Romoli stepped forward and scrutinized me with the briefest of sneers before placing himself in front of the judge.

"Honorable bargello, I am grateful for your time today. Please, please, call me by my nickname, Panunto. I am a former student of the late Bartolomeo Scappi. With extreme sadness, twenty years past, I left his employ to work for the house of the Medici. We continued a correspondence over the years, and in his letters, he shared several recipes with me. He was a man of estimable talent and a mentor who helped make me who I am today."

I gritted my teeth at his audacity. Asking the capitano to call him by such a nickname, which was the name of one of Barto's stolen recipes for oiled bread. What pride rested within that villain's breast!

Romoli continued. "I have in my hand a letter from Signor Scappi that outlines his desire for me to inherit his recipes." He waved an envelope toward the bargello. "Signor Betto is here to vouch for the validity of the document. He was the scalco for Cardinale Campeggio and for Pope Paolo and worked alongside Signor Scappi for many years."

The name I recognized. I also knew Betto and my father had no great love for each other. His journals documented many everyday arguments between them. He had seemed like a minor character in the story of Bartolomeo's life.

"Step forward and let me see the letter."

Romoli handed the letter to Ventura. The bargello scanned the document and turned to me. "Signor Scappi was your uncle?"

I nodded my assent. "Yes. He passed away in April."

"Did his will specify the recipes should go to you?"

I glanced at Francesco. I hated that I doubted him—he had administered several wills for servants of the Vaticano over the years and he knew the laws well. But I could remember nothing in the will pertaining to his recipes.

Francesco spoke up. "I was the executor of the will, and no, he did not make any specific provisions for the recipes." It was as though the floor dropped out from under me. But Francesco continued, his voice confident. "Signor Scappi did, however, confer his name, title, and position to his nephew, Giovanni, and with that typically comes all of the items of the trade."

The bargello studied the letter carefully, then waved me forward and handed it to me. "Look at this correspondence."

I opened it with trepidation, knowing with all my heart it could not be real. And yet, when I saw the scrawl upon the page, it did indeed look much like Bartolomeo's handwriting. I tried to keep my face passive, but inside me a fire raged.

The letter appeared to be a friendly note from Bartolomeo to Romoli, asking about life in Florence, then it went on to say that of late he had been feeling ill and he desired to have Romoli take possession of his recipes should anything happen to him. It was a forgery, but a clever one.

I handed the paper back to the bargello, saying nothing.

"Well, is it your uncle's handwriting?" His stare burned into me.

"It resembles his handwriting," I said begrudgingly. "However, I do not believe he wrote these words. My uncle did not care for Signor Romoli, who is a thief that stole several of Bartolomeo's recipes, then fled to Florence. I do not believe for an instant my uncle would give him the time of day, much less his most precious recipes. Signor Romoli further dishonors the name of my uncle with this charade."

"That is a *lie!*" Romoli said, his voice rising with each word. "Honorable bargello, you hold the truth in your hands. Do not listen to this mouth-stinking bastardo."

The bargello's voice rose over the court. "Signor Romoli, you will pay five scudi for this insult. I recommend you keep your mouth clean for the remainder of this hearing."

I must have appeared smug, because Ventura gave me a stern look as well. He turned to Betto and motioned for him to take the document. "Does this look like Signor Scappi's handwriting to you?"

Betto made a big show of staring at the page for far longer than necessary. He passed it back to the bargello. "I was the receiver of many written requests from Signor Scappi during my years as a scalco in the Campeggio household. This is most definitely his handwriting."

I opened my mouth to respond, but Ventura spoke over me. "This case will go to trial in one week's time. Signori Romoli, Betto, Reinoso, and Scappi, you will be placed in confinement until you come before the court once more. You will be given the opportunity to request whatever you would like from your homes, and you will also be asked to name your witnesses. Sbirri, please remove them from this court and take them to their cells to await trial."

"Bastardo," Francesco said to me under his breath as the sbirri moved to take us away. "Betto is a well-known forger. I do not know how Romoli thinks he can get away with this."

"I didn't even get a chance to tell my—"

I was interrupted by Romoli, who appeared next to Francesco. His smile was laced with contempt. "I told you, Giovanni, I would have those recipes."

I nearly swung a fist at him, but was stopped by a strong hand gripping my upper arm to lead me away.

We were almost at the door when I realized I had not had a chance to give the bargello the envelope Pope Gregory had given me. I drew it from inside my jerkin and pulled free of the sbirri. "Wait!" I shouted, waving the envelope in the air and sidestepping several people as I made my way back to the bench.

Ventura motioned to the guards to let me approach. "You asked for witnesses." I handed him the letter, my heart pounding. "You should see this."

I heard the break of the seal. I wondered what it read.

Whatever the words within the letter, they were enough to make Capitano Ventura straighten up. "This case is dismissed. The Court of the Governor will not consider a change in ownership of Bartolomeo Scappi's recipes. Please unhand the signori. You are all free to go." He waved a hand at us in dismissal, then called for the next case to be brought forward to him.

I didn't even have a second to breathe a sigh of relief when Romoli turned to me. "What did you give him?" he growled.

I began to walk away. I had not taken more than two paces when a hand gripped me forcefully and turned me back around.

"You pig-dog, what did you give to him?"

I threw up my arm to remove his grip. "Unhand me. You have no right to dishonor my uncle."

Suddenly I was on the ground, sprawled at the feet of three men who sat on one of the court benches. I felt a bruise blossoming on my chin.

"*What is this disturbance?*" Ventura's anger stunned the room to silence. He pointed to Romoli. "Remove this man and place him in a cell. You will stay there, Signor Romoli, for three nights for disturbing my court, dishonoring a man, and for violence in a place of civility."

The sbirri were upon Romoli before I could even stand up.

"You'll pay, you filthy whoreson. You'll pay!" he screamed at me as they dragged him out of the room.

"Give him two more nights for cursing!" Ventura called after the sbirri.

Francesco helped me up and we left the court in a hurry. Betto was nowhere to be seen.

"When he gets out of prison he is going to come after you," Francesco warned me as we descended the *cordonata*, the long ramp leading away from the Campidoglio.

"I know. I will be wary."

"You should leave Roma. Go elsewhere until he tires of this game and returns to Firenze."

I thought about Isabetta, about Caterina, and my work at the Vaticano. I did not want to leave. Nor did I want to give in to Romoli. "No, my friend. He will not make me leave Roma. Do not worry, *amico*, I will be careful."

We parted ways at Saint Peter's Square. Francesco urged me to take the afternoon to myself and leave my duties at the Vaticano to Antonio. Grateful, I agreed.

I walked home, my mind set on reading some more of my father's journals. The sky above me was filled with the silver-red tail of the comet burning through the heavens.

CHAPTER 17

Scappi

Roma, September 1549

Bartolomeo hissed in pain. He dropped the hot chestnut back into the pan and stuck his index and middle fingers into his mouth.

"You poor man," Stella said, pulling his hand from his lips and bringing it to her own. She took his fingers and slid them into her mouth and across her tongue. Despite the sting of the burn, Bartolomeo felt the familiar tug in his groin.

"You are a vixen," he breathed, leaning down to kiss her. He never tired of her delicate lips, the way she tasted like roses. He loved the moment when he first felt the soft pressure of her tongue against his.

A chestnut popped loudly and they pulled apart with a jolt, which sent them into peals of laughter.

"Your brother will be here soon, stellina mia. It will do you no good to lure me back into bed."

"It would do me every bit of good, orso mio." She laughed and the sound filled Bartolomeo with longing. Before he could succumb once more, he took a spoon and scooped the remaining chestnuts from the pan into a bowl to cool.

Bartolomeo loved the stolen afternoons when he did not have to work and Stella came to visit. Her brother still escorted her to and from Bartolomeo's house, taking great care to make sure they went unnoticed.

"I have some good news," he said, picking up a chestnut and peeling it apart.

She leaned over the table seductively, her breasts threatening to spill from the bodice of her corset. "What good news?" She plucked her own morsel from the bowl.

"Pope Paolo was so impressed by the feast I prepared for the Barberini wedding that he asked Cardinale Bembo if he could hire me and make me cuoco segreto." He puffed up his chest, full of pride. To be made the private chef to a pope was the highest honor any cook in the world could hope to receive.

Stella threw her arms around his neck and smothered him with kisses. "How wonderful, Barto!"

"That's not all. He also wants me to be his mace bearer."

Stella gasped in wonder. "The mace bearer is an important post, is it not?"

"An extra two hundred scudi a year, and I'm granted a room at the Vaticano."

She ran her hand down his cheek, then pulled away, crossed the room, took a burlap sack from a pigeonhole on the shelf, and began to fill it with the warm chestnuts. She paused as his words sank in, then eyed him, concern wrinkling her brow.

"A room at the Vaticano! Oh, Barto, we court scandal if we were to try anything under the pope's nose. Please tell me you aren't giving up your house!"

"No, no, stellina mia. Do not fear. But it will be nice to sleep close to the kitchen on big feast days."

She visibly relaxed and returned to the task of filling her sack full of chestnuts. "Don't you have to walk in front of the pope with the big jeweled mace? He always has mace bearers when there are papal processions."

"There is a college of mace bearers who do that. Nine of them, to be exact. They are the ones that march in all the ceremonies. For this post, I would not have to march in the ceremonies, unless he dies, then I will march at the head of them with the pope's mace. I will also have several duties for the conclave, like cooking meals, making sure no one sneaks notes or poison into the food, and a few other responsibilities. I would also carry the mace in front of his casket."

"How dour." Stella winked at Bartolomeo. "Tell me of something happier. What is the news of our boy?"

Bartolomeo squinted at her. "For agreeing we would not talk much about him, we sure seem to have a lot of conversation about the child."

She sighed. "I know. It's harder than I thought it would be. I find myself wondering if he looks like you, if he'll grow up with your voice, with your love of laughter. Please tell me he fares well."

Bartolomeo came around the table and took her in his arms again. He brushed away a golden lock from her face. "Stella, Stella, worry not. He is hale and hearty and growing faster than a stalk of asparagus. The gift you have given me in letting me be part of my son's life is one I can never truly repay. I will take great care of him, my love." He changed the subject before she could dwell too much on the arrangement. "Tell me, what other news do you have? How is the life of my stellina since we last saw each other?"

Her face darkened. "My father is talking about marrying me off again."

Bartolomeo drew in a sharp breath. Her previous husband had only been dead two years. "I thought we had too much fortune these days. To whom? Please tell me this marriage won't take you away from Roma."

She stared off into the fire, her expression hard to read. "I do not think it will. The union he proposes will bring me closer to Pope Paolo."

"What do you mean?"

"I think he wants to marry me to one of the pope's relatives." She said his name, low, even though no one was in earshot.

Bartolomeo paused. "Are you sure?"

"Do you know much of him?"

Bartolomeo snickered. "I do. I always thought his father would petition Paolo to make him a cardinale. It would be an office more fitting than that of a husband."

Realization bloomed in Stella's eyes. "He does not love women?"

He shook his head. "Well, I always see him in the company of women, but he is more interested in discussing jewels and the latest fashions than love." He smirked. "This could be a perfect union."

"I wonder if my father knows."

"Perhaps it's a gift to you."

Her laughter was genuine. "You might be right. He knows I am tired of bearing children to old men who do not love me."

*   *   *

Two months later, Bartolomeo was closing the kitchen when Betto, the scalco, came with word of Pope Paolo's death.

Betto placed a key on the table in front of Bartolomeo.

"What is that?"

"The key to the box holding the pope's mace. I will have it brought to you shortly."

Bartolomeo picked it up and put it in the pouch on his belt. A wave of sadness and confusion rippled through him when his hand touched the cold metal. "How did it happen?"

"He collapsed during dinner with his grandsons," Betto said, his face impassive but his eyes black and hard.

"On Monte Cavallo?" Bartolomeo asked. The pope's family had a palace on the back side of the hill overlooking central Roma where they often held parties.

"Yes. The body will be borne from the palace through the Traste-vere to Saint Peter's tomorrow. You will carry the mace before the bier when they bring the body into the church. The funeral will last nine—"

Bartolomeo cut him off. "Nine days, yes I know. There is a reason they call it a Novendialia." Sarcasm coated his words, but he didn't care. He was annoyed that Betto showed no emotion at the loss of the pope. Pope Paolo had been a kind man to Bartolomeo. Not to mention that with a new pope came extreme uncertainty. The two of them could both be looking for new jobs when the next pope took office.

"You will find all the hampers and the staves for carrying the hampers in the third cellar room, the one marked with the griffin carving. The travel boxes for the wine are in the same location." Betto continued to list off the various details relating to the funeral and the conclave when Bartolomeo interrupted him, unable to contain his irritation anymore.

"Do you even care that your employer has just died? Did you say a prayer or shed a single tear?"

Betto raised an eyebrow. "It is not my place, Maestro Scappi. My place is to see to the running of the Vaticano, as is yours."

Bartolomeo threw his hands into the air. "Fine, Signor Betto. Let your heart be full of ice. And fear not. I will do my duty, but know I will do it as a man who cared for the other men around him. Pope Paolo took us both under his wing, elevating us to stations higher than we might ever have again. He was kind to me and I will remember him as such. He was good-hearted, obliging, and supremely intelligent. He was a man worthy enough to be described as magnanimous. I, for one, will mourn his passing."

Betto's visage cracked into a scowl. "And he allowed astrologers to live within the Vaticano, he failed at the conciliation of the Prot-estants at the Council of Trent, he filled his court primarily with his relatives, and he excommunicated the king of England, placing a wedge between our countries. You shed all the tears you want, Maestro, but I will welcome the next pope, whomever he may be, with open arms." The scalco stormed off, leaving Bartolomeo slack-jawed, with the few remaining kitchen servants murmuring in the background.

"Get out of here," he growled. "We have a lot of work to do, with the funeral, and with the conclave. It could be weeks before you have a full night of sleep again."

The next evening, an hour before midnight, Bartolomeo performed his duty as mace bearer, carrying the elaborate gold mace with its head pointing toward the earth. He walked in front of the procession, and the cardinali followed the casket into Saint Peter's, their robes flowing in a sea of purple. The pope's body lay in Christ Chapel for three days before it was buried behind the organ of Saint Peter's.

As he walked in the funeral procession each of the nine days, carrying the pope's mace before him and leading the pope's family to their seats, he memorized the details of the enormous catafalque in the shape of a castle that was erected in the middle of Saint Peter's. The temporary monument had four sides and small torches, over 1,120 of them, along the top. Black taffeta and painted symbols of the pope's coat of arms and angels in various poses covered the sides of the catafalque. An hour of prayer and song followed, then every day Bartolomeo thanked the stars he did not have to follow the family into the sacristy for a general congregation, which lasted another three or four hours.

On the tenth day, the conclave began. Bartolomeo was not allowed inside, but he had helped Betto oversee the creation of the fifty-nine cells that would hold the cardinali of the conclave, the gathering to choose a new pope. The cells were decorated in purple, with beddings and furnishings of the same color, each cell adorned with the coat of arms of that cardinale. For every cell there was a table covered with a purple tablecloth, a rack to hang clothing, a small wooden lantern, a chamber pot, two stools, and poison-proof jars with locking lids for drinking water. Each cardinale had a secretary, a nobleman, and a personal attendant to wait upon him. Several enormous hampers carried food from the kitchen to the conclave.

The ritual of it fascinated Bartolomeo. So few were ever able to witness a conclave and he felt it was his duty to chronicle every moment. Each night he would hole up in his new room in the Vaticano and detail the events of the day in his journal. He made note of everything he could, down to the guards who checked the hampers for notes, poison, and weapons, to the number of servants each cardinale could have, to the way they tested the food, to the rule that dishes were not allowed to leave the conclave once they entered, to prevent notes from being passed back.

Writing kept him from thinking about what could happen to him when a new pope was chosen. Would he lose his job? He recorded the names of all the cardinali in attendance, except for one, the one he prayed would never be pope. Superstitious, he believed if he did not write it down, perhaps it would not be so.

The rumored favorite was Cardinale Ippolito d'Este.

*   *   *

The conclave was not a short one. A week rolled by, then another, then another. Every day Bartolomeo's routine was nearly the same. He oversaw the inspection and placement of the food into hampers, which the scalco would place in the *rotonda*, spin it around, and the assistant on the other side would remove it and bring the food to his master. This took till noon, then began all over again for the evening meal. With so many cardinali in the conclave, it was a tedious process. One of the duties Scappi held was to choose the order in which the cardinali should receive their food. Every day at the end of the night he would draw lots and make up the new list, with the exception being those cardinali who were sick—they were always on the top of the list.

And many cardinali did fall ill. On the fourth of December, Cardinale Veruli was carried out of the conclave to the Castel Sant'Angelo, where he died two weeks later. On the twentieth, Cardinale Santa Croce emerged, ill. And on the first of January of the new year 1550, Cardinale Bologna left the conclave in tremendous pain from gallstones.

Toward the end of January, as dictated by tradition, the process changed to encourage a swifter decision. Bartolomeo oversaw the reduction of rations to the conclave. Gone were the meat pies and sumptuous desserts. In their place was barley soup and a little bread and cheese. The upper-story windows of the Cappella Sistina were closed to reduce the natural lighting and fresh air. When Cardinale Niccolò Ridolfi left the conclave on January 20, dying soon after, it was rumored the poison air within the chapel was to blame.

Every time a cardinale left the conclave, Bartolomeo's gut clenched. And every time it wasn't Cardinale d'Este, he fell into a dark rage that sent the kitchen hands scurrying out of his way.

Exhaustion was Bartolomeo's closest companion during the two months of the conclave. He did not see Stella, nor was he able to send messages to her.

A little after ten o'clock on February 7, just as Bartolomeo was putting his knives away for the night, the bells rang through the chapel, signifying a new pontiff had been selected.

Bartolomeo dismissed the remainder of the kitchen hands and returned to his room to contemplate the news. The new pope would not be announced until late the next morning. The thought of Ippolito d'Este becoming pope was one he could hardly imagine. Over the years he had successfully dodged encountering him face-to-face despite Cardinale d'Este's inquiries at various banquets about the mysterious chef who made such delectable meals. Bartolomeo always had an excuse to prevent him from meeting the man who had once crushed all his eggs in the Rialto market. To imagine he might end up employed by his enemy seemed unfathomable.

He thought about leaving, going back to Venezia, or looking for employment somewhere else, perhaps in France. When the morning sunlight peeked into the room, he was still awake, considering his options. But he could not bear to be away from Stella. Reluctantly, he dressed, tied on his apron, and went to see how his world was going to change.

It was a long morning. The official ceremony to announce the new pope could not occur until the cardinali had completed their preparatory rituals, which allegedly included the ritual of the *sedes stercoraria.* Bartolomeo had heard clergy say it was to guard against the extreme aesthetics of self-castration. But everyone knew it really had to do with the mysterious Pope Joan from three hundred years past, whom the church never spoke of. She was rumored to have dressed as a man during her tenure as clergy, but when she took on a lover, she was exposed as a fraud when she gave birth. To ensure no woman would ever take the papal throne again, each prospective pope had to sit on a special keyhole chair and let a junior cardinale fondle his testicles and then exclaim for all to hear: *"Duos habet et bene pendentes."* He has two, and they hang well. Bartolomeo shuddered to think of it.

As mace bearer to Pope Paolo, Bartolomeo was expected to be present when the new pope was announced to the hundreds of faithful who waited in the church of Saint Peter's. He walked in the procession and knelt with the other mace bearers when the doors to the Cappella Sistina opened and a rush of stale air streamed forth.

Senior Cardinale Cibo stepped across the threshold, the cross in his hand. The many cardinali who made up *il collegio cardinalizio* milled about behind him, anxious to leave the confines of the chapel, but held back by protocol and tradition.

"I announce to you a wondrous joy," Cardinale Cibo said, his voice ringing across the crowd of family members and nobles who had been granted access to the inner confines of the Vaticano to hear the announcement. Bartolomeo's heart pounded. He wanted to reach up and wipe the bead of sweat from his forehead, but dared not break the frozen stance he shared with the other mace bearers.

"*Habemus papam!* We have a pope! The Most Eminent and Reverend Lord, Lord Giovanni, Cardinale of the Holy Roman Church Maria Ciocchi del Monte, who takes to himself the name Julius III!"

Bartolomeo thought his legs might give way, his relief was so great.

The sea of red parted and the new Pope Julius came forth, his long gray beard freshly combed and the red velvet cape and hood framing his long face. His eyes glittered as he scanned the crowd and raised his hand to give a blessing. Then Cardinale Cibo led him away, the people moving aside as they headed for the balcony to give the news to the citizens of Roma who waited in the dusty piazza outside Saint Peter's.

The cardinali poured out of the chapel, brushing past the mace bearers and into the arms of their friends and family. Bartolomeo found Ippolito d'Este in the throng and was pleased to see he appeared haggard and unkempt from his two months in confinement. He scowled and stormed past the cardinali walking too slowly, the force of his movement throwing more than one of the older men off-balance.

Bartolomeo stared at him, daring the defeated cardinale to look him in the eye, but the man brushed past him, his elbow sending the elaborate mace in Bartolomeo's hand flying. It clattered to the ground with a loud clang, loosening several pearls that flew across the Vaticano tiles.

Cardinale Ippolito d'Este never looked back.

* * *

Twelve days before his crowning ceremony, the new pope-elect came to the kitchen to survey the staff. Betto, in a rare gesture of kindness, had alerted Bartolomeo to the visit that morning, giving the cook a chance to make sure each of the servants was dressed in their cleanest aprons and that everyone's station was even more orderly than normal.

Pope Julius III allowed Bartolomeo to kiss his ring, then greeted him warmly. "We are pleased to hear the finest cuoco in the land will be at Our disposal," he said, already comfortable with the plural denoting the pope together with God. Bartolomeo hoped the pope did not notice his hand shaking when he bent to kiss the ring.

"We enjoyed one of your meals for His Holiness Pope Paolo a year past," the pontiff continued. "We expect you will continue to employ your talents in Our kitchen during Our reign. You will be allowed to keep your title of mace bearer if you so desire."

Bartolomeo felt lighter at the pope's words. He had not known how much worry had rested upon his shoulders until that moment. "I would be honored, Your Holiness." He bowed his head, grateful for his continued employment.

"Excellent. You will begin preparing the coronation feast. We are expecting exceptional things from you, Maestro Scappi. Do not disappoint." Pope Julius was out the door before Bartolomeo could blink.

He began to sort through the lists in his head, of the pigs and cows to be slaughtered, the bread to be made, the vegetables and fruits to be purchased. He made a mental note to stop at the spice merchant first thing in the morning. And to send a note to Stella.

My Stella, he wrote in his head as he worked. *We will meet soon, after this feast, after this pope and all the cardinali see and taste the glory that is only mine to give.*

CHAPTER 18

Giovanni

Roma, July 1577

Twenty days passed, and I had heard nothing from Romoli. I had taken Francesco's advice and, at great expense, hired two *condottieri* to escort me to and from the Vaticano and to watch over the house. I dismissed the mercenaries at the end of the three weeks. They were bored and overpaid, and I could find no reason to keep them. I kept a close eye on my surroundings, but there was still no disturbance to my daily routine.

The same day I let the condottieri go, a letter in memory of Bartolomeo arrived from a woman. The flowery script said little other than that she had loved his meals very much and she was enormously saddened by the news of his passing. It was signed by Sofia Pisani, a Venetian name. I interrogated everyone I could about Signora Pisani, but no one knew who she was.

* * *

In mid-July I received a message from Caterina that she and Cesare wanted me to come to dinner. She hated that her sons were not speaking and wanted to mend the divide. I recalled Cesare's curses and knew it was an impossible hope. Still, I responded with an invitation for them to visit on the coming Sunday, a day I rarely worked because Pope Gregory tended to fast and he liked the clergy to follow suit.

I also asked Isabetta to join us, hoping that her presence would keep my brother civil. As it was a formal meal, I suggested Rolando accompany her, which he graciously agreed to do.

I helped Dea do most of the cooking. I did not want to give Cesare any cause to complain about the meal, and I had to admit there was a certain pride that overtook me. I always thought I had to prove myself to Cesare, and now that he had decided I was not his brother, it somehow strangely seemed even more important to validate my worth in his eyes. There had always been a part of me that craved his love and approval.

I decided to serve him even more luxurious versions of the foods he had loved when we were young. The centerpiece of the meal would be braised beef shank, flavored with fennel pollen, cinnamon, ginger, and a hint of rose vinegar. I stewed it with plums and cherries and doused it with a little malmsey for good measure. Then I made a casserole of eggplant and cheese, ray fish in pastry wraps, capon meatballs, and a blackberry tourte. Dea finally put her foot down when she saw I was going to make a pizza as well.

"We'll be eating this food for a week, signore! Please, no more."

I looked at the array of dishes before me and had to admit, maybe Dea was right. Salvi had flour in his auburn hair, and butter smears and cherry juice on his apron. I had been delighted to discover that he loved to work alongside me in the kitchen. Dea had begun to enlist him for help in the kitchen when I was too busy to instruct him, and she said he took to it like a bishop to a jug of wine. It was exciting to see how quickly his skills had progressed. At eight years old, he was still so young, but already he was better than I had been at fourteen.

"Salvi, make sure to clean up a bit before our guests arrive. You look like you got in a fight with a flour sack." I flicked the dough on the end of my knife in his direction and the glob landed on his hand. He stared at it for a second and before I knew it, I had streaks of flour across my face. Laughing, I reached for him, but he lunged and hid behind Dea.

"Enough, boys!" she said sternly, but the smile on her face belied her mood. "Hand me your aprons, then run along and clean yourselves up. I'll finish here."

"You indulge that child too much," Dea said to me after Salvi had gone to change his clothes.

"Don't worry so much, Dea. I suspect few have ever indulged him in his life. So, if we do a little bit, what harm could there be?"

She looked at me thoughtfully, then waved a hand. "You are a good man, Signor Scappi. Now go, get cleaned up."

I hurried out of the kitchen. My guests would arrive soon.

While I looked forward to entertaining the Palones, I dreaded seeing my own family. I knew Caterina would do her best to keep the peace, but I could not get Cesare's words from his last visit out of my head. What would he say once he was seated across the table from me? My stomach was in knots by the time the knock sounded on the door.

I was surprised at the greeting I did receive. Caterina hugged me warmly, as always, and Cesare acted as though there had never been strife between us. He clasped my arm with a smile and clapped me on the back with his free hand. "Giovanni! It has been a long while since I've had one of your feasts."

I debated whether I should bring up his last visit. I was suspect about his motives for attending after his outburst, but the appearance of Isabetta and Rolando quickly pushed the thought from my mind and I made introductions.

"So, this is your brother," Isabetta said, her tone neutral. I knew that underneath her calm exterior she had strong opinions of Cesare—

his display of emotion on his last visit had soured her impression of him.

"I see my reputation precedes me," Cesare said, bowing and gallantly taking up Isabetta's hand for a kiss.

"It does," she said simply. She retrieved her hand and curtsied, but the tension did not dissipate until my mother swooped in to give Isabetta a hug. After greeting Rolando, the two women moved off to the dining room to warm themselves by the fire and gossip a little before dinner.

"I understand you are likely to become a father-in-law to my brother?" Cesare said to Rolando as we walked down the hall toward the dining room.

I thought my heart might stop. Behind his jovial facade Cesare had clearly not changed. He always tried to embarrass me or make me look small in a situation.

Rolando didn't pause, didn't even raise an eyebrow. "That may be true, yes. And I welcome it, for Isabetta's heart sings whenever she is around your brother."

Isabetta had surely told her father about Cesare, and Rolando, being the gentleman he was, would not shame me or give in to my brother's goading. But his words meant more than that. It was a message to me he fully approved of our union—and he was waiting for me to ask for his daughter's hand. My mouth went dry.

Salvi caught up to us, sparing me from a response. "Dinner is ready to be served," he announced with a little bow, then he disappeared down the corridor toward the kitchen.

Grateful, I ushered Cesare and Rolando into the dining room where Caterina and Isabetta were taking their places at the long table. I faltered a moment when I saw Isabetta and her eyes met mine. She smiled and the air grew warm around me.

I took my place at the head of the table, Caterina to my right and Isabetta to my left. Before the guests had arrived, I had Dea place a display of flowers at the opposite end of the table, which meant Cesare couldn't claim the spot. He settled in next to Caterina and Rolando sat next to his daughter. We had barely found our seats when Dea and Salvi swept into the room with the first course. My guests wasted no time at digging in.

The mealtime conversation was genial, ranging from Roman politics to the comet, which only seemed to get brighter day by day. After the beef shank was served, I managed to forget my animosity toward Cesare and began to truly enjoy myself. The food was perfect, the wine was lush and full, and the conversation was friendly and punctuated with laughter. I thought it was all too good to be true.

"Our uncle taught you well," Cesare said as he finished off the last of his blackberry tourte. I was surprised; he seemed to mean what he said.

"I could have eaten a hundred of those," Isabetta agreed.

"I'm happy to share the recipe," I told her, beaming with pride.

"Yes, you must," Caterina said, touching my arm. "Cesare and I were talking about that earlier tonight, about all the things Barto would make for you boys when you were young."

"You must have hundreds of our uncle's recipes squirreled away," Cesare noted.

I glanced in the direction of the kitchen, thinking about the long recipe box on the shelf near the door. "I have a few," I conceded.

"I have one of his recipes for strawberry pie somewhere at home," Caterina said, lifting her wine to take another sip. "I wish we could get strawberries this time of year."

The conversation turned to trade and how difficult it was to import foods from afar, particularly when growing seasons for some fruits and vegetables were longer in other parts of the world. Rolando was, as ever, a fount of knowledge and I hung on his every word.

"I need the privy. I'll be right back," Cesare said. I returned my attention to Rolando, who continued with his story.

A few minutes later, I heard a cry from Salvi, followed by a crash in the kitchen.

Stunned, we looked at each other for the barest of moments, then the table erupted as chairs flew backward and we all raced toward the sound.

Dea was on the floor, a trickle of blood running down her neck. She cradled her head in her hands. Rolando rushed to her side. The kitchen door stood open. I moved past Dea and Rolando to look out.

The privy and the courtyard were empty. The gate in the far wall banged in the wind. Neither my brother nor Salvi were anywhere to be seen.

I went back inside and found Caterina on the floor, cradling Dea's head in her lap. Isabetta wet a rag from the jug at the washbowl.

"She's just had a bad scare. The scratch did not go deep," Rolando said. His voice held an edge I had not heard before. "Your brother—why would he do this? Where would he have gone?"

My gaze flew to Caterina, hoping she might know. She only looked at me, despair in her eyes, and shook her head.

I lifted a hand to my head in response to the deep headache that made my temple throb. I scanned the room, wondering what my brother wanted so badly he assaulted my housekeeper.

"He took Barto's recipes," Dea said weakly. "He had just tucked the box under his arm when I came up from the cellar."

I looked at the shelf near the door for the red and black painted two-foot-square box, the one that contained all of Bartolomeo's recipes. It was gone. A great panic swept through me when I thought about Bartolomeo's knife, which I kept on top of the recipe box. Then I saw it on the floor, a few feet away from Dea. I wanted to collapse to the floor, my relief was so great. I could hardly bear to think about losing the recipes, but there are not enough words to describe how I would have felt if I had lost the knife.

Then I remembered the journal I had stowed away in the recipe box.

"I have to get that box back." Heat rose to my face, a mixture of embarrassment and anger.

"Where is Salvi?" Isabetta asked as she wiped the blood from Dea's head.

"He chased after Cesare." Dea motioned with her hand toward the door. "I told him not to, but he ignored me."

I thought of him racing through the streets in the dark.

"We need to find him."

"He was a street urchin before your uncle took him in. He'll be fine. Better than we would be in the dark of night," she warned.

I started to open my mouth, but one look from her and I kept it shut.

"Dea is right. That boy probably knows the streets better than any of us. Perhaps he can tell us where your brother went," Rolando said.

I stared into the dark. "Do you think he will go back to your house, Mamma?" I asked my aunt, mindful of how I called her my mother. She would know it was for appearances. I swallowed, guilt on my tongue.

Her eyes narrowed, and her brow creased into an angry line. "No, he wouldn't dare."

I chuckled at that. Caterina had a legendary temper. Cesare's betrayal had provoked her fury.

* * *

Salvi returned home an hour later, just as Rolando and Isabetta readied to escort Caterina home.

"I lost him." Dejection colored Salvi's words. "When I got to Piazza Navona, there were some sheep being led out of the market that got in my way. I wanted to tell you where he had gone."

"Thank you for trying."

Salvi wiped his nose with his sleeve.

Rolando put a hand on the boy's shoulder. "You did a good thing today, Salvi, trying to help Signor Scappi. I want to help too. Why don't you meet me tomorrow morning after first light at the new fountain of Neptune on the north end of Navona. You can help some of my men search the area. Hopefully he didn't go far. We'll get that box back, what do you say?"

Salvi's eyes lit up at the thought of helping the adults do something so important. I found myself smiling despite the situation.

"Thank you, signor. Thank you."

"Go tell Dea you are safe," I told the boy. "She's in the sitting room lying down. She'll be happy to know you are well."

Salvi disappeared into the house and Rolando turned back to me. "We'll find those recipes for you," he said. "I have many eyes in Roma. Someone will have seen something or know someone who did."

I worried about Rolando finding the box with the journal inside, but could not gracefully reject his help. Worse, I could not go with Salvi in the morning to meet Rolando, because Pope Gregory was hosting some bishops from Spain, and I was needed at the Vaticano to prepare the meal. If Rolando found the box, and the journal, I hoped he would do the honorable thing and return it all to me without prying.

Caterina dabbed at her eyes with the corner of her sleeve. "Please, promise me you won't hurt Cesare."

"No one will be hurt, Signora Brioschi. Don't worry," Isabetta said, squeezing her shoulders.

*　　*　　*

I lay awake much of the night listening to the sounds of the three-century-old house that surrounded me. While I didn't want Cesare or Romoli to have the recipes, Rolando leading the charge made me more uneasy. If Isabetta learned of the journal she would want to know why I had lied to her, and why I had told her it had ended up in the Tevere. Then she would want to read it; she would know that I was keeping something from her. I had no doubt that her brothers would decide that I was a worthy victim to end their vendetta.

Light had not yet begun to filter through the windows when I heard Salvi rustling around downstairs. I pulled on my night robe and went down to see him.

He startled when my lantern light broke the darkness of the kitchen entryway.

"I'm so sorry to wake you, Maestro Scappi. Please do not be angry." His voice quavered.

"I'm not angry with you, Salvi. How could I be when you are readying yourself to go help me?"

His features relaxed. I sat down at the long bench at the table in the center of the room and reached for a slice of bread leftover from last night's meal. Dea would be up soon to make a new batch, especially if she heard us stirring.

He put a piece of bread into the pocket of his coat. "I will find him. It's my fault that Dea got hurt. She heard me yell and tried to stop Cesare. If it weren't for me he would never have hit her."

Such honor in the little boy's heart, I thought.

"It's not your fault, Salvi. Cesare has never been a nice man. In fact, you did a good thing by trying to help. It shows you have courage."

Pride glittered in the boy's eyes and the corner of his mouth turned upward a little.

A cock crowed somewhere down the street. It was still dark, but dawn would be swift. Salvi buttoned his coat and made for the door.

"Salvi, be careful today. And can you also do me a favor?"

He turned toward me. "Anything, Maestro."

"In the box with all the recipes was a special journal. It was Barto's and it means a lot to me. It's also very private. Can you make sure that Signor Palone doesn't look at it?"

He nodded vigorously, and for a moment I thought his hat might fall off his head. "Sì, I promise to keep it away from him."

I believed him. He was a child so desperate to please me. I remembered my own years as an unruly teenager and wondered if his loyalty would last.

*　　*　　*

I was glad that the Vaticano kitchen kept me busy that day. When visiting dignitaries were guests, the meals were more elaborate, but nowhere near the banquets of the past. But I did what I could with the limited number of dishes Pope Gregory allowed. I made tourtes of veal, of capons, and of artichokes and cardoon hearts. I slaved over pork belly tortellini and eggs stuffed with their own yolks and raisins, pepper, cinnamon, orange juice, and butter. I made sure the pastry chef was working hard on the pastry twists made with rosewater and currants. Soups of cauliflower, mushrooms, and leeks simmered for the better part of the day. When I finally made my way home, I was exhausted.

Salvi greeted me at the door before I even had a chance to open it.

"Maestro, Maestro, I have the recipes!"

He proudly produced the box, which looked big in his arms.

I took it from him and brought it into the parlor, where I could set the box down and properly dig through it. Salvi bounced alongside me.

"We found him on Via dei Coronari at one of the houses of the Confraternita del Gonfalone."

Ahh, the charitable Guild of the Banner. The guild owned many churches, hospitals, and inns to host priests and pilgrims coming to Roma.

"We saw him coming out of the door with another man and they walked in the direction of Piazza Navona. I wanted Signor Palone to send his men after them, but he told me to wait, and to be patient. Do you know what happened?"

His excitement tempered my worry and I grinned in spite of myself. "Tell me, Salvi."

"Signor Palone has a cousin in the Gonfalone! Once he explained what happened to the men inside they searched the rooms of Signor Brioschi and his friend. They found the box in the other man's room and they gave it to Signor Palone. The other man came back alone just as we were leaving. He saw us with the box and immediately turned and ran. Signor Palone's men followed, but he was very quick."

"Who was the man?" I asked. "Did Signor Palone find out?"

Salvi nodded. His eyes sparkled with the knowledge. "Signor Romoli. He is in service to the Medici and was visiting from Firenze. I guess he gave them a lot of extra money to stay there, even though he isn't a pilgrim."

Of course Cesare knew Romoli. A weight descended upon my shoulders. I sighed and shook my head.

"What's wrong, Maestro?"

I forced a smile. "Nothing, Salvi. You did well." I ruffled his hair. "Thank you."

I turned to the box. I undid the latch and lifted the lid, half expecting to find it empty. I released a heavy breath when I saw that the recipes were there.

But the journal was missing.

"Remember the journal I mentioned this morning?" I asked Salvi. He faltered, staring at the box. "Yes," he finally said.

"It's not here. Was it missing when Signor Palone recovered the box?"

Salvi's words came out in a rush, in the way that they did when he was afraid he had done something wrong. "We looked in the box together. It was not there."

Damn Cesare! Damn Romoli! I said nothing, just closed the box and put my head in my hand, wishing that I could turn back the clock to the day before. They must have split up the journal and the box when they went their separate ways. But which one of them had the journal? How long would it take for the contents to be deciphered? What would happen then?

They would go straight to Rolando and tell him what my father had done.

And then Rolando and his sons would come for me.

*   *   *

The next morning, Salvi woke me from a deep sleep with a knock on the door. Groggy, I asked him what time it was.

"The cock crowed only a little bit ago." His voice was muffled by the heavy door and I stopped my movement to hear. "But Signor and Signora Palone are here to see you."

The hold that sleep had on me vanished. Had they found the journal and decoded it already? No, it couldn't be.

They waited in the little courtyard, the summer sun already warming what was left of the flowers. Both were dressed for travel. Isabetta looked like she had been crying.

"Oh, Gio."

I stepped forward to hold her, looking over her shoulder to Signor Palone for an explanation. It was unlike Isabetta to be so taken by emotion. Her body tensed at first, then relaxed into me.

"It's my niece," Rolando said, squinting in the sun. "We got word last night that she has taken quite ill. We are on our way to Lucca to be with the family."

I held her tight and kissed her forehead. "How long will you be gone?" I asked.

"I don't know. At least a month, but we know little about the illness that she has." Isabetta's voice was soft in my ear.

The thought of being away from this woman made my heart sink like a stone in the Tevere.

"You will write to me?"

She lifted her head and nodded, her eyes solemn. I stared into them, memorizing their every spark.

I looked at Rolando. "Thank you for your help in recovering Bartolomeo's recipes."

Rolando shook his head. "It was nothing. I am only glad that you have your family treasure back in your own hands."

"When you return, I would like to speak with you about your daughter."

Isabetta hugged me again, tight. I felt her tears wetting my neck.

Rolando took Isabetta gently by the shoulder. "Yes, Signor Scappi. I look forward to that conversation."

He smiled and shook my hand, his grip full of energy.

Isabetta followed her father out of the courtyard to the waiting carriage. She waved at me once, just before she climbed in and closed the door, the curtain fluttering. I watched them go. Part of my heart was in that carriage and I knew I would not be the same until it returned.

But their departure also gave me great hope. Perhaps I could recover the journal in that time. To have the Palones away from Roma could only be a good thing, I thought.

* * *

After my duties at the Vaticano that day, and to distract my mind from Isabetta's departure, I decided to decode another journal, this time for the year 1555. I would have been eight and still living in

Tivoli. At that age I already worshiped Bartolomeo. He was the happiest man I knew, with a laugh that filled me with joy. Would I find myself in these pages?

I flipped open the journal and began to decode. The date of the first entry was March 23, 1555.

Today Pope Julius III died from the gout that riddled his body. I am somewhat conflicted about his passing. In his service I did some of my best work—feasts that I may not ever surpass in my lifetime because of the extraordinary expense that he lavished upon me. And yet, he was a terrible man, given to terrible vices. He loved beauty and he loved pleasure and he loved that damn Innocenzo! He was a beggar boy on the streets when the pope took him to his bed. I hated sending my kitchen boys up to the pope's bedchamber with sweetmeats and wine, but what choice did I have? Now that beggar boy is the most powerful cardinale in Roma, rich beyond measure. He flaunts his new status.

I pray that the papal conclave will take him down a notch. Who will protect him now this his lover is gone? Certainly no one that I know. Many of my servants would love to put a dagger in his breast. I myself have considered it.

Bartolomeo never talked about the vices of Julius or his lover. I had heard all about the feasts, but nothing more. I knew the rumors, of course, but when Innocenzo died last year, the clergy at the Vaticano were ripe with all the stories of his more egregious crimes. This included murdering two men while on the way to a third conclave from Venice. The men, a father and son in Nocera Umbra, had uttered ill words about him. Several years later, he raped two lowborn women near Siena. Each of these crimes was worthy of imprisonment and potentially death, but in both cases, friends of the late Julius let him go free.

I skimmed through the descriptions of the conclave until I found the paragraph with the outcome.

Pope Marcellus II has ascended. I am greatly relieved that it only took four days to bring this new pope to power, not months on end as in the past. Today the preparations begin for the feast to celebrate his coronation. I hear rumors that Marcellus is of weak constitution. I remember him leaving the 1549 conclave with quartan fever. I will need to learn which broths he may prefer.

But right now, it is Stella that fills my thoughts. Stella.

CHAPTER 19

Scappi

Roma, April–May 1555

Stella. I cannot wait to see her and hold her in my arms once more. I long
for my stellina. I worry that the distance between us will someday create
cracks in our love that cannot be mended. Our time together sometimes seems
thin, like a spice or other flavor is missing. I need to think of something I
can do more to seal our love together, to rekindle our fire so we will always
long for each other.

For now, I must exercise patience. It will be two weeks before the cor-
onation activities are complete, then Easter and the feasts leading up to
the Ascension. Seeing her will have to wait until the banquet planned for
the cardinali and their families on the first of May, the day of St. Joseph.
Her second husband's uncle is a cardinale, and will most certainly invite
his relatives, which means I will have to be very clever to steal a moment
with my Stella while she is here at the Vaticano. I have a maypole I am
sure she would like to wrap her ribbon around.

Bartolomeo put down his quill and picked up the pounce pot
with cuttlefish bone powder and shook it across the journal to dry
the ink. When he was satisfied, he put away his writing supplies,

then locked away the journal in the cupboard behind his desk. He blew out the candle and took to his bed.

He had almost drifted off to sleep when he heard a rustle in the wall below his head. He sat up, startled, and jumped off the bed. The creature on the other side of the wall, perhaps a mouse, scratched in earnest. Although hearing mice in the walls was common, this scratching sounded like it came from the room. Puzzled, Bartolomeo made his way to the hallway, where a lamp was lit near his door. He took a flame for his own light and returned to his room as the culprit skittered across the floor.

He pulled the bed from the wall. The wall was adorned with a simple fresco depicting various saints of food and drink. Each panel was separated by a long red stripe from floor to ceiling. It was in the bottom corner of one of the stripes that he found the hole the mouse had made.

He took a loose tile to patch the wall temporarily, but as he bent to place it against the wall, he saw something unusual. Along the bottom of the wall a thin crevice had formed above the hole. On a hunch, he put his finger in the hole and pulled, and, sure enough, the wall began to crack open. It was a door!

"Madonna!" he exclaimed.

The door wouldn't open more than a crack and Bartolomeo soon realized he would have to find the opening mechanism. After a few moments of pounding various parts of the fresco with the palm of his hand, he stood back and surveyed the wall in the dim lamplight. Finally, at the far left end of the wall, he noticed a small, unused tapestry hook set by itself in the wall, what seemed like a remnant from an earlier tenant. He wiggled it, then turned it counterclockwise. A click sounded.

Returning to the door, he could see the crack had widened; he slid his fingers in and moved the door aside. A rush of cool air hit his face, but he could not see in the darkness. He retrieved the lantern and locked the door of his room, just in case.

He stood at the edge of the dark corridor, holding the light in front of him, deciding if he should go in. All his senses warned him of folly.

The narrow hallway was made from brick and plaster, hardly wide enough for one person, and Bartolomeo had just enough room to stand up. At times, his hair brushed the ceiling. He was grateful he had never experienced claustrophobia. Fifteen feet into the corridor he encountered a set of steep stairs. He ascended them carefully, thankful for the recessed handrail built into the walls. At the top, small beams of light crisscrossed the passage in front of him.

When he came to the first hole, he peered through the tiny aperture, and he almost gasped when he discovered he was looking down on an internal barrack room of the Vaticano guard. A lamp on a desk in the corner of the room illuminated a man reading at the desk as well as the sleeping forms in the bunks below. If he pressed his ear to the wall he could hear the soldiers snore. The walls of the Vaticano were high, and Bartolomeo noticed that he walked across the top half of these vaulted rooms, just above the doors and windows, close to the rafters. Every step in the dim corridor brought a jolt of fear, and every view through one of the peepholes left him in awe.

He pressed on until he reached another small opening. Looking through the hole he could see part of a torchlit hallway lining the Courtyard of San Damaso. He guessed if he continued he would come across the now unused chambers of past pope Rodrigo de Borgia, who had taken the name Alessandro VI, directly below the apartments Pope Julius II had occupied.

What were these secret passageways for? He noted he left footprints in the dust as he walked—at least this part of the network of hallways had gone unused for a very long time. He wondered if a previous pope had used them to spy on others within the Vaticano, or if someone used them to do the same to a pope.

The passage was long, but eventually he came to a bend to the left. A rope spanned the narrow space, preventing him from falling down another steep staircase to the floor below. His options were a narrow ledge that would allow him to continue forward, or the staircase to the first floor. He chose to go down.

At the bottom of the stairs the passageway became quite short, with one peephole, but also a mechanism to open a door into the room beyond. Bartolomeo peered into the peephole to see if his suspicion was right. He had never seen the Borgia apartments before because they had been sealed when the pontiff died in 1503. The furniture in the moonlit room beyond was covered in sheets, and cobwebs clung to the corners. The gold of the room's frescoes glowed in the light as he moved his gaze from one to the next.

The switch to the door was connected to another part of the wall by a long bar, which he thought must connect to the interior switch to open the door. Bartolomeo activated the switch and the door opened with a creak that almost made his heart stop. Then he admonished himself—at this hour there wasn't a soul in this part of the Vaticano.

The Borgia rooms were beautiful, even by lamplight. He gasped as he took in the scenes of the Annunciation and the Nativity painted in brilliant colors. The paintings didn't have the glory of the frescoes Raffaello had executed in the rooms above, but there was a golden glint that gave the works an ethereal glow. In one fresco of the Resurrection, the chubby, elderly Pope Alessandro knelt in prayer beneath the resurrected Christ. Bartolomeo stared at it for a time, mesmerized by the level of detail the great artist Pinturicchio had used. The hypocrisy of the scene was not lost on him. Pope Alessandro was lusty and full of vice. He, like so many of the clergy Bartolomeo knew, pretended to be one kind of man, but was in truth another.

The rooms themselves were filled with dusty, covered furniture. He made his way carefully through the space, lifting the corners of the sheets to peer beneath. He marveled that he might be the first person to see the apartment in over fifty years.

In the corner of one room, Bartolomeo discovered a credenza with dozens of maiolica plates, all finely decorated with Pope Alessandro's crest and symbols of his papacy. He ran his finger along them, wondering what the banquets of that time were like. Through the next door he found the pope's desk, drawers empty save a few pieces of vellum. Couches, chairs, and tables were in the same position they must have been during the pope's life.

He returned to the room where the pope's elaborate bed was still standing. Under the protective sheet it was still made up as if waiting for one of his lovers to climb in. He lifted the sheet and sat on the edge of the mattress, his heart thudding as it creaked with his weight. *Now this was a pope's bed,* he thought. Celibacy had not been one of Alessandro's strong suits, and his lover Giulia Farnese was said to have been one of the most beautiful women in Roma. Bartolomeo briefly wondered if this was the bed in which Stella's friend Laura della Rovere was conceived. At minimum, the bed was surely riddled with untold stories of lust and sin. The thought filled him with pleasure, and it was then the idea came to him. He would bring Stella here, to these magnificent apartments, to this den notorious for forbidden love. Together they would add one more passionate story to the tale.

He lay down, the luxurious pillow still comfortable after all this time. The curtains of the window opposite him were cracked open, and through the slit he could see a brilliant star low on the horizon.

Yes, he would bring Stella here. It would be a moment to sear their souls, to bring them closer together than ever before. Yes, he would find a way.

*   *   *

For the next two weeks he slept little, torn between the worlds of the kitchen and the preparations he was making to surprise Stella with a stolen moment hidden behind the walls of the Vaticano.

During the day, he cooked for the pope, for cardinali, and for the many foreign dignitaries who had arrived for the banquet. At night he explored the corridors, swept away dust that could reveal where his footsteps began and ended, and planned for a brief evening tryst, which he knew was reckless. But, he reasoned, everything he and Stella did was reckless, was it not? He thought about how Stella would feel sitting on the edge of that lustful bed, his hands up her dress, her hands tangled in his hair.

In one of his nighttime wanderings, he discovered another secret door in a servant corridor off one of the main halls. If Stella could find her way there, perhaps under the guise of going for a long walk with her brother—which was plausible—it would be easy for her to slip away through the secret door into the hidden passage to the Borgia apartments. They would not have much time, but what time they had would be blissful.

Planning this escapade gave Bartolomeo an unusual fire in the kitchen. He worked at a feverish pace. He experimented with all manner of pies: tortoise, eel, chicken, frog, mushroom, artichoke, apricot, cherry, and his favorite of all, a luscious strawberry pie. He made omelets, stuffed eggs, and poached eggs with rosemary over toast. There were soups galore: fennel, tortellini, Hungarian milk, millet, kohlrabi, pea, and his famous Venetian turnip soup, which this time he made with apples instead. He molded jelly into the shapes of the cardinali crests, colored with wine, carrot, and saffron. He delighted most in the moments when he worked with his favorite knife, carving and slicing roasted cockerel, peacock, capons, turtledoves, ortolans, blackbirds, partridges, pheasants, and wood grouse. Every slice of the knife gave him greater confidence and belief in his power to make the world his.

Most of all, he dreamed of Stella, her golden hair, her dark brown eyes, the feel of her breast in his hand.

Three days before the feast, he took a few spare moments and met with Stella's brother in the osteria they often frequented. He explained the walk they should take through the Vaticano and the door where he would meet Stella. Her brother impressed upon him the hazards of their actions.

"We have engineered our lives around danger, my friend," Bartolomeo told him.

"Sì, that is true. But I think I will need a few more favors after this one."

Bartolomeo downed his wine, then motioned for the tavern keep to bring him another. "As many as you need." He nodded. The tasks Scappi did for Stella's brother always varied. Sometimes they were special meals prepared for the noble and his lover. Sometimes it was procuring something through one of the many merchant networks to which he was connected. This time it was an introduction to a prestigious guild member. The favors were rarely monetary—Stella's family was not one for want.

*   *   *

On April 29, the Vaticano was a whirlwind of activity. Betto, a man of few words, came to the kitchen early to confer with Bartolomeo on the evening's proceedings.

"In attendance tonight at the feast will be the Duke of Urbino and the Duke of Ferrara. Additionally, the pope wishes to especially honor Cardinali Alessandro Farnese, Ippolito d'Este, Louise de Guise, and Ascanio Sforza."

Bartolomeo bristled at Ippolito's name.

The scalco noticed. "What's wrong, Maestro? Are you unwilling to cook for these cardinali?" he asked, his voice sour.

"My apologies, I'm just considering the dishes they might prefer."

"Good. I will make sure they receive the proper place settings of honor. You see their food is adequately adorned."

"Noted," he said, thinking over his stock of gold leaf locked away in the strongbox in his office. He would have to spend extra time gilding the sugar sculptures and the sumptuous pies for those cardinali. He gritted his teeth and set to work, his mind turning to thoughts of Stella.

When the time for the feast came, it was Bartolomeo's duty to accompany the sculptures honoring the pope's favored cardinali. All afternoon he had dreaded the moment when he would don a clean apron and cap and follow the servers in procession to the pope's table.

The sculptures the pope had ordered were replicas of the new medal commemorating his reign and featured an image of him in profile. The medals Bartolomeo created were larger, made of sugar, and painted with vegetable dyes and gilded to make the pope's eyes bright, the jewels on his robes shine, and the letters of his name glitter in the light of the afternoon sun.

As Bartolomeo walked through the courtyard, he felt Stella's eyes upon him, but he dared not look for her in the crowd. He was not going to make the same mistake he had years ago during the dinner for the emperor.

The pope's table was long. Two favored cardinali sat on either side of the pontiff. As the pope mentioned each cardinale, Bartolomeo placed a tray with the medal before the clergyman. Ippolito d'Este was the last cardinale to be honored.

Bartolomeo kept his eyes to the ground as he brought the tray in front of the man who had ridiculed him in the market thirty years past. The years had not diminished his fury—on the contrary.

Ippolito's voice broke through the memory of the basket of eggs on the market stones. "It's beautiful, Maestro Scappi."

Bartolomeo was expected to respond. He took a deep breath and looked into the eyes of his nemesis. "Thank you, Your Eminence," he managed to say.

Ippolito's brow furrowed, and his long nose seemed to shrink a little with the gesture. "It seems the Lord has blessed you with extraordinary talent."

Bartolomeo could only nod. He did not believe the cardinale was sincere.

"Where did you learn such skills?"

At this Bartolomeo did not hesitate. "In Venezia. In the kitchen of Cardinale Marino Grimani." He held Ippolito's gaze.

Cardinale Sforza responded before Ippolito could say a word. "The world is a darker place without him. He was one of our very best."

Bartolomeo did not turn from Ippolito. "Yes, he was." He knew he should keep his voice neutral, but his simmering anger slipped forth. Ippolito raised an eyebrow but said nothing.

Bartolomeo broke eye contact and turned to the pope. "Your Holiness," he said deferentially, then he bowed and stepped back a pace before turning back toward the kitchen.

He did not return to his station. Instead he went straight to his studiolo, shut the door, and collapsed into the Dante chair at his desk. He lowered his head into his hands and didn't return to the kitchen until he could catch his breath and slow the beating of his heart.

*　　*　　*

The rest of the afternoon went without incident. Finally, at the appointed time, between the dessert courses and the digestive liqueurs, Bartolomeo, careful to avoid notice, slipped away into his bedroom, locking the door behind him. He lit a lantern and stole through the corridor, up and down several sets of stairs until he reached the door to the rarely used hallway. He peered through the tiny eyeholes until he saw Stella and her brother approach, then released the latch, his heart pounding.

"How ingenious!"

Stella punched her brother in the arm. "Shh!" she admonished.

"I'll return when I hear the bell strike again," he whispered as she slid into the opening where Bartolomeo waited.

"That does not give us much time, my stellina. Come, let us hurry. We must be very quiet as we go." Bartolomeo latched the door and led the way through the darkness. He could feel her close behind him, her hands against his back, along his side.

There were several staircases that enabled them to traverse over and around doors and windows without anyone knowing. Finally, Bartolomeo opened the door that led into the Borgia apartments.

Stella gasped when he led her inside. "Is this . . ."

He knew exactly what she would say.

He nodded. "It is, indeed. They sealed these rooms fifty years ago. Judging by the dust I think I was the first person to explore the rooms since then."

The late-afternoon sun lit up the golden frescoes, and even though Bartolomeo had seen the frescoes several times during his nighttime journeys, they were even more breathtaking in the light.

"Shouldn't there be more dust?" She eyed him, puzzled.

"I didn't want your beautiful gown to be ruined." He motioned to the red and yellow brocade dress she wore. "But just in case, perhaps I should carry you."

He smiled, then swept her off her feet and into his arms. She giggled and buried her face into his neck, which she began to nibble.

Bartolomeo carried Stella through the sumptuous rooms, past the covered couches and tables, to the bedroom where Pope Alessandro had once made love to his mistress Giulia night after night. He laid Stella down across the bed, her legs dangling off the edge. She gave a low laugh.

"Are we about to sin where the best of the Lord's sinners did?"

He hiked up her skirts and ran his hands up her thighs. "Why yes, Madonna, we are about to do just that. The Lord blessed this bed once, why not again?"

He let his fingers tease her until she uttered soft cries. Stella spread her legs further and wider as his hand explored, touched, and pleasured every part of her womanhood.

She untied her outer bodice and lifted her breasts so they spilled from her corset. Her hands rubbed and played with her nipples. She knew what excited Bartolomeo. He continued to pleasure her while she touched herself, and he stroked his erection until he was near to bursting. Finally, he pulled her forward and slid into her, and her exclamation was louder than either of them expected. She clamped a hand over her mouth, wide-eyed.

He did not release her. Instead, he slowed his motion, and once he felt sure no one could have heard them, he began to rock against her, deeper and harder. The bed began to creak, but he was lost in the depths of his desire.

When she reached her climax, her cries more urgent and sustained, he lost control and spilled into her, his hips bucking a few more times. His legs threatened to give way with pleasure and exhaustion.

"When you are quite finished, you will join me in the next room," a voice directed.

Bartolomeo thought his heart might stop. Stella's eyes went wide with fear. That voice was unmistakable.

Bartolomeo pulled away from her and they cleaned up with a cloth he had brought for the purpose. He wiped away her tears with his hands, kissing her cheeks. He knew they were both wondering if it might be the last time they would ever have together. They dressed, and with mighty dread, Bartolomeo led Stella into the sitting room.

Pope Marcellus stood at the window.

"We will not defile these sacred chambers more than you already have. We will return to my room, where we will discuss your indiscretion."

He motioned toward the secret door from which they had entered. They marched in shame through the door and into the dark corridor, where the pope immediately told them to halt. He bade Stella to hold the lantern to close the door to the Borgia rooms. He did not move down the passage but instead unlatched a door on the other side of the narrow corridor that led to a simple sitting room. A bedchamber was visible beyond it.

"They are repairing the windows in my chambers. I could hear you from my temporary room here. And yes, all popes learn about the corridors." He turned to Stella. "Madonna, please, will you bring us some wine?

"Sit," the pope instructed. He motioned to the four chairs positioned around the fireplace.

Stella poured two goblets of wine at the sideboard. She handed each of them a glass, then returned to fetch herself a portion before taking the seat next to Bartolomeo.

Pope Marcellus did not sit. He paced, occasionally stopping to take a small sip of wine. "You have broken one of the Lord's commandments. You have crossed lines of class, you have defiled a pope's bed, and you must pay the consequences."

Bartolomeo thought about how many times Pope Alessandro had broken his vows and committed adultery with another man's wife in that very bed, but said nothing. His mind raced to find a way to get out of this situation. He did not want to lose his life for this transgression. But if he struck first . . . Perhaps he could strangle the pope? It would be easy enough to kill him with only a little physical effort. But if the noise did not rouse the guards outside the chamber, it likely wouldn't be long before they found the secret passages and followed them back to the kitchen.

"In the morning, I expect to see both of you before the altar in Saint Peter's. You will confess your sins before the Lord. You will ask forgiveness of God and of the community in which you live. Then you will be free to go."

Stella gasped. "In front of everyone?"

"Surely, Your Eminence, there must be another way," Bartolomeo said.

The pope leaned against the back of one of the chairs. "There is only one other way. Excommunication and deportation. You, Signor Scappi, will lose all heavenly aspirations and I will have my guard see you to the borders of the papal state. The principessa here will not have that option. She will face excommunication and beyond that, her family can decide her fate."

"Both options will get us killed," Bartolomeo said.

"Perhaps not. I will advocate for mercy if you declare your sin at the altar."

He downed the rest of his wine and set the glass on the little table in front of them.

"You know that is not true." Bartolomeo ran through other possibilities in his head. He could snap the pope's neck, he could slam his head to the floor, he could push him to his bed and suffocate him.

"We won't do it," Stella said, her voice low, almost too low for Bartolomeo to hear.

The pope cleared his throat, his words seeming a little labored. "You do not have to. But it saddens me you do not want to know the love of God in the afterlife. For that is your other choice."

"You don't understand," Stella said to the pope. "We won't do it because we won't have to."

Bartolomeo gawked at Stella.

Pope Marcellus pointed at his glass, then suddenly pitched forward, his face red. He fell to his knees, then hit the floor with a thud.

Stella stood. She appeared calm, but he heard the quaver in her voice. "Help me get him into bed."

Bartolomeo rushed to his feet. "I don't . . ."

Stella held out a shaking hand, eyeing the ring he had given her.

"Thank you, love, for my ring and the gift of cantarella. It seems to have proven useful."

"I had not thought it would prove *this* useful," he said, waving his hand at the incapacitated pope. He leaned down to feel for Marcellus's heartbeat. It was faint, but he was not yet dead. Good. If he died in the night, it would be thought he merely died of old age.

Pope Marcellus was tall but thin, and Bartolomeo picked him up easily. Together, he and Stella stripped the pontiff down to his undergarments, then laid him in the bed, leaving his clothes in disarray, to make it appear as if the pope had peeled them off himself before crawling between the sheets.

Bartolomeo led Stella to the doorway where her brother had left her. She handed him the towel she had used to wipe clean the wine goblets.

"Burn it," she suggested before she threw her arms around him. He kissed her, wondering if it would be the last time he tasted the sweetness of her lips.

"Ti amo, stellina mia," he breathed as she slid through the door. He watched through the crack until she slipped her arm into her brother's.

*　　*　　*

Two hours later, Betto appeared in the kitchen.

"Maestro, please cook your most healthful broth. When I went to prepare the pope for sleep I found him ill."

Bartolomeo turned to look at the scalco, hoping shock did not register on his face. "Ill? What are his symptoms . . . so I know what broth to make?"

"He is in a stupor," Betto explained. "We are not sure he will wake, but I want to be ready in case he does."

"He seemed fine when I saw him at the banquet this afternoon," Bartolomeo said, choosing his words carefully.

"He was. He left the meal early to rest. When I found him, however, he could only moan. It does not look good, I fear."

"I will make a concentrate of capon right now. And a cinnamon potion too." He snapped his fingers at his secondo, a wiry man with one drooping eyelid. He hurried to Bartolomeo's side.

"Thank you. Please pray for Our Eminence."

CHAPTER 20

Giovanni

Roma, late July 1577

The night Pope Marcellus died was one of the longest of my life. I have never felt such terror, not even the night when they interrogated me for the murder of Giacomo Crispo. Francesco and the cardinali that held vigil with Our Holiness thought my worry was only concern for Pope Marcellus. I turned over every bit of the evening in my mind—had anyone seen Stella and her brother coming or going? What if someone decided to finally, after all these years, enter the Borgia rooms?

I fretted, but forged on as though nothing was wrong other than the pontiff's illness. The physician said he suffered from apoplexy and likely would not wake. The potions and broths I made could not be administered, as I suspected might be the case—it was rare that anyone woke from a dose of cantarella. So when I heard Pope Marcellus did so briefly near the break of dawn, I thought my heart would leap out of my chest. Fortunately, he spoke in a jumble and the only words anyone could make out were "sleep" and "madonna," neither of which implicated Stella or me. Then, they told me, at the seventh hour, he gave a great shudder and convulsion, and at the end of that day, his twenty-second since he was chosen by il collegio cardinalizio, he breathed his last breath.

As far as I know, no one has suspected a thing.

I put the journal and the cipher wheel down, my hands shaking. I gazed out over the courtyard from my chair in the sunlit loggia. A strange, small murder of black and white crows swept over the Vaticano in the distance, and the shock of what I had read hit me. My mother had killed a pope. A pope! And she had killed him with a poison ring my father had given her. Dio mio!

I did not consider religion much, and I was surprised to find the implications of this crime bothered me beyond the legal ramifications. Was my mother doomed to hell? My father? If the sins of the parents were my sins as well, where did that leave my immortal soul?

Salvi appeared, startling me. I snapped the journal shut and pushed it aside.

"Signor Carpi is here to see you." Salvi gave a little bow, pulling off his cap with a flourish, and despite my anxious mood, I could not help but smile at the boy's enthusiasm. I had tried to convince him not to be too zealous, but this advice usually fell on deaf ears.

I was relieved to hear it was Val who had come to call. "Please, show him in."

Valentino appeared as he always did, as though he were on his way to some luxurious banquet. His clothes were spotless and his hose unmarred by any wear. Even his shoes were devoid of the dirt of Roma. I never understood how he managed to appear so impeccable. I looked down at my own worn tunic and had to laugh. "I appear a pauper next to you," I said, clasping Val on the shoulder.

"There are enough princes in this world, Gio. Roma would be better with more men like you and fewer like me." Valentino deposited himself in the plush chair on the other side of the table from me.

"What brings you here?" I asked, sitting once more.

"I've not seen you. Your lady love has all the attention." He affected a pout.

"Ahh, you just miss me lugging you out of the bordello at the end of a drunken night."

He laughed. "The women of the bordello miss you more than I do. It's been months since you were there." His eyes fell on the journal and the deciphered pages in front of me. He leaned forward to pick up the page on top.

I placed my hand on the papers. The thought of what rested within those pages chilled me.

He pulled back, a wounded look in his eyes. "What's wrong? It's only me, Gio. I would never share your secrets."

I sighed. I trusted Val with my life, but the truth of Marcellus's death was too heavy a burden to share. "I have learned something terrible. I know not whether I should tell you, or anyone."

He rolled his eyes. "What about Isabetta? Surely you will tell her? What exciting pillow talk the two of you must have."

"This is not a secret I would share with her."

"What could Maestro Scappi have done that was so terrible? Did he steal a peacock from someone's larder? Did he screw a cardinale's sister? How bad could it be? It's not as though he killed the pope."

I froze and could not breathe for a small beat of time. "Yes, he did," I said, hoping to be funny, but the delivery was too awkward and my voice squeaked with the admission.

Val's mouth dropped open. He knew me far too well. I had never been good at lying to him.

He leaned in. "Wait, do you mean to tell me it is true? Your father killed a pope? Which one? Wait, I know. Marcellus, it had to be. He died so quickly," he whispered across the table, his eyes bright.

"Val, I . . ." My words trailed off. I did not know if I could say them aloud.

"He did, didn't he?" He leaned back, his eyes roaming the sky.

"Dio mio. Dio mio." He stood and paced for a moment, cursing, his hands running through his black hair.

"Dimmi, Gio. Tell me the truth," he said, stopping before me once again.

I sighed. Valentino would not rest until he knew the whole story. "Val, what I know could land me facedown in the Tevere."

He reached for the papers, pulling on them despite my heavy hand. "Then we will land in the river together, Gio. You should not bear this burden alone. Maestro Scappi was like a father to me too."

I was angered by his persistence, but also relieved. To know such a secret alone would be a weight upon my shoulders.

"Very well." Reluctantly, I pulled my hand away. He nodded at me, thanking me without words.

I watched as he read my scrawled notes, marveling that he could decipher my handwriting. Amusement lit up his features as he read about the tryst, then darkened when he discovered how Stella had slipped the cantarella into Marcellus's wine.

"It was your mother," he whispered.

"The mother I do not know," I agreed.

He handed the paper back to me. I quickly folded it up and slipped it into my shirt where I would not forget to destroy it.

"But you want to know of her, do you not?"

"I do, but now I am not sure I should seek her out." I felt such conflicted emotions at the prospect of the sin she carried. It was dangerous, it was terrible, and I knew not how to reconcile the idea of my mother doing such a deed.

Valentino waved his hand at me. "This changes nothing, Gio. Your father and mother had a love that seemed, at least to me, to transcend everything. They would have done anything to keep that intact. Didn't you tell me Bartolomeo killed for her in the past?"

"He did," I admitted.

He pulled his feathered cap from his head and set it on the table in front of him. "I've got an idea," he said, running his hand through his dark hair as he often did when his mind was racing. "I'll help you find her."

I burst out laughing. "You? Since when were you one for solving mysteries?"

He frowned. "You doubt me! But I am in earnest. Let me help. Perhaps I will think of something you have not."

I had never been able to resist Val. He always managed to coerce me into his plans. And never, in the decades we had known each other, had he betrayed me or let me down. I asked him one more time.

"Knowing what I know will put you into grave danger, Val. Are you sure you want to help me? Perhaps it is better that some things are left in the dark, my friend."

He leaned forward. "This is serious, Gio. Start at the beginning. Let's solve this puzzle."

And so, it began. I told him everything. All the details of my birth, what I knew about Isabetta's mother, and everything else I knew about my father. I paused only when Dea brought us some crusty bread, a thick slab of cheese, and a carafe of wine.

When I had finished, he sat back and smiled at me. "I know what we shall do, Gio."

"And that would be?"

"By the Madonna, I can't believe I hadn't thought of this ages ago. Can you gain reprieve from the pope's kitchens for a month or so?"

"Yes, it should be easy enough. I'll ask today and let you know."

"Good. You make sure the pope will spare you for a few weeks. I'll put a few things in order and on the morrow, we will travel to Venezia. It will be hot as all of Dante's hells, but it can't be helped. Don't worry about a thing, Gio. I'll take care of everything. We'll take one of my carriages. Bring your cards and dice. It will be a long journey."

Venezia. I had always wanted to see the city of water, but never had I thought it might be like this. "What do you think we'll find in Venezia?"

"We'll find out who married the Duke of the Archipelago all those years ago. We will go to see *Il Libro d'Oro*."

The Golden Book was kept by the Council of Ten in the Palazzo di Doge and recorded all noble births, marriages, and deaths in the city. Why hadn't I thought of that before?

"In the book, we will find your mother's name," Valentino said.

Hope rose within me, light as baking bread, growing, building.

*   *   *

That afternoon I requested an audience with Pope Gregory to let him know of my travels.

To my surprise, he did not seem willing to let me leave. "And what, pray tell, is in Venezia, Giovanni?" The pope pursed his lips. "That is a long distance to go."

I faltered. I could not begin to tell him the truth. And I had not anticipated I would need to lie. I had no story prepared.

"It's for Bartolomeo," I managed. My mind raced.

Pope Gregory squinted at me. I could not discern what he was thinking.

"Um, there are some personal items he left behind he wanted a relative of his to have. I do not trust a messenger, Your Holiness. I also want to visit some of the palazzo kitchens and let his old friends know of his passing."

"You do plan on returning, do you not, Giovanni? We are reminded of another time when a favorite maestro had requested time away to visit family and did not come back. Pope Julius—may the Lord bless his soul—spent considerable time convincing Michelangelo to come back from Firenze to paint La Cappella Sistina. This is not a similar type of excursion, is it? We know you must feel considerable sadness at your uncle's passing. Tell Us truly, Giovanni, are you happy enough working here? You would not leave Us, now, would you?"

My mouth and my brain raced to process what the pope was saying. He thought of me as a favorite? How could that be when he had not tasted even a fraction of what I was capable of making?

"Your Holiness, I am very happy in your service. And I cannot think of living anywhere but in Roma. My heart and all of its hopes are here. But I am compelled to make sure my uncle's wishes are carried out so his soul may rest in peace." I took a deep breath, hoping I sounded believable.

I had. The pope waved a hand at me. "Very well. We will grant this to you. May the Lord bless you with safe travels."

*   *   *

Before I left the Vaticano I decided to pay another visit to the library.

Bishop Avito was in his customary spot, his nose in a dusty book, quill and parchment by his side. He glanced up as I approached and seeing me, his expression soured.

"Giovanni."

"Your Excellency. I came to get your advice." Why I had come, I did not know. I didn't expect the bishop to tell me anything, and if he did it wasn't likely to be anything I wanted to hear. But he was the person who took Bartolomeo's confession, and perhaps I would find a glimmer of my father in the bishop's words.

The old clergyman harrumphed and raised an eyebrow at me. "And what, pray tell, could I give you advice about? I suspect you ignored the last bit I gave you."

"My life might have been easier if I had listened," I conceded. I lowered my voice. "My father was not always the nicest man." I wondered then, had Bartolomeo told the bishop about his hand in murdering Pope Marcellus?

"You are right. He made some very poor choices."

"I know how I can find my mother. She will be listed in *Il Libro d'Oro* in Venezia."

Avito put his book down. "You want to know if I think you should go."

I nodded.

"Will you listen to me if I tell you what I think?"

Would I? Why had I come?

"I wouldn't be here if I didn't want to listen," I said.

He put a hand to his temple and rubbed for a moment before speaking. "When you came to me the first time, I thought that you were just distraught, and that perhaps this was a sleeping dog you would let lie once you were able to let some of this grief go. But now, seeing as you are clearly not going to rest until you discover the truth, I change my mind. I think you should go."

I had not been prepared for him to say those words. I had expected him to vehemently oppose the idea. The fuzzy layer of disappointment I felt gave me the answer as to why I stood before him. I had hoped he was going to talk me out of it.

"You should go and find out the truth. Get it out of the way so you can move on with your life. And so you can stop pestering me. Go, Giovanni. Go with my blessing to Venezia. The Lord knows if you don't you will always wish you had."

I sat down on the bench and put my head in my hands, letting the darkness wash over me and the decision before me. I fervently wished I had listened to Avito the first time and burned the journals.

When I pulled my hands away, the bishop was shuffling away from me down the aisle of chained books.

On my way home, the comet in the sky burned hot and bright,

but I thought perhaps it was not so bright as it was the day Isabetta had left for Lucca, my heart trailing in her wake.

*   *   *

Two days later, I penned a note to Isabetta and left it with Salvi and Dea in case she returned before I did. Then I climbed into Val's carriage and away we went, through the streets and fields of Roma, past the cows grazing in the ruins of the Forum, beyond the Colosseo and the beautiful Lateran Basilica, until we were outside the walls, the hill town of Tivoli visible in the distance.

I had brought with me a few of the journals. It was risky to travel with them, but it was such a long stretch of ample time, and with Valentino's many guards on the trip I decided to take the chance. I showed Val how the code worked and we took turns deciphering my father's text.

"This passage is about you and Caterina moving to Roma. It's dated 1557, two years after Pope Marcellus died," Val said to me when we were nearly to the ancient village of Spoleto, where we had planned to find an inn for the night.

Finally, I will have my son here with me in Roma. I should have arranged for it long ago, but I thought too much proximity would lead to too many questions. So much time has passed that it should seem now he is truly Caterina's son. I have purchased a house for them not far from the Pantheon, in a good part of town where my sister can continue her work as an herbalist. She will be far enough away from me that we can maintain our sibling relationship, but I hope it will not be apparent the connection I have with G. And yet, he will be close enough for me to see as often as I would desire, and perhaps I will influence him to think about the world of food as I do. I have dreamed about passing on my secrets to a true apprentice. Perhaps G. will be the one.

It was strange to read these words from my father. He had wanted me to carry on his legacy from the beginning. I warmed at the thought that he had such high hopes for me.

On the road the next day, I found the passages that discussed this further. Bartolomeo's journals in his later years were spottier, covering many years in one volume, unlike the fervor with which he wrote in the journals of his youth. The passage was dated several years later, in 1564.

Cardinale Carpi suggested to me today that I take on G. as an apprentice. I am conflicted. It is everything I desire, and yet if he is too close will people begin to wonder and to guess? He has not been of working age long—if I take him on will his connection to me be obvious? I suspect Stella knows who he is, but she has never once asked, and I know she will not. She does not want her hopes to climb so high.

"I thought you didn't become his apprentice until later," Valentino said.

"I didn't. I would have only been seventeen then. I didn't join the Vaticano kitchen until I was nineteen, after Pope Pius IV died."

I skimmed through the journal looking for the correct date. Finally, I found it: April 1566.

I did it. I did what Cardinale Carpi, may he rest in peace, suggested I do years ago. Today Francesco Reinoso and Giovanni Brioschi joined me in the Vaticano kitchens at the urging of Pope Pius. They worked with him when he was still Michele Ghislieri, and while he recommended them highly to me, he was kind enough to give me the option to decide. And the answer is yes. Giovanni will be my apprentice, finally. My heart sings with the thought of my son being so close to me. The world is a strange one in which we live, is it not? No suspicion will come of this—it was the pope who recommended him, and how could I say no to the pope? My heart is light today. I cannot wait to show my son everything, to teach him all I know.

"I wished I had known him as my father while he was still alive," I said, closing the journal.

"I think he would have treated you much the same."

I smiled, thinking of all the ways my father cared for me over the years, but not just me—he was kind to so many people. "He doted on you as well," I told him.

"Because I was your friend," Val said.

CHAPTER 21

Scappi

Roma, October 1566–January 1567

"We will outdo all the other anniversary feasts, my boy. Even the decadent Leo X will smile down upon us from the heavens when he sees what I have planned." Bartolomeo clapped Giovanni on the shoulder. He was pleased by the progress his apprentice had made over the last few months. Little did Giovanni know that the grandeur of the feast to celebrate the anniversary of the coronation of Pius V was less about the pope and more about Bartolomeo wanting to show his son what marvels could be done through mastery of the kitchen.

"How many platters did you say we are serving?" Giovanni asked.

Bartolomeo glanced at the parchment in front of him. "One thousand, one hundred and sixty-seven."

Giovanni peered at the paper. "Fifty dozen pieces of light white bread? A thousand cockles with orange peel? Pastry castles with live birds? And a gelatin with the pope's face? *Mi dispiace*, Uncle, but is making this much food even possible?"

Bartolomeo waved a hand as though the quantities were nothing. "Bah, the feast I did for Emperor Charles was far more elaborate.

You have never imagined how many sugar sculptures we did for that luncheon!"

"So I've heard." Giovanni did not seem convinced.

"Worry not, Gio. We have 150 men between the Vaticano kitchen and the pope's private kitchen, and I am asking the Roman cardinali to send men from their palazzi as well."

Giovanni ran his hand through his dark locks, a nervous habit Bartolomeo knew well. "And we do this every year? Dio mio. I'm never going to remember all this," the young man fretted. "How do you keep these details straight?"

"Someday you'll feel comfortable managing even bigger feasts." Bartolomeo remembered how nervous he had been the first time he had to execute a large banquet for Cardinale Campeggio. Now it all seemed a simple feat, but back then he had bitten his nails to the quick with worry.

"Where do we start?"

"You oversee the pasta," Bartolomeo told his apprentice. "We can make much of it in December and hang it to dry. I also want you to arrange for the snails and for all the fowl deliveries, which we should start on right away. Most of the birds should be delivered live unless they come in the day or two before, but I do not recommend that—it's too unpredictable. Have them delivered to the Vaticano farm and we can slaughter them when we are ready."

Giovanni took the paper and scanned it. "What of molds for the sugar sculptures and the gelatins? Don't those take time to have carved?"

Bartolomeo smiled. "Worry about the pasta, snails, and the fowl. I'll worry about the rest."

"Sì, sì." Giovanni shuffled off, his eyes still on the paper. Bartolomeo smiled after him. It was a lot for someone so young to manage—he was barely twenty—but Bartolomeo had faith in his apprentice. Giovanni perched himself on a stool at his regular table in the kitchen. He began scratching notes on another piece of parchment as he scanned the list he had just been handed. Bartolomeo was so proud of his son, the son who would only know of him as an uncle. The thought of it pricked at the edge of his heart, but he pushed away the idea, turning back to the task at hand, determining how much flour a dozen four-feet-high pastry castles might require.

*   *   *

Three months and one week later, when the final days leading up to the anniversary feast had the entire Vaticano in a frenzy, Giovanni and Bartolomeo met with Francesco to go over the seating arrangements for the elaborate meal. They sat at the enormous wood table in the *tinello*, the staff dining room.

"We are preparing for tables in eight rooms and two of the grand hallways," Francesco said, laying down the map of the palazzo.

"Has the pope given input yet?" Bartolomeo asked. The pope had been away for the last two months, occupied with a synod he had established with Cardinale Carafa, one of his favorites. Bartolomeo worried a little—this new pope was bent on church reform and might not like to see such indulgence in a feast of this scope. So far, the kitchen had been spared the cutbacks of the rest of the papal court—the elimination of a goodly number of the clergy's personal servants, extra library attendants, stablemen, and other positions—but he didn't think such luck would last much longer.

Francesco shook his head. "He returns from Milano on the morrow. I imagine he will make changes to this arrangement, but I have a good idea of his primary alliances." He pointed at the large room in the middle of the map. "At the first table, we will have the twelve principal cardinali: Gonzaga, Colonna, Delfino, Sforza, Orsini, della Rovere, Medici, Pisano, Carafa, and Strozzi. We'll place the pope here"—he pointed to a spot in the center of the long table—"and Cardinale d'Este and Cardinale Farnese to either side of him."

Bartolomeo rolled his eyes at the mention of Ippolito d'Este.

Francesco continued. "In the hallway leading to this chamber there will be two fountains with naphtha water on their top level, lit to signal the pope's arrival. I'll have the harp and lute players set up on either side of the doors leading into the room. After everyone has been seated, the musicians will move into the room and play in the far corner."

"I will have the servers ready in the back corridor with cold platters from the credenza," Bartolomeo said. "Did you let the harp player know to signal with the bells?" Bartolomeo had provided a small set of hand bells to Francesco to give to the harpist. Having an aural signal to start the meal meant the kitchen staff could stay largely out of sight until the precise moment the food was to be delivered.

"Which sugar sculptures will be on the tables during the first course?" Francesco asked.

"Each room will have a large sculpture of Diana with five nymphs gamboling across the tables."

"And each place setting will have a *ciambella* pastry inside a napkin," Giovanni added.

Francesco stared at his list. "Two first courses served from the credenza, correct?"

Bartolomeo nodded. "Yes. Nuts, marzipan, melon, mostaccioli, and a few small cold savory items to start. Ten items per platter, 110 platters."

Giovanni consulted the list in his hand. "The second course from the credenza is triple that amount: 264 platters of salad, mushrooms, olives, and all the pastries with the pope's crest, plus the gelatina with his visage."

Francesco checked that off his list. "And the pastry castles are first or second course from the kitchen?"

Bartolomeo squinted. "First."

Francesco paused. "What's wrong with the castles, Maestro?"

He sighed. "Nothing. They are gorgeous. It's the finches. I think I cannot house them inside the castles or they might peck them apart before I can release them. I think we will put them in the napkins instead. We are working on tiny birdcages from which they will fly up as the diners unfold them."

Francesco raised an eyebrow. "One bird for each diner? That's a lot of birds, Bartolomeo." When the maestro said nothing, he sighed and continued. "I'll have servers ready with new napkins as soon as the birds are loosed. And the boys with nets will follow."

Bartolomeo had to chuckle. The last time he had attempted this feat, the birds had been kept inside an enormous pie shell until Pope Julius III sliced into it, sending twenty nightingales all over the room. They had no plan to capture or release the birds, so they flew all over the room during the meal, causing a tremendous fright to the women in attendance and leaving white streaks across the backs of more than one diner.

The men continued this back and forth, going over every detail until all three were sure there was nothing amiss. The second course would feature six butter statues, one of which was an elephant, and another Hercules fighting the legendary monster Cerebus. A monstrous pastry stag was the centerpiece of that course, with red wine gelatin bleeding from where an arrow had pierced its side.

The final course included six monstrous statues made of pastry: Helen of Troy; a nude Venus; a camel with a king upon its back; a unicorn with its horn in the mouth of a serpent; Hercules holding open the mouth of a lion; and Poseidon and his mighty trident. There were 361 bowls and plates of candied fruits: coconuts, apricots, grapes, pears, and melons, as well as plates of almonds, pistachios, pine nuts, and a variety of cheeses. At the end of the meal, each guest would receive perfumed toothpicks and a small bouquet of flowers to take home. Fifty musicians and one hundred acrobats were scheduled to perform between courses, including five renowned Venetian chorus singers brought to Roma specifically for the event.

"Do you feel ready?" Francesco asked as he checked off the last item on his list.

"This will be the most exquisite banquet I have ever served," Bartolomeo boasted, sitting up straight and puffing out his chest in an obvious display.

Giovanni laughed. "Mine as well, but I do not yet have the confidence of Maestro Scappi. My legs are like wet pasta when I think of the scope of what's ahead."

"The hard work is nearly over," Francesco assured him.

"When it is finished, Gio, you will have something you can boast about to your children."

Giovanni put down the glass of wine he was about to drink. "Children? Aren't you thinking a bit far ahead, Uncle Scappi? And why are you asking me? Why didn't you ever wed, Maestro?"

His booming laugh shook the kitchen. "Me? Married? Now that's worth a chuckle, I say."

Francesco nudged the big cook. "Honestly, what's the reason? We've known each other a long time and I've rarely seen a girl catch your fancy along the way."

Bartolomeo raised an eyebrow. "Francesco, my old friend, I could ask you the very same."

Francesco shook his head and rolled his eyes. "I think you know the truth of the matter."

Another belly laugh rolled across the kitchen. In a lower voice Bartolomeo added, "You have been discreet about that Zeno fellow. I must give you credit."

"So?" Francesco waited for an answer, patient as ever.

"I have had lovers, but none who I would wed. And that is that."

Francesco smirked and departed, leaving Bartolomeo to think about the woman he could never marry.

*   *   *

The following morning, as Giovanni and Bartolomeo worked along-side the kitchen servants folding several large napkins together to make elaborate birdhouses, two Vaticano guards swept into the room, followed by Pope Pius V with Francesco following behind. Everyone in the kitchen stopped their work and bent toward the floor.

"Maestro Scappi!" the pope's voice pierced the silence. It was not the sound of a man in a good mood.

Bartolomeo wiped his hands on his apron, removed it with haste, knelt, and kissed the ring the pope extended to him.

"Stand, Maestro."

Bartolomeo stood.

"I have just heard about the feast you are devising for Our anniversary. You are to immediately cease preparations on this feast. Distribute all the food you have prepared among the city's poor. Then you will cull this staff down to no more than twenty. Moving forward, We will not have need for more than bread, apples, and broth. The Lord needs not this display of wealth and ostentation. Are We understood, Maestro?"

It took everything he had to keep from gasping aloud. As his own stomach clenched at the thought of all the preparations coming to a halt, Bartolomeo could sense the panic of the hundred men and women in his kitchen. If this proclamation shook him so, he could only imagine how some of his best cooks were feeling with the pope's words. "Understood, Your Holiness. May I ask a question?"

Pius gave a nod, and his white beard touched his chest, leaving a few long hairs against the red velvet.

"There are many people here who have worked hard in these kitchens for the pope over the years. Many of them may not find it easy to find another job. I do not want these loyal people to worry how they will feed their families, Most Holy Father."

Pius softened with these words. He paused for a moment, looking across the crowded kitchen. When he spoke, a note of kindness had replaced the irritation previously exhibited. "Admirable, Maestro, for you to look out for your staff so. We grant you permission to give your staff a small stipend, a percentage of their salary for the year, to provide for them while they look for other work. Scalco Reinoso will aid you in this determination. Please make sure this kitchen is transformed before the end of the week."

Bartolomeo bowed, glad for the opportunity to hide his face from Pope Pius. It was a small win for a very large loss. His mind raced through all the waste from the feast—the magnificent sculptures, the beautiful pastries, the hundreds of animals slaughtered that week.

Bartolomeo stood when he heard Pius turn to leave. The pontiff shuffled toward the exit, but pivoted a few feet from the door.

"On the anniversary of Our coronation, you will prepare a simple meal for the cardinali. Bread, a little fruit, and perhaps a few capons."

"Yes, Your Holiness." Bartolomeo bowed again. When he rose, the pope was gone, the guards and Francesco along with him.

The kitchen burst into curses, tears, and the crash of a few thrown dishes. Bartolomeo couldn't move. He stared at the door, still in disbelief.

Giovanni put his hand on Bartolomeo's shoulder. "Uncle, I am sorry. It would have been a grand feast indeed."

Bartolomeo pulled Giovanni to him in a sudden bear hug, clasping him to his chest. Then he left the kitchen to lock himself in his studiolo, leaving his apprentice alone to quell the angry staff.

*   *   *

Two days later, the pope gathered his cardinali together in the yearly celebratory meal—not a feast, for in Bartolomeo's mind it could no longer be called that. The same guests attended in their original seating arrangement, but they were not greeted by sugar or pastry statues. There was no peacock, no venison, no pork. The candied fruits and elaborate pies had been shared with the families of the kitchen staff and then distributed to Roma's poor. Bartolomeo prepared the simple foods with a distinct lack of joy. He rarely spoke to anyone, not even Giovanni. Francesco made sure the departing staff received the small amount of money the pope had promised.

As the dinner ended and the cardinali began to move about the room in conversation, Bartolomeo sent his few men to clear the dishes. He stood at one end of the salone grande, and for a moment he imagined the banquet as it should have been, glorious and decadent, a testament to the greatness of the highest Lord of all. He did not know if he would ever cook up a truly magnificent feast again.

Cardinale Flavio Orsini paused momentarily to acknowledge Bartolomeo as he passed on the way out of the room. The cardinale was one of the younger clergymen, still in his thirties.

"Maestro Scappi, I was delighted by your meal tonight."

Scappi managed a brief smile, his thoughts still on the feast that never was. How delighted would Cardinale Orsini have been to see the finches flying up from the napkins?

"Your Eminence, I am humbled by your words," he said, trying to muster some enthusiasm.

"My cousin, Pier Francesco Orsini, is looking for a cuoco for a very special dinner on his grounds in Bormazo, to the north of Roma. It will not be a big feast, not like those to which you are accustomed, but I promise you, it will be a dinner of *monstrous* proportions," the cardinale said, with a glint of mischief in his eye. "I promise you will be well compensated."

"I don't know, Your Eminence . . ." he began, unsure at the underlying joke the cardinale seemed to be making.

"Worry not. It is nothing for you to be afraid of!" he said, noting the concern in Bartolomeo's eyes. "There will be monsters in this garden, but all are made of stone! It's a marvelous, mystical place for a meal. I'll have Signor Orsini send a man with all the details on the morrow."

Bartolomeo bowed his head in agreement and the cardinale moved on.

He jumped when he felt a touch on his arm.

It was Cardinale d'Este. The familiar flash of anger rose within Bartolomeo. It was the first emotion that had broken through his gray blanket of sadness in the last two days.

"Your Eminence," Bartolomeo said, daring to look the cardinale in the eye. The cardinale looked at him oddly, and Bartolomeo wondered if his feelings toward the clergyman were too transparent. He willed his face to remain impassive.

"Maestro Scappi," the cardinale finally said, the corners of his mouth turning upward into a warm smile. "I cannot begin to tell you how saddened I am that your feast was canceled. It is truly a travesty, and a waste of the talent God gave you. The rumors of what you had planned have had me salivating for weeks."

The anger Bartolomeo had harbored toward Ippolito for the last forty-one years dissolved like sugar in hot water. Out of all the things he expected to hear from Cardinale d'Este, it was not praise.

"Thank you, Your Eminence. You are kind to say so."

"I have admired your skill in the kitchen for decades and modeled my own banquets after yours. One of my favorite meals was the feast when you were working for Cardinale Campeggio, with the hundreds of black eggs. Every plate was exquisite. Such artistry! That meal has remained with me as a favorite in my memory. My chef has always hoped to outdo you, but I don't believe it could ever be possible. You are the finest chef in the land, Maestro Scappi."

Bartolomeo pinched his thigh, hard, convinced he must be dreaming. The cardinale had liked all those eggs—those eggs meant to send a warning that he had not forgotten that day in the market all those years past? But no, he was not imagining things. Ippolito stood before him still, a kind light shining in his brown eyes.

"I am honored," Bartolomeo said. And he discovered that he *was* honored. He was delighted, in fact. The cardinale patted him on the shoulder once more.

"I imagine you must be concerned about the austerity of our new pope. But I think you should put this time to good use. Perhaps you should write a cookbook? One for the ages? If you cannot cook the feasts yourself, please, I beg of you, share your talent with the world. Leave the tastes of the Lord's bounty as a legacy for others to enjoy."

He held out his hand and Bartolomeo shook it, the idea of a cookbook already taking deep root in his mind.

Something compelled Bartolomeo to ask the question that lingered in his mind. "Do you remember meeting me in Venezia, many years ago, when we were both boys?"

The cardinale cocked his head and gazed upward to the left, clearly searching his memories, confusion wrinkling his brow. "No, Maestro. I can't say that I do. I only visited Venezia a few times when I was young, but never for long. How did we meet?"

Bartolomeo thought about responding truthfully, telling the cardinale he had dashed a basket of eggs to the ground, and had told Bartolomeo he would amount to nothing, but he didn't. Those things no longer mattered.

"I served you a few times, that is all."

Ippolito smiled. "I was very self-centered as a young man and did not pay much attention to those around me. But I am glad to have spent time in the presence of your great genius over the years. Be well, Maestro."

Bartolomeo watched him go, wonder filling him. What a fool he had been! And yet, it was foolishness that had led him to that moment. The man he once thought was a rival turned out to be, instead, an inspiration.

Giovanni appeared in the doorway and a bright happiness coursed through Bartolomeo at the sight of his son. He waved him over.

"He will not be pope forever." Bartolomeo motioned to Pius with a jut of his chin.

"True," Giovanni said, puzzled. "*Morto un papa, se ne fa un'altro.*"

One pope dies, they make another. Indeed, Bartolomeo thought.

CHAPTER 22

Giovanni

Venezia, August 1577

As we bumped along the road to Venezia, I thought about what I had just read. The cookbook had been Ippolito's idea! I marveled the cardinale had maintained such unknown power upon my father, fueling Bartolomeo's drive for greatness. For nearly fifty years he worked to prove the cardinale wrong—and he had. The memory of that feast was so bittersweet for me. It was the first large banquet that I had worked on with Bartolomeo. And it marked what would largely be the crushing of much of my culinary dreams. For most of my career as a cook after that I made more soup and gruel than I would care to admit. Only on rare occasions was I able to work on feasts held by other nobles, on special request. But I did have my father's *L'Opera*, the handbook ready and waiting for me when the day came that these pious popes were no more.

*   *   *

The days passed slowly, and by the twelfth day, when we could see the campanile of San Marco in the distance, I was weary of travel.

We had deciphered two journals and played dice and cards until we were sick of looking at them.

"Finally," I said. "If I had to spend another day playing frussi with you . . ." I trailed off, staring at the city across the water. The comet was still visible between the thickening clouds, but it was smaller and more distant.

"Yet here you are. You are taking the biggest gamble of all traveling here with me," Valentino said as we stood on the shore waiting for a boat to take us the rest of the way to the 118 islands that made up the city. We had boarded the carriage at the city stables on the mainland and left our luggage with the stablemaster. Our plan was to go into Venezia for the day, find lodgings for the week, then send for our belongings. I wasn't sure I wanted to be there for that long—I was desperate to hear from or see Isabetta—but Valentino was my host and he wanted to spend time exploring the city. I had to admit I was a bit thrilled at the prospect of seeing the famous canals and the place where my father had begun his career.

I watched the approaching gondola and the two boatmen steering their craft toward us. "Val, I am not sure about this anymore. The closer I get to the truth, the more afraid I become," I blurted.

"After all these miles? Dimmi, Gio, what is bothering you? Don't you want to know who she is?"

"Of course I do, but then what?"

He nodded, understanding me. "You don't need to do anything, Gio. But at least you will know the truth."

"But Barto didn't want me to. Maybe it was for a good reason."

"Maybe, but he isn't here now, and you are. If we turn away, you will always wonder. Until the end of your days, you will wish you had gone to look at the book."

"Let's not go today. Can we explore Venezia a little first?" The suggestion was cowardly, but when I thought of standing in front of the magister to ask about the *Libro d'Oro*, I felt only panic.

My friend sighed. "Just wander? Or do you have somewhere in mind?"

I did. "I want to go see the palazzo where Bartolomeo worked when Crispo died." I kept my voice low—the gondola was nearly to the shore and I did not want my words to travel across the waves. "Maybe I'll find some answers there. We can look for an inn on the way, and maybe we can go to see the book in a day or two."

"Sounds like we have a plan, amico." A fog had formed, low across the water, blurring our view of Venezia. The gondola slipped up to the dock and the two boatmen waved at us to come on board.

*   *   *

Venezia is an impossible city. Everything about it seems implausible: the palazzi rising from the waves, the boats of all shapes and sizes bobbing across the water, and the narrow bridges crossing the gaps between the islands. How could such a city exist? I remembered Bartolomeo's stories about the famous Rialto market, about the banquets at Palazzo Grimani, and how, on very rare occasions, the highest of tides seeped up through the stones of the city. It was hard to believe I stood in the same city where my father had cut his teeth as a chef. I tried to picture him as a young man, strolling the calli of Venezia, his head full of thoughts of his new love, Stella.

Valentino had paid the boatman a little more to take us directly to the docks closest to the Palazzo Ducale. It was still early in the morning and the city was just beginning to wake. The clouds above threatened rain. We disembarked, and I asked a stocky, well-tanned dock worker for directions to Palazzo Grimani. The man laughed and pointed.

"Go in that general direction. You will get lost if you try to follow any instruction I could give."

"Surely your directions cannot be all that bad."

The man laughed harder. "You've never been to Venezia, have you? Even if you had a mapmaker make you a map, you would still become woefully lost. Just go that way and keep trying to go that way. Keep the campanile at your back. You'll eventually run into the palazzo or the Grand Canal."

"Ready to get lost?" I asked Valentino as we walked. We passed from the doge's grand palazzo, in which the *Golden Book* was housed, into the magnificent Piazza San Marco, where a market was already in full swing.

"What are you hoping to find at Palazzo Grimani?" Valentino asked me as we ducked into a dimly lit calle on the opposite side of the piazza.

I shrugged. "I know not, but there is something compelling me. I want to see where my father began to learn his trade. Perhaps I will learn more of who he was so long ago. We came all this way. We might as well see what stones we can overturn while we are here." I pulled out my pocket watch. It was just a little after ten o'clock.

We headed in the direction the dock worker had suggested. It was not long after we had left the wide piazza and entered the warren of little Venetian walkways before I realized how right the man had been.

We kept the campanile behind us as the man had suggested. After following several calli to their abrupt ends, Val suggested we stay with the wider paths. We stopped passersby to ask directions a few times, but it was a maddening warren of streets. In some places, little arrows had been painted on the sides of the buildings to indicate direction, but they were few and far between. Eventually, we found ourselves at the base of a large, somewhat rickety wooden bridge crossing the width of the entire canal, with a movable section in the middle that opened to let some of the larger ships traverse beneath it. We joined the throngs of people crossing, and on the other side found ourselves in a bustling market lined with shops. We had found the Rialto Bridge.

I had never seen such a market. There were dozens of vendors selling fruits and vegetables, and even more offering all varieties of shellfish and other creatures of the sea. There were women selling paper and cloth and stalls full of toys and all manner of items for the home. Everything about the market was overwhelming, especially the smells of fresh bread mingled with the stench of the sea and the wafting scents from the perfume stalls. At the end of a long gallery, I found several gold shops and stopped in one to buy a necklace for Isabetta. Val asked the goldsmith for directions to Palazzo Grimani.

"Giuseppe needs to deliver a package to Cavalier Grimani, so he can take you." The goldsmith tilted his head toward a boy of fourteen or fifteen standing in the doorway, his dark hair tousled as though he had just woken up.

I couldn't believe our luck. As he led us back across the Rialto Bridge, I wondered how long it would have taken us to find the palazzo without a guide. It was a short ten-minute walk from the Rialto, but the path Giuseppe took us on was confusing. Retracing our steps would not be an option.

"Cavalier Grimani . . . is he the head of the family now?" I asked Giuseppe as we walked. The title of cavaliere meant Signor Grimani was a knight of high regard in the ranks of nobility.

"Yes. After Cardinale Marino died, his nephew inherited the palazzo. They say Cavalier Grimani might be doge someday."

"He is a good man?" I asked. In his journals, Bartolomeo had thought Marino Grimani to be a kind, generous employer and I wondered if his nephew was the same.

Giuseppe laughed. "That matters not, signore."

"I don't understand."

The boy rubbed two invisible coins together with his thumb and forefinger. "He can buy his way to anything he wants, signore. Cavalier Grimani is a powerful man. What do you want with him, may I ask?"

"Nothing. I was hoping to speak to some of the staff from the kitchen. Someone I knew used to work there," I said.

"We'll go by the servant entrance. You should meet Bruno. He has been working for the Grimanis for going on fifty years now. He probably knew whomever you are looking for."

Bruno, Bruno. The name turned over in my mind as I struggled to remember if he was someone my father had mentioned in his writings.

The main entrance to Palazzo Grimani was on the canal side, but the back entrance was a towering door next to another small waterway. Apartment buildings and palazzi clustered around the immense house.

"This shouldn't take long," I said to Valentino.

"You go," he said, waving me forward. "I'll wait for you out here."

I gave him a grateful smile. I had been thinking that finding out more about my father at the Grimani residence was something I wanted to do on my own, but I did not know how to voice those words without offending him. But he knew me well. He took a seat on a bench under a tree in the tiny piazzetta and nodded at me.

The door guard was familiar with Giuseppe and let us in without a word.

The kitchen was off a hallway not far from the entrance. It was big but still not large by my standards—the Vaticano kitchens were immense and it was hard to compare anything to them. Dozens of men and women worked over simmering pots, counters with thinly rolled dough and knives fast at work deboning the meat for that night's meal.

"Bruno!" Giuseppe led me to a grizzled man who sat in the corner making rosettes out of dough. He paused when he saw Giuseppe.

"What brings you here today?"

"The scalco ordered new candlesticks," the boy said, holding up the carefully wrapped bundle. "But signore here tagged along with me. He wanted to meet you. Someone he knew used to work here."

252

"Go on, Giuseppe. I'll take care of him." Bruno waved the boy off and he departed without saying good-bye. The kitchen hand turned his attention to me. He said nothing, waiting for me to speak first.

I held my hand out. "I'm Giovanni. My uncle was Bartolomeo Scappi. I wanted to see where he worked when he was young."

Bruno didn't shake my hand. Instead, he pushed a lock of gray hair out of his eyes and sized me up. When he spoke, he didn't sound happy. "Your uncle? Are you sure you aren't his boy? You look just like him. Too much like him."

My heart jumped. "No, he, he . . . he was my uncle," I stammered.

"You are a mirror image. I never forget a face, and your face is just like his. Bartolomeo taught me how to make these goddamn roses." His eyes alighted on the pastry flowers. Then he peered back at me and smiled, exposing a mouth of yellowed teeth. "I'm glad you are here. I have something for you." He set the rosettes aside and stood up.

"Come." Bruno motioned in the direction of the door. "My house is nearby. I have something there I saved for your father in case he ever came back to Venezia. You should have it."

"My uncle," I corrected him. I wondered if he was senile. And I wasn't sure I should believe him. "You kept something for him for fifty years?"

"Not exactly. I just discovered it a few years ago. But I still have it, and now it should be yours."

"What is it?" I asked, wary.

"It's not easy to explain. Better you should see it," he said.

He looked a bit younger than Bartolomeo, which put him under seventy. His forehead was lined with age and he had deep wrinkles around his eyes that made him look tired. Like many who worked in the kitchen, he did not wear a beard, but a day's worth of stubble stood out from his tanned face.

"You worked here with Bartolomeo? You must have been young."

He looked at me, his dark eyes unreadable. "I was fifteen."

"He passed away a few months ago. He always spoke fondly of Venezia to me when I was a boy," I said.

"Did he now?"

I wasn't sure how to respond—his tone seemed to carry disbelief—so I remained silent as he led me out of the palazzo and into the piazzetta. He did not see Valentino look at us askance from his spot on the bench at the far side of the piazzetta. I waved my hand to convey to him to follow but remain unnoticed. I didn't look to see if Val understood, instead hurrying to keep up as Bruno led me down the tiny calle next to the palazzo toward a four-story apartment building not more than a stone's throw away. There was something about the way Bruno had spoken to me that made me distrust him.

Out of the corner of my eye I caught Valentino walking by us as though he was heading to some specific destination. Bruno ushered me into his first-floor home with a small push on my shoulder.

He closed the door behind me.

"Did you know Bartolomeo stole the maestro's knife before he left for Roma?"

My mouth fell open and I quickly closed it. My father had written about so many more terrible things, but his journals said nothing about stealing a knife. I wasn't sure I believed Bruno. Despite other things he had done wrong in his life, I knew Bartolomeo had intense respect for his trade—stealing another chef's knives was something I could never fathom him doing.

Bruno closed the sitting room curtains and lit a lamp, gestures that caused the hairs on the back of my neck to rise. "I knew your father when he was a favorite of Maestro Claudio's. Then he up and left, taking the knife with him."

"My uncle," I reiterated, "moved to Roma. He worked for several cardinali there and later, he worked in the Vaticano kitchens."

"I know," the man said flatly.

"He would not have stolen the maestro's knife." I struggled to keep the ire from my voice.

"It has a handle of ebony. It's shorter than a carving knife and the blade looks like rippled water. Doesn't it?"

Porca miseria! Bartolomeo had taken the knife. After holding it in my hand, I understood the allure. I might have done the same if I were him. Yet it still surprised me, as I did not think of him as a thief. But I said nothing.

I was beginning to think I should not have followed Bruno.

"It's in here," Bruno said, pulling open a closet and removing a chest. He set it on a nearby table and motioned me forward. He pulled a key from a pouch at his belt.

He fumbled with the lock for a few moments. I offered to give it a try.

As I bent over the chest, opening it without issue, I felt a hand on my shoulder, turning me around, and a long knife at my throat. He reached down with his other hand and pulled my rapier from its sheath, tossing it behind him.

"Your father killed my older brother, Piero. He let him hang for a murder he himself committed. You will fulfill this vendetta, Signor Scappi. Vendetta—that is what I have kept for him." Spittle hit my cheek.

"Bartolomeo is dead!" I said between gritted teeth, knowing it would not matter.

Bruno leaned in. His breath smelled of rosewater and garlic. "A vendetta cares not. Someone needs to pay for his crime."

Cristo! Why did Bartolomeo leave me saddled with his vendettas? Then I remembered that he had not—it was I who had failed to burn the journals and the letters. It was I who had decided to walk this path.

Keep him talking, I thought. I wanted to stall him till Valentino decided to check on me—he was an expert with the blade and could quickly end this altercation. And I wanted to know what he recalled about that day.

"Who did he murder?" I asked. The blade pricked my skin, and a trickle of blood ran across my collarbone. I felt strangely calm although my mind raced.

He squinted at me and the folds around his left eye twitched. "The Duke of the Archipelago! They questioned each of us, but, oh, Barto was the one who had done it. And I knew it! That night, I came upon him throwing something wrapped in a napkin in the canal after they carted my brother away. I remembered it because it was so strange."

"I don't understand what a napkin in the canal has anything to do with a murder," I said. I winced with the pain of the knife.

"I didn't understand it either, until a few years ago, when I heard about Caterina de Medici. Then I understood what Bartolomeo was doing at the canal."

That puzzled me. "The French queen? What does she have to do with this?" Blood trickled down my neck as I croaked out the words.

He grunted. "I told the capi dei sèstiere Bartolomeo had thrown something in the canal. They went to the spot and fished around but came up empty-handed. I told them the current must have taken it, but they would not believe me. They thought I was lying to save my brother. Even then, I did not want to believe it myself—Barto was my friend. But he was wearing gloves when he threw that napkin in the canal. Gloves in the heat of Agosto! So, years later, when I heard how Caterina de Medici was rumored to have poisoned the queen of Navarre with her sweet gloves—the poison in the fabric itself—then I knew why Barto was wearing gloves. He did not want to get the poison from the napkin on his skin. Which is how, dear boy, Giacomo Crispo died. And it was my brother who hung for Bartolomeo's crime. I vowed to end him if he ever returned to Venezia. Instead, you'll have to do." He pushed the knife closer and pain lit up the side of my face. "Say your final words, son of Bartolomeo."

I had no words for him. Instead I leaned back into him to relieve pressure from the steel against my neck. Then, before he could react, I spun my shoulder away from the knife, lifting my left hand to grasp his hand that held the blade, pushing it away from me, while at the same time slamming my right fist into his face. He fell back, giving me space to grab his shoulder. I kneed him as hard as I could in the groin. He whimpered, but I didn't pause. I pushed his knife arm backward as he doubled over and moved my other hand around to grab his thumb so he couldn't let go of the blade. I kicked him in the face, twisted his arm around, and pushed his wrist forward, hearing a crack as it broke. I yanked the knife away. Bruno fell to the floor, cradling his broken limb.

"Bartolomeo taught me well," I said, backing away from the aged kitchen hand. When I was a teenager, Bartolomeo had taught me how to defend myself, which had come in handy more than once in the rough streets of Roma. But never had I been so near to death as I was moments before.

A knock came at the door. The noise from the struggle must have summoned Valentino. But Bruno did not seem to hear the noise at the door. Instead, he rose, gave a loud cry, and rushed me. He was on me before I knew it, shoving his body into mine and into the knife I still held in my hand. It sunk into the space in the center of his chest, just below his breastbone. Warm blood rushed across my hand. He gasped, shock widening his eyes. I pulled away the blade and it slid free with a terrible slurping noise.

Bruno fell to the ground and blood gushed from the wound across the floor. He did not move.

The door opened then, and I looked up, seeing only a dark figure framed in the brilliant sunlight of the doorway.

"*Madonna!*" Valentino swore. He stepped forward and hastily pushed the door shut.

I backed up until I was as far away as I could get from the fallen man. He stared past me and blinked, his mouth working soundlessly.

"Dio mio, Gio. What happened?"

I looked at the bloody knife in my hand. "His . . . his . . . brother hanged for killing Giacomo Crispo. He attacked me."

When I looked back at Bruno, the life had gone from his eyes.

I stared at the dead body for a moment, my heart still beating so loud it felt like a roar in my ears. Every part of him burned itself into me. The stubble on his chin, his eyebrows all askew, the mole below his right ear, the hole in the knee of his black hose, and how he still had his apron on and it was covered in flour.

"You must have caught him in the heart," Valentino breathed. He was white with shock.

Bartolomeo did this, I thought. He set this wheel in motion long before I was born. It was because of him I had just killed a man. And yet, if Piero had not died, if Giacomo Crispo had not died—I myself would not be alive.

"He somehow puzzled out it was Bartolomeo who killed Crispo. He wanted revenge for his brother," I explained.

A noise in the house above made us both jump. "We have to get out of here," Valentino whispered.

I surveyed the body. The blood had pooled below the old man and outward by a foot or so. One arm was curled under him, his hand a little away from the wound. Careful to avoid stepping in the growing circle of red, I placed the knife downward in his hand. I thought perhaps someone might think he fell on the knife. I found the key to the chest and replaced it in the pouch within his doublet, leaving the money that was there, then returned the chest to the closet. I wanted no one to think there was any cause for this death.

I still had blood on my hand.

I found a napkin in the kitchen. I wet it in a water bucket sitting on the counter and cleaned what I could from my skin and fingernails. I wrapped the damp, bloody napkin into a clean one and tucked it into the inside of my waistband, hoping it would not wet through.

The irony that I was following in my father's footsteps did not escape me.

Valentino peered through the curtains and, deeming it safe enough, moved to the door.

"*Andiamo*," he announced.

As I picked up my rapier and prepared to leave, I spotted a scale and a series of iron weights on a table. I slipped one of the weights into my pocket and followed Valentino out the door. We did our best to walk at a normal pace away from Bruno's house and the Grimani palazzo toward the large calle that Giuseppe had first led us down.

"Did you tell anyone who you were?" Valentino asked.

"Only Bruno."

"Good."

He didn't need to say what I too was thinking—that we didn't want anyone to decide to come looking for me as the last person to see Bruno alive.

At the end of one long calle, when I was certain no one was around and nearby windows were shuttered, I had Valentino pause. I tied a knot with the blood-soaked napkins around the weight I had taken from Bruno's house. I threw the bundle into the center of the little canal and together we watched it sink. I thought of Bruno's words, about how he had seen Bartolomeo do the very same thing. I shuddered, remembering Bruno's face in death and the blood around his body. I knelt off the edge of the dock, emptying my guts into the muddy brown water. Valentino said nothing. He just held his hand on my shoulder so I would not fall.

CHAPTER 23

Giovanni

When we once again started forth, rain began to fall. I had never been so happy for it. It meant I could pull up the hood of my cloak without notice.

"Do you think anyone saw us?" I resisted the urge to look over my shoulder; it would be the obvious action of someone guilty of a crime.

"No, I don't think so."

He did not sound nearly as worried about our situation as I felt. I wondered if my heart would ever stop its thunder.

"Tell me, Val, I don't look much like Bartolomeo, do I?" It bothered me the man had kept calling Barto my father. If he could see the resemblance, had others? Francesco was the only one who had ever mentioned our similarities.

"A little, but only if you were standing close to each other, and one really stared at you. Maybe you looked like him when he was young, who knows? But fear not, Gio. Many nephews resemble their uncles."

He sounded so sure, but I did not feel the same confidence.

The storefronts became more familiar as we approached the Duomo di San Marco, and then, as if bursting forth from dark tunnels, we were out of the warren of narrow alleys and crossing the immense piazza.

Val led the way toward the docks, but when we passed the guarded door of the Palazzo di Doge, I stopped him.

He looked around, nervous. "What, Gio? We must get away from Venezia. We cannot dally."

"*Il Libro d'Oro*." I looked toward the doorway of the palazzo.

He started to protest, then saw the look in my eye. "Are you sure no one learned your name back there?"

"I am sure. And you said yourself that you don't think we were followed. I doubt they will even find Bruno for a day or two."

Valentino gave me a heavy sigh, but he turned in the direction of the palazzo.

*   *   *

The guards gave us little trouble, only requiring us to state our business before they let us pass. Valentino, to protect our identities, surprised me by answering for us both. "I am the lawyer for la famiglia Chigi and this is my assistant. We are here to peruse *Il Libro d'Oro* for a case we are examining."

The Chigi name was a means of easy entry. Even hundreds of miles from Roma the name was still an influence.

"The office of the State Advocacies holds the book," one of the guards said, jerking his finger toward a staircase on the far side of the internal courtyard.

"Grazie," Valentino said, doffing his cap to the guard before strolling into the palazzo.

I hurried to keep pace as he strode ahead with an air of superiority, practically ignoring me. I knew this was only for show and I hoped any memory we left behind was not one of two men who would bother murdering a kitchen hand. I looked down at my hand, sure I would see blood in the cracks around my fingers, but there was none—I had scrubbed clean.

If only I could scrub my memory clean of the blood as well.

When we reached the attorney's office we were greeted by another contingency of guardsmen. Again, Valentino explained himself and we were let to pass without incident.

The chamber was decorated with paintings of the Avogadori, the men who safeguard the principles of law. The Avogadori were nearly as important as the doge, the ruler of all Venice.

"And you are?" the clerk behind the long counter asked us. This time Valentino sounded less patient.

"I am here representing the Chigi family, investigating some claims for monies owed to them by the Crispo family of the Archipelago."

The clerk sat up straighter at the Chigi name. "Ahh. How can I be of help?" He was a portly man, with a nose reddened from what I suspected was a bit too much drink.

"My assistant and I would like to see *Il Libro d'Oro* to verify that certain weddings took place. We have several cases of property we are investigating."

The clerk's chin bobbed against his chest. "Yes, yes, of course. Please come with me."

He led us across the room to an ornate door. He slid a key into the lock and pulled it open. The room was of much plainer decor. It was lined with wooden benches, and in the back lay several big chests with heavy locks. It was to one of those chests that the clerk brought us.

I had to press my hand to my heart, it was hammering so hard. The clerk unlocked the chest and extracted a large, gold-painted book. He brought it to a podium in the center of the room and laid it down carefully.

"Please tell me who you are looking for. If you have a date that would be even more helpful."

Valentino's voice was slick. "I assure you, signore, we are capable of looking on our own. These cases, you see, require discretion."

The man's head wobbled back and forth. "No, that won't do. I must remain in the room with you."

Valentino smiled. It was the same charming smile I had seen win over many a woman and turn even the hardest heart of a man. "Are you quite sure about that, signore?" A hand went into his money pouch and extracted several scudi. He placed the coins into the clerk's palm and closed his fingers over them. "I promise you we will not alter or harm the book in any way. We will only need a quarter of an hour and we will be gone."

I held my breath, willing the guard to agree. We could not risk someone knowing we looked at the Crispo record, then later tying that to Bruno's—and Piero's—death.

He looked at his hand, then bobbed his head in the affirmative. "Ten minutes. Not a second more," he said as he left us alone with the *Libro d'Oro.*

"Please, Gio, have the honor. It's your mother we are looking for, after all." Valentino held a palm out toward the heavy volume.

The book was two hands high and half a hand thick with page edges gilded in gold. Shaking, I opened up the cover of the book and began thumbing through the illuminated pages. The fine vellum was decorated with the coats of arms of the various patrician families and inscribed with countless dates of weddings, births, and deaths.

"I don't know how I'm going to find Stella in all of this," I said as I stared at all the names, hopeless.

Valentino looked over my shoulder. "It's likely not to be in the newer pages. Go back about a hundred pages and start there. Just look for the Crispo name; ignore all the rest."

I did as he suggested. Page after page made mention of the Fabbi, Foscari, Mocenigo, and Barbaro families, but nothing of Crispo or the Dukes of the Archipelago.

"Wait," Val said, darting his hand forward to stop me from flipping the page. "I see it."

"Where?" My eyes scanned the pages in front of me.

Val gasped. "*Madonna,*" he whispered.

"Where, where is it?" I looked everywhere but saw nothing that looked familiar.

He looked up to the sky, as if searching for an alternate answer from God. "Gio, you will not believe it. I myself do not believe it. Dio mio, Dio mio."

"Show me where the name is," I said, exasperated.

He put his finger on the bottom of the right page. "There."

I read the words: *Agosto 28, 1528, Palazzo Ducale. Il matrimonio di Giacomo Crispo e Serafina Chigi.*

For a moment I could not breathe. When I finally turned to Valentino, his eyes were wide. His mouth was still open in disbelief.

"It's your mother," I said in a rush, causing Valentino to raise his eyebrow at me. He gaped for a second, then continued my thought.

"And if Stella is Serafina, that means my mother was your father's lover. And now . . ." he said, nodding his head.

I felt strangely giddy as this puzzle unlocked between us. "You . . . are my . . ."

"*Fratello.* Yes, it appears so." He stared down at the page again for some time, long enough I wondered if the news was unwelcome. Then he broke out in a wide grin. "It has always been so, that I have thought of you as such." He threw an arm around my shoulder and hugged me.

"So much more makes sense now," I said, thinking back to all the ways Bartolomeo had doted on Valentino as much as he had me. A thought came to me. "Did he ever call you his cipollino?"

My friend—no, my brother—laughed, then his expression turned to curiosity. "Hmm. Not when I was older, but actually, now that you ask me, I do remember that he would call me that when I was very young. Probably before you moved to Roma. I always assumed he stopped when I was older because it would be strange to call me that when he was not part of our family. How did you know?"

"In the journals, he mentions a son, and that's what he calls him."

As the words passed my lips, I remembered the conversation I had with Isabetta about the date of the birth of that child, in 1546.

Valentino was a year older than me—it was his birth we had read about. I had one unread journal in my pack, from 1547, which we had decided to save to decode on the long way home. I wondered then, would that journal tell me of my own birth?

The clerk's voice cut through our conversation. "I trust you have completed your investigation."

Valentino straightened next to me. I closed the book before the man could see what we had been reading.

"Grazie for the time, signore. Now let us be on our way. Come now, Bernardo. We must be getting back to Ferrara before it is too late."

"Sì, Maestro." I shuffled out after him, glad he had the where-withal to conceal our true identities. I was still in a state of shock, the image of the names on the illuminated page glowing against my thoughts as we walked.

"Say nothing else of import until we are back at the inn," Val said in a low voice as we passed out of earshot of the palace guards. He hadn't needed to warn me. I had no words for what was going on inside my mind.

*   *   *

Soon we stood in front of a gondola waiting for passengers. There was only one boatman when we arrived. "Alonzo should be here shortly," he assured us. When we had arrived, I wondered why the boats needed two boatmen, but with the water starting to become choppier with the weather, I now understood. I slipped into the felze and settled against the cushioned seat while Valentino paid the fare. The rain was starting to fall harder, and I was glad for the cover. "Andiamo!" I heard another voice say as Valentino took his seat across from me.

Val looked grim. He spoke to me so low I could barely hear. "The second gondolier is the man who gave you directions to Palazzo Gri-mani. Speak only of benign things on this trip and keep your hood up when we disembark."

I nodded. "What a miserable day. I'm so glad we had the chance to spend time with your cousins before the rain started to fall," I said in a loud voice.

"Lisa has such a sharp wit. I warned you not to play her at cards!" he responded.

We continued the banter, making up the details of our "day" as we traversed the rough waters of the lagoon.

When we were about halfway to our destination I heard shouts on the right side of our bow. *"Férmate! Férmate!"*

The gondola slowed. "What is going on?" Val peered through the curtains of the felze.

"Can you see anything?" I whispered.

"No, there is too much fog and rain."

The voices grew louder until it was clear the other boat had drawn up next to ours.

"We're looking for two men who committed a crime. How many have you on your gondola?"

The hairs on the back of my neck stood up. How did they find us? And how could we get away?

I held my breath as the gondoliers confirmed there were two men on board. Next thing I knew the doors were opening and a burly man with a sword at the ready was peering in. "Your names, what are your names?"

"I am Valentino Pio da Carpi, the son of a Chigi daughter. I am traveling with my friend, Giovanni Scappi. May I ask who you are looking for? Perhaps we saw them when we were in the city?"

I hated that Val had given the officials our real names, but knew he was right to do so. If they wanted identification and found out we had lied, things would go much worse for us.

The door shut just as quickly as it had opened. I heard a grunt from one of the voices and a gruff explanation to the gondoliers. "We're looking for two Englishmen, not Italians. They robbed and strangled one of the other guests at their boardinghouse."

I think that if I had been a woman I might have fainted from relief.

The rest of the boat trip was blissfully uneventful. When we reached the mainland we both kept our hoods up, but it likely mattered not.

"Do you think we need to leave now?" Valentino asked after we were out of earshot of our gondoliers. "We can stay at the inn and go in the morning."

"No, no," I said, panic rising within me. "We must go."

"Very well." My friend saw the worry in my eyes and clapped me on the back. "Please do not worry, Gio. There's an inn in Mesola. That should be far enough away. We can get there by dark if I can round up my guard quickly. I hadn't told them to be ready to leave so soon."

I tried to calm my breathing. "Thank you, Val. Thank you."

We left Venezia within the hour, and thank the Lord, there were no more incidents to bar our journey. Only when we were on the road, the rattle of the carriage covering the sound of our voices, could I relax.

I changed clothes in the carriage, and after we cleaned the cut on my neck with water from a water skin, I wrapped my neck with a scarf to conceal the wound. It wasn't deep, but it was noticeable.

Valentino uncorked a bottle of wine from the small rack under the seat. He took a swig and handed it to me. I downed the sour liquid gratefully.

"Fratello mio. I know I keep saying this, but so much makes sense to me now. So much," he said.

He was right. Suddenly many things were clear. In thinking back, Serafina had always appeared much like Bartolomeo had described in his journals. Golden hair and chestnut brown eyes. Other puzzle pieces fell into place. In the journals, Stella had helped Bartolomeo secure his first job in Roma—in the service of Cardinale Rodolfo Pio da Carpi. The journals had only mentioned Stella was married to the brother of a cardinale, and with many dozens of cardinali, that could have been anyone. Now I understood. Stella had been married to Ludovico, Cardinale Carpi's brother. The journals had said Serafina had six children—including il cipollino. Valentino had a brother and sister—both grown and married off. Serafina's other three children had not survived childhood. And Serafina was a Chigi principessa.

From the moment I arrived in Roma, Serafina had let Val play with me and had always encouraged him to learn from Bartolomeo. It occurred to me that had not been the case with the other Carpi siblings—I had thought it was because Val was the one who had befriended me, but now I understood the deeper connection.

Over the years, Serafina had not shown me any favors. When I recalled the times we had met, talked, and dined together, she treated me only as though I were Val's good friend.

"If she knows I'm her son she has never let on," I said to Val as we rattled along the road toward Mesola. "Perhaps Barto did a good job of convincing her otherwise—I seem like someone who would have been obvious for her to suspect."

"You might be right," Val concurred. "She always thought you were *un buon ragazzo*, but she really only seemed to think of you as my friend. If you were Caterina's whelp, then any similarities in our looks could be explained away easily."

"In the journals Bartolomeo wrote that he never planned to tell her where I ended up. Maybe he never did. She probably thought I truly was his nephew. Even so, it seems so strange to me that she didn't guess."

Val stretched across the bench of the carriage. "She might have. But my mother is good at not concerning herself if she does not need to. And I think that even if she had guessed, she might have told herself she should not ask, should not assume, should not wonder."

I could not understand how anyone could be so insulated. "She is not curious?"

Val thought about this idea. "She is, but when it comes to people, she keeps to herself. I have never known her to gossip, or to presume she understands the motives of another person."

"Perhaps it is because she has had so many secrets in her own life."

"Clearly." He tilted his head backward over the cushion to look out the window upward at the passing sky. I could see the red tail of the comet in the distance, still bright during the day but faded from its former brilliance several weeks ago. Perhaps the end of the world wasn't nigh.

A thought occurred to me. "Why did they split us up? Why did I not grow up with you and Serafina?"

"There is so much to this story I do not understand. That I can hardly fathom. I just realized, Gio, my mother is Stella, and that means my mother"—he lowered his voice—"killed a pope."

"I have been thinking much of that too," I said, knowing his fear.

"Do you think—"

I cut him off. "No, no. I do not think the sins of our parents are our sins. The Bible also says as much. It is all in which of those damned words you choose to believe."

He looked at me, momentarily shocked at my blasphemy, then burst into laughter. He knew I did not always think much of religion, having been jaded by the excesses of the church.

"I know not why I question it. I have never been so pious myself, have I?" He lifted the bottle of wine in toast and we shared a swig. "But the thought of my mother, doomed to the depths of hell . . ."

"We know nothing of that," I said quickly, but I felt the same. "Should we tell her we know the truth?" My heart skipped as I said the words. What would we say? If her family ever found out what she had done . . . I couldn't finish that thought.

"I don't know. I find I don't know if I want to see my—our—mother when we get back."

The carriage hit a bump and I knocked the back of my head against the polished wood. I rubbed it, wondering what I felt about Serafina. She had been on the fringes of so much of my life, but I did not know her well enough to determine how she might feel about learning I was her son. Would she be angry we had discovered the truth? What if she pushed me away?

"You never really knew Ludovico," I reminded him. "Doesn't it please you to learn he was not really your father?"

He stared out the window at the comet in the distance. "It does, but it bothers me that she let me believe he was."

"She was protecting you, Val. Surely you know that. If anyone had found out you were not his son, the family might have cast you both out or worse."

"I am no longer a child, Gio. There has been nothing to prevent her from telling me now."

I could say nothing to that and turned my attention instead to Barto's journal from 1547, the year I was born.

CHAPTER 24

Scappi

Fara in Sabina and Monterotondo, August 1547

Bartolomeo paced the long hallway. Behind the closed door at the end of the hall he could hear Stella screaming in agony. It was a sound that cut to the very core of him, and though he hated that he was not the one holding Stella's hand, he was grateful for Laura della Rovere. She had graciously offered them aid, including the ancestral Orsini hunting lodge high in the hills beyond Roma in the ancient town of Fara in Sabina.

He began his pacing anew. Everything about his and Stella's presence at the hunting lodge had to be kept a secret. It was the reason there was only a small, very trusted staff of servants. It was also the reason both he and Stella had arrived under the cover of darkness and why Laura's armed guards were chosen from those who were most loyal.

So many secrets, Bartolomeo mused as he wandered the empty halls. There was the secret of his son, Valentino, the boy Stella had given birth to eleven months ago and was at home with his nurse. Everyone believed he was Ludovico Pio da Carpi's legitimate son. As soon as Stella had thought she might be pregnant, she made certain to spend some time with her husband. He was not any the wiser for it. With this child, Ludovico would not know at all.

That was the other secret, a terrible one Bartolomeo would hold as close to his heart as he did with Giacomo Crispo. Ludovico Pio da Carpi had died several months ago of an unknown illness. No one suspected anything.

Murdering Ludovico was not something that any of them had planned to do, but when Stella realized she was with child again it was during a time when Ludovico had just left for Spain on business. By the time he returned three months later, the pregnancy was beginning to show. She could hide the evidence of her adultery with the right clothing, but there was no way she could seduce him and make him believe the babe was his. Stella and her newborn would be shipped off to a cloistered nunnery, never to be seen by any man ever again. Stella had been distraught. They discussed a myriad of ways to terminate the pregnancy, but in the end, it was Laura who came up with the plan to end Ludovico once and for all.

Although the idea had been Laura's, it was Bartolomeo who had secured the black hellebore tincture. As a close friend, Laura spent a lot of time visiting Stella, and it was easy enough for her to slip the poison into Ludovico's wine one night while dining with them in their garden. Ludovico was not a young man, so when he complained of vertigo twenty minutes later, no one thought of poison. Stella accompanied him to his bed and Laura dumped the remaining wine into a hedge. He died of a heart attack less than an hour later. Stella sent the other children to spend time with their cousins and Laura whisked Stella away to her hunting lodge for the spring and summer to recover from the "loss" of her husband. And if she came home with a child? What a blessed miracle it would be to have been carrying the memory of her husband. No one would be the wiser.

*   *   *

A little guilt about the decision sometimes crept into Bartolomeo's consciousness, not because he felt any sympathy for Stella's husband, but because the man had helped Bartolomeo secure a position with his brother, Cardinale Rodolfo Pio da Carpi, who had been a good employer thus far. But Stella herself was delighted to be rid of her husband. He had never been someone she cared for, and as he aged he had become more easily aggravated, and sometimes even violent.

Bartolomeo stared out of the high window down to the little village below. It pained him that he might have another son who would grow up in a household without his fatherly love. Bartolomeo might connect with little Valentino in various ways throughout their lives, but it would be as a servant to a prince. This separation left him desperate for a child with whom he could share his life. Most of all, Bartolomeo wanted a son who would learn his trade, would know the wonder of delighting hundreds of diners at once, and of holding sway with kings through the most basic of desires—food.

Stella's shrieks subsided for a few minutes, then began anew. Bartolomeo studied the dozens of paintings of Orsini princes lining the walls and wondered if they had ever been in such a predicament. Laura herself was a bastard daughter, borne of the blasphemous relationship between Giulia Farnese and Rodrigo Borgia, Pope Alessandro VI. But she had been lucky. Giulia's husband, Orsino Orsini, had accepted Laura as his child and heir. It was a choice that had made her very wealthy indeed, as she, and her husband, Niccolo della Rovere, inherited the entire Orsini fortune, including the lodge where they now stayed.

Bartolomeo turned his mind toward the elaborate plan he had finally convinced Stella to accept—to let him raise the child instead of her. It was dangerous, but the more he thought about it, the more he believed they could make it work. Laura had proven herself to be loyal, and her well-paid men would keep quiet. Caterina and the midwife were the only unknowns.

Bartolomeo had stopped in Monterotondo to see his sister on his way to Fara in Sabina. He was not prepared to discover her in mourning; hours earlier, she had given birth to a stillborn boy. She had lost her husband, Nazeo, to the plague only a month before. Bartolomeo hadn't even known she was with child. The midwife had greeted him at the door and only begrudgingly let him in. Caterina was understandably distraught. "God is cruel," she told Bartolomeo before she turned on her side away from him. "So terribly cruel." He stayed with her for only a night—the tragedy made him even more desperate to get to Stella before the baby was born. The thought of something happening to Stella or their child filled him with terror. He could see the grief in his sister's eyes and did not know if his own heart could take such heartbreak.

That's when the idea had come to him. Perhaps Caterina would be willing to raise another child?

Stella howled again, louder this time. Bartolomeo hurried toward the door. Would she be all right after this birth, her seventh? Just as he pressed his ear to the door he heard the cries of a newborn child.

His child.

To hell with this door, he thought. He turned the knob but met with resistance. Locked. He pounded on the door.

"Calm down, Barto." Laura's voice filtered through the wood of the door. "Stella is fine. And so is your little boy. Let us get them cleaned up. Be patient."

Another son? Thank the heavens. While he would have been delighted to have a little girl, he was relieved to have a potential heir to his culinary legacy.

The child wailed again. For a moment Bartolomeo thought about breaking down the door. Instead, he turned back down the hall and began his pacing again.

When the door finally opened, it seemed like an eternity had passed. Laura appeared holding a little bundle in her arms. Bar-

*   *   *

Later that afternoon, just before Bartolomeo planned to depart for Roma, four armed men rode up to the gates of the palazzo. Laura's guard went to meet them, and finally, after it was clear the men were not going to leave until they spoke to the head of the house, they returned to summon Laura. The men came from the Palone household, the guard reported. Laura told the guard to send them away.

"Why are they here?" Bartolomeo asked when she returned to the library where he waited with Stella and Giovanni.

"They are looking for the midwife, who never made it home," Laura said, peering out the window. She seemed unconcerned.

Realization hit him. "You had her killed?"

Laura turned to him. "I had no choice."

Bartolomeo looked away, bile rising in his throat. The midwife had kept his family safe. She had children of her own at home.

There was a shout from downstairs—the guard calling to Laura. Bartolomeo peeked out the curtain and saw the path was empty. Noise from below confirmed that the men were inside.

"We are lost." Stella looked down at her son and began crying. "Lost before his life really began."

Laura stroked the sleeping baby's head. "Worry not. You will hide and I will lie. I am not pregnant, and that will be quite evident. I will tell them the Palones are confused—I did not send for a midwife. All will be well. I do not expect them to demand entry, but if they do, you'll need to hide behind that bookcase."

She pointed to an ornate bookcase on the library wall opposite them. She moved a hidden lever that was nearly invisible in the detailed oak carving. A loud click sounded and the side of the bookcase moved forward just enough for a person to slip inside.

Laura ushered them into the passage and handed Bartolomeo a small lamp that had been flickering on the desk near them. She was closing the door just as a frantic servant entered to request her presence downstairs.

"They may not deter easily, but rest assured, they will be deterred," she said before the bookcase closed with another click.

They wound their way through the passage to the little room at the end of the short hallway, furnished simply with a bed, a desk, and two chairs. There were no windows in the room. He set the lantern on the desk and he helped Stella to the edge of the bed. He kissed the top of her head, and though clearly weary, she smiled up at him, calm, as though it were perfectly normal to be holed up in a wall behind a bookshelf just after giving birth. He held her close and they ceased their whispers to listen for the Palone guards.

It was an interminable wait. The hunting lodge was large and the guards seemed to be scouring each room carefully. Just as the voices came closer, the baby began to stir. Stella rocked him, but it only succeeded in waking him further. She struggled with the ties on the front of her gown, but not before the child let out a short, piercing wail. She moved him quickly to her breast. Thankfully, he latched immediately.

There was a loud crash in the room beyond. Bartolomeo had never been a praying man, but he flung a prayer heavenward, hoping the boy would stay quiet. Bartolomeo stood to block the corridor in the event the Palones' men discovered the hidden bookcase. He knew not how he would protect his lover and their son without any weapon, but he was not going to let them near without a fight.

When he heard the bookcase click and Laura's voice telling him it was safe to return, he could almost taste the relief.

"What happened?" he asked.

"We were lucky. In their search, they scared the cat that was sleeping on the top of the case. She must have climbed up there after you hid. One of the men accidentally bumped the bookcase and she screeched and flew off the bookcase, landing on top of him.

That filthy donkey broke the vase I just bought." She pointed to the remnants of a huge maiolica vase.

"I will cook that cat the biggest fish it will ever eat," he said, looking at the fluffy beast in admiration.

"Alas, I'll have to feed the cat. You should leave before first light," Laura said as they went down to the salon.

He considered Stella and his son, wondering if he had made the right choice. But wondering mattered not—when the midwife lost her life it was in exchange for the secrecy of his son. He would not have her die in vain by letting Stella go back to Roma pretending the babe was Ludovico's.

"Understood. Tell the night guard to rouse me at the first sound of the birds' dawn chorus."

Laura put her hand on his shoulder. "All will be well, Bartolomeo. You'll see."

*   *   *

Bartolomeo rode the fastest horse in the Orsini stable. Monterotondo was not far, about an hour's ride on an open plain. In the dark morning, he had to trust the horse to keep a straight line on the dirt road. Giovanni was blissfully quiet, and it wasn't until the first edges of light began to peep through the clouds and they neared the edge of the town that the babe began to fidget. By the time he reached Caterina's door, Giovanni had begun to scream, a terrible wail Bartolomeo was sure the entire town could hear.

Fortunately, Caterina lived on the outskirts of the village and her nearest neighbor was on the other side of a vineyard. She was awake. She peered out the window of her modest house to see as he banged on her front door. When she saw it was him, she came running. Cesare appeared a few moments later, wakened by the noise.

Bartolomeo waved at Cesare. "Go back to bed, little man. I'll come tuck you in shortly."

Cesare disappeared behind the door.

Caterina turned back to her brother. "Why are you here? Who is the babe?"

Bartolomeo unwrapped the infant from his chest and passed him over to Caterina. She held the boy, stunned.

"He needs milk. Pray tell, sister, you must still have some?"

Caterina sat down on the nearby chair, holding the boy and looking at him in wonder. "I . . ."

"Caterina, do you have milk? If not, we need to find him a wet nurse. He's only a day old."

She began to undo her robe. "I don't know. It's been a few days. I will try." She lifted out one of her breasts and pressed the baby against her. He found the nipple immediately and took it without hesitation. Caterina eyed Bartolomeo in wonder.

"I don't understand. What is going on? Whose child is this?"

"He's yours, *sorella mia.* His name is Giovanni. When anyone asks you, he's yours. Born from Nazeo."

"But the midwife knows I birthed a stillborn, so do a handful of others in the village."

"You only need keep him hidden for a couple of days. Then I'm moving you to Tivoli. I am buying you a house and will provide for you all."

Caterina's eyes grew wide. "This makes no sense, Barto. Who is his mother?"

"You are, Caterina. And I am his uncle. Do this for me, sorella mia. His life, and probably mine, depend upon it."

She tried again. "Who birthed this babe, Barto?"

But he would not be swayed. He could see the look Caterina had when she beheld the child; this was a precious gift he had brought to her.

"I told you, Caterina, you are his mother."

Three-year-old Cesare's voice interrupted the moment. "Who is that baby?"

Bartolomeo swooped up the boy from the doorway. "I see you didn't listen to your uncle, Cesare. He's your little brother. His name is Giovanni."

The puzzled look on his face would have been cute in any other situation, but his voice was accusing. "Mamma, you said my brother was in heaven!"

Bartolomeo didn't miss a beat. "He came back. The angels wanted to play with Giovanni for a little bit. And now he's here so you will have a playmate of your own."

"Remember how you told me yesterday you hated it here? That you didn't like the smell from the fields up the road?" Caterina spoke up. Bartolomeo saw the wetness in her eyes. She had never been one who liked to lie.

Cesare nodded.

"We're going to leave Monterotondo and go to Tivoli," she said, a bright smile on her face. "It's a better place for little boys."

"And I'm going to make sure you get some riding lessons too," Bartolomeo added.

Cesare's eyes lit up. "Riding? I want a horse!"

Bartolomeo ruffled his hair. "Maybe someday. For now, why don't you get dressed? It seems you aren't going to get any more sleep this morning." He set the boy down upon the ground and he ran up the stairs.

"I am not a good liar, Barto."

He sat down in the chair next to Caterina and rubbed Giovanni's head as he nursed.

"You will be," he told her.

CHAPTER 25

Giovanni

Roma, September 1577

I woke Valentino as soon as I had deciphered my father's words.
"I won't let Isabetta know," he said when I finished telling
him the story.

I stared out the window of the carriage. Ravenna loomed in the
distance, its terra-cotta buildings jutting up beyond the marshes that
surrounded it. "I know not how I can live with this knowledge. My
very birth is the reason for her mother's death."

He leaned over and smacked my knee. "Stop that nonsense. You
yourself had nothing to do with it, Gio. You cannot blame yourself
for the things your father did."

"Your father too," I reminded him.

He paused, thinking about the import of my statement. "Our
father, then."

"How can this be? That I fall in love with a woman who, if she
knew the truth of our connection, should hate me? I think God must
be playing a trick on me."

"You know as well as I do that the greater someone's station is,
the fewer people they need to keep up with. Bartolomeo was well
connected with the right people—like Laura della Rovere."

"But this happened in Fara in Sabina! There are barely more than a few goatherds there. What are the chances that my lover's mother was my midwife?" I shook my head. "It is a cruel fate, a cruel one."

"Roma is not the big city it once was. The Sack, the plagues—these days, it is all too easy for us to be connected to the most unlikely of people. Besides, Fara in Sabina is only a day from Roma." Valentino leaned back into the seat and stared at me. "How is your hair wavy and mine is not?"

I shrugged. "Barto had curls in his beard? But I have always thought it odd that our noses are the same."

Val and I continued to go back and forth, comparing memories and how they fit between us. Everything from banquets we attended where our parents spoke to each other, to how we sometimes seemed to have matching toys as children. There were several things we had written off as insignificant or coincidence that suddenly seemed poignant.

Valentino's face lit up with a realization. "That ring!" He lowered his voice. "The one with the cantarella, that she used on the pope . . ."

"I've never seen her wearing a memento ring," I said, racking my brain to recall if I had ever seen Serafina wearing such specific jewelry. That type of ring was big and hard to miss.

"No, she's never worn it. But I found it once, when I was a youth, snooping through her things. I opened it and it was empty. I wanted to ask her why she didn't put anything inside it, like a lock of hair from me or my siblings, but then she would know I had been where I didn't belong."

He laughed. "Fratello mio. My best friend, this secret brotherhood will not undo us."

I ran my fingers across the worn leather cover of the little book. "We should burn this journal. It is too dangerous for us to keep it."

"Sì. We should burn them all. Bartolomeo was right in telling you to do so, but if you had—"

"I wouldn't have known you were my brother," I said, finishing his sentence.

I thought of all the hours I had spent poring over our father's words. The thought of burning his secrets filled me with trepidation— these journals were an intimate piece of Bartolomeo I did not want to lose. But then I thought of Isabetta and the bond we had built unraveling the story of Stella. It had seemed like a puzzle, an elaborate game, not something that would tear apart our real lives. This was not just about me. Isabetta's face loomed in my memories. My mother. I had so much to think of.

"Do I tell Isabetta about you? About Serafina?" I put my head into my hands and let the carriage jostle me in the darkness behind my eyes.

"Can you keep any of this from her?"

I looked up at him. There was no anger or frustration in my brother's eyes. Only a quiet reassurance we would weather whatever storm came our way.

"I know not," I said, turning my sight to the world beyond our carriage. "I know not."

* * *

By the time we reached Ravenna, I was anxious to get back, and it didn't take much to convince Val we'd be better off on horseback than taking the slow carriage. We rode as fast as we were able, nearly halving the time it took to travel to Venezia. Still, eight days on horseback left me barely able to walk when we finally returned. It was early afternoon and clouds threatened to make good on the pattern of Roma's tradition of September rains.

We dismounted at the Farnese stables near the Campo dei Fiori.

"Are you returning home?" I asked Val.

He sighed. "I must. My mother is probably worried about me.

I do not know how I will be toward her. I am angry, and I am sad. Perhaps I will seek out the bordello tonight. A little comfort would do me good."

"Val," I began, but he anticipated my words.

"Fear not, fratello. I will say nothing to her, I give you my word. If we decide to tell her what we know, we will do so together."

We parted with the customary kisses and I began the walk back to my house near the Vaticano. I thought of stopping by to see Caterina, but I was not sure if I was ready to talk with her. Should I tell her the truth? She deserved to know whose child she had raised.

I kept walking and did not turn down the long street leading toward her home. Instead, I followed the bustling via Giulia, dodging out of the way of running street urchins and carts laden with goods. As I neared the end of the street a man stepped out of a shop without looking, and I almost knocked him over.

"Sorry," he said, reaching down to retrieve his hat, which had fallen in the effort to avoid knocking into me. I recognized the voice.

"Tomaso!" I reached out to Isabetta's brother to embrace him, my heart rejoicing in the thought that Isabetta must be home.

He turned toward me. He paled, making the strawberry mark around his eye appear brighter than it normally was. "It's you," he sputtered.

Then, to my surprise, he turned from me and ran. He ran as though his life depended on it. I called after him, but he did not slow. I stood in the street, watching his diminishing figure, wondering what had made him run.

*   *   *

It wasn't long before I discovered the source of Tomaso's consternation. I had been home less than an hour when Dea told me Isabetta's brother was in the courtyard waiting to speak with me. I assumed it was Tomaso, but when I came down the long marble stair into the open courtyard, I found Richo pacing the lemon-tree-lined walkway.

He didn't notice my approach. His brow was furrowed, and he stared at his feet as he walked. He held his hand ready on his sword, which I assumed was a nervous habit.

I assumed wrong.

"Richo, is everything all right? I saw Tomaso earlier . . ." I began.

He whirled at the sound of my voice, drawing his sword. He advanced toward me. Startled, I stumbled backward.

Richo thrust his sword toward my chest, stopping short of touching me.

"Richo? What are you doing?" I said. My mind raced through the possibilities. Did he think I had dishonored Isabetta in some way?

"You know something about my mother's death."

Dear God, the Palones had the journal that mentioned the vendetta poem Bartolomeo had seen on *Pasquino*. For the second time in a week I was about to be the victim of a vendetta meant for my father. I had a fleeting thought—if I had never opened those journals, none of this would be happening.

But it was.

"I'm not sure I understand." I scrambled backward, but hit the wall next to the stair instead. His sword caught on my doublet, snipping the threads of a button. It fell to the tiles and caught in a crack.

"You do! You hid that journal from Isabetta. You kept it from her. You filthy worm-head!"

"I can explain, Richo." I tried to stay calm despite the increasing pressure of the sword against the padding of my doublet.

"There is no explanation! Isabetta was with my father when he recovered the journal and the recipes from the casa di Gonfalone! When she saw the journal, she assumed you had to be hiding something. She decoded it when we were in Lucca. You betrayed my sister! You betrayed us all. Your uncle knew something of our mother's death. And I suspect you know something too. Mamma will be revenged, and as your uncle is not here, you will have to do." He spat out the words with a ferocity and rage I had never seen in another human being.

He raised his sword and I closed my eyes, waiting for the blow.

It didn't come. Instead I heard a thump and the clang of Richo's sword on the ground. I opened my eyes, my heart thundering in my chest.

Richo was sprawled across the tiles, his sword flung a fair distance from his hand. A rock the size of my hand rested at my feet.

Salvi rushed toward me.

"Maestro Scappi! Maestro Scappi! Are you all right?"

I pushed myself off the ground and dusted off my breeches.

"I'm fine, Salvi. Thank you for your fast thinking."

Fast thinking that might have killed my lover's brother. I leaned down to feel for his pulse and thankfully found one. I felt the back of his head to see if the rock had broken it open, but there was no blood, only a bump smaller than an egg that had started to form. I surmised he would have a large headache when he woke.

Seeing Salvi next to Richo made me wonder about our conversation after he brought me back the recipes the first time.

"Salvi, after we recovered those recipes, you told me you and Rolando inspected the box together and the journal wasn't there. Was that true?"

His mouth opened, then closed, then opened again, his eyes wide as he tried to find the words to say.

"It is true. When we looked into the box together, the journal wasn't there."

"Who took the journal before you opened the box?"

He stared down at his feet.

"Isabetta was the one who went inside to get the box. She took the journal out. She made me promise not to tell you. She made me swear it on my heart. She told me the Lord would strike me down if I told you." He shivered.

I was disappointed but could not fault him for fearing the Lord's retribution more than mine. It was not the time to reprimand the boy. I needed to figure out what to do.

"Help me get him into the house," I demanded. I motioned for Salvi to take up Richo's legs.

"Are you mad? Why would you bring him into the house?" Salvi burst out.

I had never heard him speak so. He seemed to realize this and hastened to pick up Richo's feet.

"If he's hurt, we must tend to him," I explained.

"He was going to kill you, Maestro. He will still want to kill you when he wakes up."

I hoisted him up and moved toward the main door to the house. Salvi lifted his feet. If we could get him into the parlor to a couch, then we could decide what to do with him.

When we reached the door, Salvi briefly set down Richo's feet to open the door. Dea gasped as we entered.

"What happened?" she asked, moving items out of our way so we had a clear path to the couch.

"He wanted to kill Maestro Scappi!"

We lifted Richo onto the couch. Dea put a pillow under his head and feet and covered him with a thin blanket.

She gawked at me. "What does he mean, Maestro? Was he trying to kill you? Why?"

I sighed, looking down at the man who so closely resembled Isabetta. They had the same nose, the same dark eyelashes—even the curve of their mouth was similar.

"It's a very long story, Dea." I turned to Salvi and asked him to fetch Richo's sword.

I fell into the Dante chair opposite the couch. I stared at Richo, wondering what I should do next. Salvi was right. He would still want to kill me. Tomaso probably wanted to see me gone, and Rolando had the power and money to send assassins in my direction. All of this was terrible, but not nearly as terrible as the idea Isabetta had been the one to discover my betrayal; that I hid the journal from her, and that I knew Bartolomeo had information about the death of her mother. If I had never been born, none of this would have happened.

I couldn't bear the thought of Isabetta hating me. It left me with a dark hollow nestled in the pit of my stomach.

Salvi returned, breathless, sword in hand. "Maestro, Signor Palone is entering the courtyard. You should slip out the back, hurry!"

I needed time to consider what to do. If I explained it wasn't Bartolomeo who killed their mother, would that be enough? Would they seek out the surviving children of Laura della Rovere? Did I want more blood on my hands for leading them down that path?

"Take Richo's sword and hide it under my bed," I instructed the boy. "Then the two of you should find a safe place to hide. I know not what might happen."

The housekeeper blanched. "Oh, Maestro, please, it can't be so bad as that."

"I think it is."

A look of steely resolve settled on her face. "Hurry, Salvi. We will go to my sister's house."

A noise at the open door startled all of us.

"*Salve!* Giovanni! Giovanni!" Rolando Palone's voice rang through the entryway. Panic filled his voice, not anger, which puzzled me. Still, I motioned to Dea and Salvi to hurry.

I went to meet Isabetta's father, and what I was sure might have been, quite probably, my death.

Rolando had just crossed the threshold into the house. "Giovanni, we must go! Isabetta . . . your brother kidnapped her!"

His words slammed into me like a horse rushing at full speed. "What? What do you mean? My brother did what?"

He peered past me into the house, as if looking for someone. "Bandits overpowered our carriage as we made our way home from the market. They killed my driver and the guard, and Cesare appeared. He ripped Isabetta from the coach and took her! He told me if you didn't turn over Bartolomeo's knife and recipes before tomorrow at noon, they will kill her."

I couldn't believe what I was hearing.

"Where is Richo?" Rolando was frantic, his cap missing, his cape haphazardly thrown across his shoulders and a wild look in his eye. I had never seen him thus or imagined he could become so flustered. Behind him in the courtyard were a dozen hired condottieri, awaiting Rolando's command.

"He's inside," I said, blocking the door to the parlor. "How did you know he was here?"

"One of the servants said he was coming here to talk to you. Get Richo, get your uncle's knife and his recipes, and do not tarry!"

I gritted my teeth. Cesare had sunk to a new low. I wondered what Romoli had promised my rotten cousin. While I cared a great deal about my father's recipes, the thought of losing the knife cut into me, deep, nearly as much as the thought of losing Isabetta. He hadn't cared about the knife before, why now?

"There will be a messenger waiting by the Fountain of the Dolphins in Piazza Navona at four today. You are to give them to the messenger. You need to go alone, without weapons, and they will not tolerate being followed. They will wait twenty-four hours, then they will release Isabetta and send her home in a coach. Here," he said, handing me a folded piece of vellum. "They shoved this into my hand as they took her." He tried to look past me. "Richo!" he called, frantic. "Where are you?"

I saw Dea and Salvi out of the corner of my eye, listening to the conversation. I cursed to myself about how they couldn't manage to listen to a simple direction.

"He tripped and hit his head. It knocked him out," I lied. "He is in the parlor on the couch. Dea has been attending to him."

Rolando pushed past me to the parlor. I scanned the note from the kidnappers, but it said little more than what Rolando had conveyed. Before I could turn to follow him to the parlor, another familiar face appeared in the doorway: Valentino.

"I couldn't go home," he explained. "What in the devil is going on here?" He motioned to the guards waiting in the courtyard.

I yanked him inside the house. "Salvi," I said to the boy. "Let Rolando know I went to get the knife and the recipes. I'll be right back down." I turned back to my brother and motioned to him to follow.

As I led the way to the kitchen I told Valentino what I could about Isabetta's kidnapping.

"I'm coming with you, fratello mio."

"I had hoped you would say that." Val was an experienced swordsman whom I would be only too glad to have at my side. He might also help give me a fighting chance of saving face with the Palones—and with Isabetta.

I thought of her enduring such captivity. I knew not what Cesare and Domenico Romoli were capable of doing to her. The thought spurred me to move faster. Rolando was waiting for us when we returned.

I lifted the document and knife boxes and hooked them under my arm. I jerked my chin toward Val. "This is my friend, Valentino Pio da Carpi."

"I want to help," Valentino said, holding out his hand in greeting to Rolando.

Rolando took it and pulled him in for a congenial hug. "Thank you. A friend of Giovanni is a friend of mine."

So he didn't know about Bartolomeo's confession—that my father knew something about his wife's death. I wondered why Rolando's children had chosen to keep the truth about the journal that mentioned Sandra from him.

I checked my pocket watch. We had thirty minutes until four o'clock. I had an idea. The messenger might be watching for one of the condottieri or one of the Palone brothers, but they would not be looking for a child.

I gestured to Salvi, who was listening in the doorway to the parlor. "Salvi, we need your help. I want you to go ahead of us now. Take one of my caps and put on a different jacket, one you do not wear so often. Hide in the market and watch the fountain for the messenger. After I give the man the box, I need you to trail him and find out where he goes."

"Do you have a few coins I can have, Maestro?"

I hesitated, shocked at the request.

"Not for me!" he protested. "I have friends who wander the market. I can have them help me know how many men he has, and where they might be hiding out. Signor Brioschi does not know them like he knows me."

Salvi, Salvi, always thinking. He was right. Cesare wouldn't be on the lookout for street urchins. I dug into my coin purse and handed him several scudi. "Go now, hurry."

"Tell them if they help and are not detected, there is more where that came from," Rolando added. "A lot more."

Salvi rushed off to get a new jacket and cap. I handed the document box to Val while I fastened my cape. Rolando looked beside himself.

"We'll get her back," I told him. "I promise."

He didn't look like he believed me.

CHAPTER 26

Giovanni

I left Rolando Palone and his condottieri at the edge of Campo dei Fiori, not far from Piazza Navona, on the corner where chestnut vendors hawked their treats in autumn.

Valentino left when Salvi did, and we arranged to meet afterward at one of the osterias lining the piazza. Two of the condottieri went with him, leaving behind their swords in favor of hidden daggers. I gave them two of my most tattered doublets, so they might blend into the market better. Their job was to watch for the people who might be watching me.

The Fontana del Delfino, designed by the famous artist Giacomo della Porta, was the newest addition to the bustling Navona market, added only two years ago to the southern section of the piazza. A dolphin and the surrounding four Tritons sprayed water. I approached the fountain with trepidation. I knew nothing of what Cesare's messenger might look like, nor did I know on which side of the fountain he might be waiting. Would I be accosted? Killed? Would they honor their word to let Isabetta go?

I surveyed the crowd but could not see anyone paying attention to me, nor could I see Salvi. Then, just as I grew closer, five dirty street urchins ran past, kicking a pig bladder ball. They stopped near the fountain to play catch. I almost smiled. These must be the boys

Salvi had enlisted to watch the comings and goings of the market around me.

The sky was gray, but a small break in the clouds showed me the faint reddish tail of the receding comet. I sat down on the edge of the fountain, the recipe and knife boxes on my lap and my back to the water, so I could not be surprised from behind.

Not that it would stop an errant dagger, or worse: someone from a window with an arrow.

I waited, the minutes ticking by. The piazza was still busy despite the late-afternoon sunlight glowing across the market stones. The merchants had not yet begun tearing down their stalls, but their calls no longer rang out over the crowd. Instead they were busying themselves with the final customers haggling over the last of the day's bread and vegetables.

The urchins played tag, racing back and forth through the stall area and around the fountain. They never stopped in one place, hopping from one area to the next, seemingly oblivious to me standing at the fountain.

Or to Cesare walking through the crowd.

He approached me, hands outspread to show they were empty. I stood, the blood beginning to pound at my temples. A slow rage began to build, a fire hotter than the hearth at which I had spent so many days of my career.

"Cesare." I did not try to hide the anger in my voice.

"Giovanni! I knew you would be here. Your little whore didn't think you would come. For some reason, she thinks you are dead. Why would that be?" His lip curled with a sneer.

I willed myself to stay calm. This was not the moment to throw things away. I could not give in to my anger. I thought of the heat of my rage and of Bartolomeo, standing at the stove, stirring a pot of risotto with endless patience and silence. "This is like meditation, Giovanni," he used to say. Slowly, slowly, he would stir.

I paused before I spoke, focusing on a tiny mole on the side of Cesare's nose. He was not one for silence, so I channeled the patience of Bartolomeo and said nothing.

"Well? You aren't dead, it seems."

"I am not," I agreed.

"It probably won't be long before you are."

"You wish me dead, Cesare? Why? I have ever tried to be a good brother to you."

He burst into laughter. "A good brother? You cannot be serious. As a child, you hid behind my mother's skirts. And when you weren't being cowardly you were taking everything. All the attention. All the gifts. Bartolomeo doted on you. You had nothing to want for."

"He loved us both like sons," I said, knowing it wasn't exactly true.

"No, he loved *you* like a son." He said the word as though he was talking about excrement. "Because you are his son."

I said nothing, only stared at him, wondering how this exchange was going to end.

"You are. When he gave you everything in the will, I knew it was true."

"Cesare," I began, but he didn't let me continue.

His voice rose. "I remember him bringing you on his horse. They tried to tell me you were the baby who had died, but I was too smart for that. Bartolomeo told my mother to keep you safe. He promised me riding lessons. It was the first of many promises to me he broke."

I remembered reading about that in Bartolomeo's journal. I was surprised to learn he didn't follow through on his promise.

"I think of you as my brother, Cesare. I always have."

"No!" he shouted at me. A drop of spittle hit my brow. I resisted the urge to wipe it away. "Valentino is the one you thought of as brother. You have never treated me like we were of the same blood."

I shook my head. I struggled to keep my voice even. "I became friends with Valentino when you would not be a friend to me. You never gave me a chance, not once."

"You weren't worth the effort." He spat at my feet.

"What do you want, Cesare? I swear, if you have harmed Isabetta . . ." My grip on the boxes tightened. As I stared at my false brother, I was overcome with a sudden urge to turn around and leave with the knife, despite Isabetta, its hold on me was so strong. The thought of cooking without that knife filled me with despair. I kicked myself about the recipes too. After their previous theft, I should have set myself to scribing copies of them. I never once thought Romoli would try for them again, not after the court case. I pushed those thoughts from my mind and pictured Isabetta, her dark locks framing her face, her clear blue eyes piercing deep into me. It sealed my resolve.

"I want you dead, but in lieu of that, I'll take your humiliation. Hand over the recipes. And the knife," he said.

"You don't care about them."

"Ahh, but I know someone who does. And he's making up for the fact that you sucked up all the money in Bartolomeo's will."

I patted the boxes. "If I give these to you, Isabetta goes free? I want your word you'll release her immediately. This has nothing to do with her."

"You don't get to negotiate this, Giovanni. She will be released in twenty-four hours, after we are sure I have not been followed. Now hand me the boxes or I will walk away and she will die."

I handed them to him. "Your jealousy makes you ugly, Cesare. I am surprised your wife even deigns to sleep with you unless you force her."

His dagger flashed in the last dregs of sunlight. "You leave Maria out of this."

"Giovanni! Cesare! How fortuitous to run into you both."

We both turned at the sound of the familiar voice. Dottor Boccia, the old dwarf, came toward us, arms extended, immediately cutting through the tension. I hadn't seen him since Bartolomeo's funeral.

I was relieved to see him. He had been such a dear friend to me in my youth, particularly when Cesare himself was not. As he approached, I noticed the children nearby had scattered.

"Dottor Boccia," Cesare said, his voice tight. "I must go. Good-bye, Giovanni. Don't do anything stupid."

He tucked the boxes under his arm and left, making his way through the depths of the remaining stalls of the market.

I sat back down on the edge of the fountain. "Oh, Boccia, I wish this meeting was a happier one."

He came close and held out his hand in greeting. I shook it, puzzled at the gesture after my words to him.

"Smile a little as we speak," he said in a low voice. "Salvi told me what happened. He sent me in your direction in case you needed help. Cesare always had a dark cloud about him—I am only too happy to make sure he goes along on his way."

"Thanks, old friend."

"I'm to escort you to the osteria, you know, as jolly old pals."

I marveled at Salvi's foresight. No one, much less Cesare, would ever suspect the old jester, who was known mostly for his stupid antics and frivolity in the court of Pope Leo, as a distraction.

"Romoli doesn't have as many spies as he would like you to think," he said as he leaned in. "He is more bluster than anything else. There are only two men watching us. I suspect they will follow us to the osteria. When we enter, we'll have a drink, then a pretty woman will come to the table. Act as if you do not want to go with her—you are too distraught about what happened, but eventually let her coerce you."

I let Dottor Boccia lead me through the piazza to the nearby osteria where we proceeded to take a table, order a drink, and talk about everything except what mattered to me most in that moment— finding Isabetta. I did not bother trying to hide my misery, and the man made a grand show of trying to cheer me up. I even managed to crack a smile at a few of his jokes despite myself. Two men entered, eyed me briefly, then sat at a table near the door. They were dressed like laborers with tunics, trousers, and rough jackets rather than doublets and hose. As my eyes passed over the crowd in the osteria, I noticed three of Rolando's condottiere drinking and playing cards—and keeping an eye on that table.

Finally, the woman Dottor Boccia had warned me about appeared at our table. She was dressed in a yellow gown—marking her as a courtesan—which was missing its chemise and sleeve, her bodice unlaced to a salacious level. She wore her curly auburn hair down, framing her face, which was accentuated with too much rouge. She slid onto the bench next to me and slinked an arm around my waist.

"No, signorina," I said, perhaps too loudly. She pretended she was wounded but did not back away.

"Come now, let me make everything better." She ran her hand up my shoulder and began massaging my neck. I let her for a moment or two—by God she knew what she was doing—but then lifted her hand away.

"I cannot, signorina. Please, leave me in my cups." I lifted my mug.

She leaned in again and her hand traveled down, in between my legs. If she was pretending, it was not evident to me. She ran her fingers along the side of my codpiece, teasing the edge of my thigh through the fabric of my breeches. My body responded, and I hated myself for it.

"Come with me now," she whispered in my ear. Then she pulled her hand away, letting it run up my side and across my chest. She turned my head toward her and planted a deep kiss on my lips. I let her, stunned.

When she pulled away, she reached for my hand, ready to lead me away. I looked to Dottor Boccia.

"Go, polpetto mio! Go and have a good time. You seem like you need it." He waved a hand at me. "I'll be here when you get back."

I let her guide me through the tables toward the staircase lead-ing to the bedrooms upstairs. We went to the farthest room and she opened it and pulled me in.

Valentino and two condottieri sat on the chairs and the bed inside. Richo sat on a chair in the corner. His lip snarled when he saw me.

"You took your time," Valentino said.

"What is he doing here?" I stared at Richo. He must have woken just after I left. I wondered how fast into this plan he was going to slash my throat with his dagger.

"Rolando sent him here."

"I hope he wasn't followed."

One of the condottieri spoke up. "He wasn't."

"You are going to save my sister. Or you will die at my hand," Richo said, his eyes never wavering from mine.

"And if we save her?" I asked.

"Then I will let her decide."

I hardened my resolve with those words.

The younger condottiere handed the courtesan a pouch of coins. She opened it and peered in with a smile.

"Hello, honey," she said, turning back to me. "Time to take those clothes off."

I gaped at her.

"You heard her," Val said. He motioned toward the man who had handed the courtesan her coins. "You too. You know the plan."

He nodded and began to remove his outer garments. The mer-cenary was the same height as me with the same curly dark locks. Then it hit me—we were going to exchange clothes. I unclasped my cape and pulled off my breeches and doublet.

We swapped clothing, and I was forced to admit he resembled me once he was buttoned up and he had put on my hat and cape. I hoped he appeared enough like me to get by the men sitting at the door.

"The dwarf and I will go back to your house and wait for word."

A knock sounded on the wall next to Richo. Valentino rose and pushed upon a panel in the wall. A door opened. Salvi stood there with another young boy.

"Salvi, there you are, you little spy." I grinned. "What a plan you have cooked up with your street friends."

His face lit up. "Maestro! Were you surprised to see Dottor Boccia?"

I nodded. "I was. What a brilliant idea."

"We'll get Signorina Palone back, you'll see." He held a determined look in his eye. It was a look that said he wanted to fix things. I wondered how much he understood that Richo's desire to kill me had to do with Isabetta finding the journal.

Valentino ushered them into the room. The older condottiere made room for the boys to sit on the bed.

"Do you know where Cesare went?" Valentino asked Salvi.

"Sì, he returned to the Confraternita del Gonfalone."

"You must be jesting," I said. "Why would they go back there after we stole the recipes there the first time?"

Richo spoke up. "The confraternita fired my cousin, the one who let Isabetta into the rooms before."

Salvi had told the truth. It had been Isabetta who recovered the box and discovered the journal.

"They made him return the keys," he continued. "But he had made a spare set. When Romoli and Cesare stole the recipes the first time, Cesare was staying on the second floor. We'll try that first and work our way up each floor until we find them."

"Do we know if Romoli or Isabetta will be there?"

"No. We only know that's where Cesare took the recipes."

The courtesan patted the young condottiere on the back. "Come now, caro mio, let us return you to your dwarf friend. He must be wondering about you."

"Be careful," I said to him as they were leaving. The idea that someone pretending to be me could lose his life in my stead appalled me.

"We'll be watching the streets," Salvi said, jostling the young boy with him.

"Sì!" the boy said, his voice just a squeak. "Nothing gets past us. We're like the wind. Like spirits. Invisible. No one looks at us, ever."

He said those words proudly, but they made me feel sad.

"It's nearly dark. Salvi, take your friend and go." Valentino pressed upon the panel and the door opened up once more. "We'll follow you when you give us the sign."

The door closed, leaving the four of us—Val, Richo, the older condottiere, and me—to wait, and to plan the possibilities of what we would do once we reached the confraternita.

The sign, I soon learned, was a rock tossed against the window. We sprang into action, our beating hearts the only sound as we slipped through the secret door and into a corridor leading to the street.

Night had fallen, but unfortunately, the temperature had not. I wiped the sweat from my brow. Our lanterns gave off very little light, and the candles lighting the Madonnas on each corner were more of a marker in the dark than any source of illumination. I couldn't make out the features of anyone I passed, which meant they could not do the same for us. For the first time in months I realized the comet above did not light up the night like it used to. I could barely make out its tail, now just a slim red blur amid the constellations.

When we reached the Via dei Coronari, Richo stopped us. "There are two guards stationed at the inn. We'll go ahead and distract the guard in front before you arrive. Go straight until you reach the next street, the Via dei Tre Archi, which runs parallel to this one. Underneath the second arch you'll see a big door on the right. Take this key and go in. You may need to be ready for a fight. There is a small stairway on the east side of the house that will take you to the other rooms."

He handed me a key tied on a leather cord, then leaned in and hissed, "Bring her back, Giovanni. Or you will wish you had." Richo and the condottiere ran ahead into the dark.

CHAPTER 27

Giovanni

The tiny street was empty and silent, save for the scuttle of rats across the stones. Valentino and I encountered the first arch, which connected two buildings, the moment we turned onto the street. The buildings to either side were illuminated by candlelight from high windows, too high to easily see into, a cautionary measure against burglary.

The second arch was not more than a long stone's throw away. It was too dark to see how much farther down the street the third arch was.

The space under the arch was dimly lit by another high window, next to the big wooden door Richo had described. Several of the rooms in the adjoining buildings were lit by candles, their glow flitting on the edge of the shutters. We would have to be very quiet to not be heard.

I crossed through the arch and looked up, hoping to see a bit of the comet, which was, for me, a fading memento of Bartolomeo. If it weren't for the slight variance in color, I might not have even known what it was. *Watch over me, Father,* I thought. *Help me get out of this alive.*

My heart rose to my throat when I heard voices above.

"Here, hoist me up," Val said. I moved to the wall beneath the window and laced my hands together so he could step up and peer into the sliver of light at the clouded glass.

"I couldn't see a damn thing. But I only heard voices for two people inside that room," he whispered once he returned to the ground.

"If I can open the door without any noise, we might be able to surprise them," I replied.

"Lord protect us," he breathed as I inserted the key in the lock.

I turned it slower than I had ever turned a key before. I could feel the pins catching on the tumbler. At one point the lock made a loud *click* and I froze. The voices also stopped. I waited, my hand like a statue, afraid to release or move forward on its turn. After an interminable silence, the voices continued. I waited for a long time before I continued the turn of the key. When I felt it give way to freedom and the voices did not stop, a rush of accomplishment and relief flooded through me.

I pulled out the key and stood back.

"Bravo!" Valentino whispered to me. He moved toward the door and prepared to pull it open. "Are you ready?"

I nodded, but in the darkness I'm not sure he saw me.

"*Uno, due, tre!*" he whispered. The door flew open and we rushed in, swords drawn.

Two men sat at a wooden table playing a game of bassetta. I noted they were playing with *ducats*, not scudi—a high-stakes game. They wore doublets embroidered with the insignia of the Confraternita del Gonfalone. Shock registered in their features for only a moment, then their hands flew to their swords—which were not there.

The bigger of the men glanced at the rack on the far wall where he had placed his sword; Valentino's sword was already at the man's back, and mine was at the throat of the young man sitting across from him.

Val winked at me, then crashed the hilt of his sword against the burly man's head. He fell over with a thud, unconscious, taking half of the cards on the table with him. The man in front of me squeaked.

"Not a sound," I warned him. "You talk only when I ask you a question."

Valentino set about gagging and tying up the unconscious man.

I applied pressure to my blade. "Is Domenico Romoli here? Or Cesare Brioschi?"

The man nodded, his sandy brown hair falling into his eyes. "Sì, signore. On the fourth floor in the big room."

"Who else is staying here tonight?"

Tears tumbled across his ruddy skin. He could not be older then sixteen or seventeen. I pulled the sword away but held it at the ready so there was no illusion of escape.

"There are ten travelers in the inn tonight. Most on pilgrimage."

"What's your name?" I asked the boy.

"Venzi," he sputtered.

Valentino finished his knots, stood, and faced Venzi. "How many of Signor Romoli's men are there?"

"They have two men staying in the room below Signor Romoli and two men on watch out front. They paid us well to stay here and keep our mouths shut about anything we see or anything that happens."

I waved the sword at him. "Are you telling me the truth? That's all the men he has?"

The boy's tears increased in volume. "Yes . . . yes, signore."

"Is there a woman with them?" I asked.

"I don't know!" Venzi sobbed, his breath coming in large, heaving gulps.

"Such dramatics," Valentino murmured. "Let me take care of him." He moved to the boy and shoved a cloth into his mouth, then began to tie him up.

I felt sorry for the lad. I swept up the ducats and dropped them down the front of his doublet. Val threw a nearby blanket over him to further muffle his sobs, then turned back to me.

"Now what?"

"Wait here," I told him. Quietly I stole from the back first-floor room to the front of the inn. The entryway was empty. An oil lamp lit up the small space. I turned the corner and found myself at the foot of a long, narrow staircase carved into stone. I crept up to the first landing. Looking up the center of the stairwell I could see, just as the boy had indicated, there were three floors beyond the ground floor. I went back to Valentino.

"We don't want them to bar the door from the inside. We'll have to knock or find some way to get them to answer the door. Fighting in that stairwell will be difficult—it's only one person wide. I'll knock, and you guard my back in case anyone from the lower floors rushes to their aid. Hopefully we can find a way in without that happening."

"What about the other rooms?" he asked. "We know nothing of the people within."

"We take our chances, I suppose. Let's hope they are just pilgrims to the Vaticano and will stay behind their shut doors."

We climbed the staircase slowly, with as little noise as possible. We could hear voices from a few of the rooms, some sounding more amorous than others. I was grateful for the stone beneath our feet, which would not creak and give us away.

When we reached the fourth floor, I moved forward the four paces to the door at the front of the building. Valentino took up the rear, facing the stairwell. We stood for a moment to catch our breath and listen. I couldn't make out the words, but it was clear there was more than one man in the room. I didn't hear the voice of a woman.

I looked at Valentino and he nodded. I knocked lightly.

"Who is it?" I recognized Cesare's voice at the door.

I tried to make my voice a slightly higher pitch without sounding too ridiculous. "Venzi. I have some news to share with you."

There was the sound of the door being unbarred and then it opened. Cesare's eyes widened and I pushed my way in, my sword at his breast.

"Back up, slowly . . . brother."

I had a feeling it would bristle Cesare to call him by that name. He sneered at me but did as I asked. Val was right behind me as I moved forward. We appeared to be in a sitting room with a few chairs, a settee, and some tables. There was a door next to the one we entered that likely went to a bedroom.

Then I saw Isabetta. She sat in a simple chair near the shuttered window, her hands bound but her feet free. She wore no gag. Her clothes were intact and her hair laid loose around her shoulders. It was evident she had been crying. Her eyes pleaded with me.

She didn't dare speak because Romoli stood next to her, Bartolomeo's knife at her throat. My heart sank. I knew exactly how sharp that knife was, how it felt in the palm of one's hand.

"Don't be stupid, Giovanni." Romoli was calm. "You wouldn't want your lady love's neck to be marred by my blade."

"It's not your blade," I said, seething.

"Dio mio! This blade does feel good in the hand, doesn't it?" He smiled and licked his lips. Isabetta made a noise as the blade pressed closer.

Cesare chuckled, and at the sound I instinctively pushed the sword tip against his chest.

"Didn't he tell you to not be stupid?" he said, lifting his hand up to the sword. I let him push it away, knowing that if I carried through it would be Isabetta's spilled blood I would mourn.

"Come on in, Gio. And your friend too. Be good boys and toss your swords to me."

How was I going to get out of this mess? I put on my best mask of calm, but inside I was a mixture of burning rage and fear. Romoli had what he wanted. There was no reason for him to spare any of us.

"Now!" Romoli's features screwed against one another, his brow furrowing and making his eyes small, his nose wrinkling, and his cheeks reddening as his rage flew across the room in that one word.

The shout was likely to draw Romoli's men from the floor below. I threw the sword toward him and it scuttled across the floor to stop at Isabetta's feet. Val did the same and it came to rest against her slipper with a clatter against the tiled floor.

"Now you two, sit yourself down on those chairs. And don't you dare make a wrong move. Cesare, get the door, then tie up these rogues."

Cesare began with Valentino, tying his hands and feet to the chair. Romoli removed the knife from Isabetta's throat and picked up one of the swords. He strode toward me, the menacing blade pointed toward my heart.

As soon as he did, Isabetta began to move as well. Without looking too closely in her direction I noted she had freed her hands. Blood coated her wrists where they had rubbed against the rope.

"Maybe we don't need to bother tying you up," Romoli said with a sinister grin. "I have the recipes. And I have this exquisite knife." He waved it in the air. "The knife that made Bartolomeo Scappi famous. What I don't need is you or your friend coming after me."

"You do know who I am, don't you?" Val said as Cesare tied his right hand to the chair.

Romoli waved the knife again, this time more dismissively. "You're a filthy prince, I know, I know. I'm not impressed by your title. Besides, I'll have returned to Firenze before anyone realizes you are dead. I have a prince of my own to protect me. The Medici are more powerful than your paltry family."

Val had to be thinking what I was, that the Chigi family—Serafina's bloodline—and the Farnese family to whom he now belonged were far wealthier and more resourceful than the Medici. And the Carpi family believed Valentino was a true son, which made